SEAWEED UNDER WATER

Stanley Evans

TouchWood Editions
#108 – 17665 66A Avenue
Surrey, BC V3S 2A7
www.touchwoodeditions.com

TouchWood Editions
PO Box 468
Custer, WA
98240-0468

Library and Archives Canada Cataloguing in Publication
Evans, Stanley, 1931–
    Seaweed under water / Stanley Evans. — 1st ed.

ISBN 978-1-894898-57-7

1. Coast Salish mythology—Fiction. 2. Coast Salish Indians—Rites and ceremonies—Fiction. I. Title.

PS8559.V36S43 2007   C813'.54   C2007-904914-1

Library of Congress Control Number: 2007931910

Edited by Ed Strauss
Proofread by Marial Shea
Book design by R-House Design
Cover design by Jacqui Thomas
Front-cover photo by Miguel Angelo Silva / iStockphoto

Printed in Canada

TouchWood Editions acknowledges the financial support for its publishing program from the Government of Canada through the Book Publishing Industry Development Program (BPIDP), Canada Council for the Arts, and the province of British Columbia through the British Columbia Arts Council and the Book Publishing Tax Credit.

BRITISH COLUMBIA
ARTS COUNCIL

Canada Council
for the Arts
Conseil des Arts
du Canada

This book is dedicated to Xanthe Evans

THE WARRIER RESERVE DOES NOT EXIST. The Mowaht Bay Band does not exist. All of the characters, incidents and dialogue in this novel are products of the author's imagination. Any resemblance to actual living persons or to real events is coincidental. Depictions of Native mythology and religion are based on ethnological research and do not necessarily reflect the present-day observances and practices of Canada's West Coast Native people.

The author is grateful for the expert help and advice of Dr. John Marsden, Dr. John Tibbles, James Clowater, George Easdon and Michael Layland in the preparation of this manuscript.

CHAPTER ONE

PC came into my life last winter. Her private life is none of my business, although she acts like she was brought up in an alley. Sleek, black, alluring, PC has a way of suddenly appearing. Sometimes I feel a presence, look up from my desk and there she is, eyeing me seductively from the door with her legs crossed and toes pointing out. We make eye contact and the next thing I know she's sniffing around as if she owns the place.

I knew she was a hussy, so it didn't surprise me when she started coming on. Office romances often end in heartbreak, although like most men I occasionally give way to quixotic impulses. The next time PC shook her tail in my face I reached out and grabbed her. Big mistake—I ended up scratched and bleeding. I haven't laid a hand on her since.

After that I should have known better, but—as must be evident—I lack restraint. So there I was, a 40-year-old Coast Salish cop, head over heels with a tiny black female with God knows how many children, every one of whom—I'll bet my pension on this—has a different father. One day I brought a carton of milk to work, drank most of it, poured what was left into a saucer and placed it by the door. Within a month, I was PC's primary caregiver, my wastebasket was her principal residence and she was making increasing demands upon my wallet.

One hot summer's day, PC was dining on salmon (two dollars a can at Thrifty Foods) and I was doing nothing when somebody knocked on my door.

"Come in," I said.

A young woman entered, wanting to know if I was a policeman. I told her I was. She asked me why a Victoria policeman was wearing jeans and a black shirt with Harley Davidson patches instead of a uniform.

"I'm a neighbourhood policeman," I told her. "Sometimes I monitor public parks and shopping malls for pickpockets and rowdies."

"What's *monitor* mean?" she asked. She seemed sleepy and a little lost.

"That's a very good question. All it means is, I keep my eyes open."

She was wearing a faded blue T-shirt, baggy corduroy shorts and tennis shoes. Glossy black braids hung halfway to her waist. I judged her to be aboriginal, like me, except I'm a full-blooded Coast Salish Native and she was half white, at least. Instead of sitting, she leaned against a wall with her hips cocked. Posed like that, tall, loose-limbed and beautiful, she looked sexy enough to lure a senator from his soapbox. I had an idea she was a hooker; I get a lot of them in here, usually when the weather's bad. Her name was Terry Colby. She was sweet, gentle and not very bright. She seemed to be the kind of person of whom the unscrupulous might easily take advantage.

PC chose that moment to stick her nose inside the doorway. Terry gave PC a passing glance, half-turned toward me and said, "My mother . . . " Words failed her. She broke into sobs, chest heaving, and tears running down her cheeks. Then it got worse. I stood up as Terry's eyes rolled back in her head. She swayed a little. With colour draining from her pretty face she went limp and slid to the ground. I reached her fast enough to stop her head from smacking the floor, cradled her in my arms and felt her pulse—her heart was beating too fast. Even though the sun coming through my windows was hot enough to melt floor wax, Terry's wrist was clammy beneath my fingers. Moments later she opened her eyes, pushed me away and tried to stand, but her legs were rubbery and she couldn't manage it on her own.

"It's all right," I said, helping her into a visitors' chair. "Take it easy for a minute."

Terry pulled herself together at last and said, "I'm looking for my mother."

These words started another flood of tears. I grabbed a box of tissues from my desk, handed it over, laid a comforting hand on Terry's shoulder and made vague paternal tutting noises with my tongue while Terry blew her nose and wiped her eyes. "Tell me about your mother," I said, after she calmed down.

Terry raised her lovely face and stared at me directly for the first time. She didn't smile, and something in her eyes reminded me of a mistreated dog. "Something happened to my mother," she whispered.

I felt the hair on the back of my neck rising eerily, but I shook off the feeling and asked calmly, "What happened to her?"

Terry shook her head. "I don't know."

After some patient questioning, I learned that Terry lived in a care home in James Bay. Terry didn't know her mother's address and couldn't quite remember the last time she'd heard from her, or had seen her.

"We'll find your mother," I promised, speaking with more optimism than truth, because sometimes mothers with difficult children just run away.

PC jumped onto my desk. Before I could warn her that PC scratched, Terry had reached out and was stroking her neck. Purring like an engine, the cat rolled over, waved its furry legs in the air, closed its yellow eyes and let Terry rub its belly. Terry had calmed down nicely by the time I took her out to my car and drove her home.

PC wanted to come too. I wouldn't let her.

ARCHITECTURALLY, VICTORIA'S JAMES BAY district is a hodge-podge—houses and bungalows alternate with modern apartment towers and corner grocery stores. Terry lived at 25 Crowe Street—a large Italianate mansion replete with bay windows, ornate jigsaw fascias, balustrades, turrets and brick walls ornamented with stucco. It had been built with fur-trade money in the days when servants worked cheap. During the Second World War, it fell into the hands of a gambler, who operated it as a girly joint. Today it was a residential care home.

Terry and I entered the grounds through wrought-iron gates and tramped together up a pathway between well-tended lawns and flowerbeds. As we neared the house, Terry began to drag her feet. I pressed a button beside the front door and heard brassy chimes echoing inside. Waiting for somebody to answer, I noticed that every window in the house had bars across it. The door opened eventually, and a calm middle-aged nun stood gazing at me. She was wearing long black robes and a stiff white collar. Long silver hair flowed from beneath a starched head-covering like a snowy owl's outspread wings. An ivory crucifix the size of a postcard dangled from a silver chain around her neck. Tall, willowy, serene, she reminded me of a nurse who had mothered me at boarding school.

"Good morning. May I help you?" she said, smiling as if she meant it.

I was saying "I'm Sergeant Seaweed, VPD" when she spotted Terry cowering behind.

The tiny lines wrinkling the nun's forehead smoothed. "Terry, my dear!" she cried. "We've been so anxious." Taking Terry's elbow, she ushered her into a large reception hall. I slid inside too, before an automatic door-closer shut me out.

"Whatever is the matter, Terry?" the nun was saying, "You ran off without eating your breakfast, or taking your pills."

Terry's eyes flicked from the nun and then to me, back and forth like a cornered animal. Sagging with despair, Terry looked ready to faint again.

The nun turned her smile on me again. "I am sorry. Who did you say you are?"

"Sergeant Seaweed, Victoria Police Department."

She told me that she was Sister Mildred, and asked me to wait. Her arm around Terry's waist, Sister Mildred steered her across the polished hardwood floors, through an inner doorway and out of sight.

That high-ceilinged house felt distinctly cool. Small tulip-shaped light bulbs, shining dimly from wall sconces, lit the hall fractionally. A red settee faced a marble fireplace. A coloured lithograph of Christ, wearing His crown of thorns, hung above the mantel. A polished brass crucifix as long as a walking stick stood on an oak credenza. I moved to a writing desk in an alcove near the door. Undelivered mail filled its many pigeonholes. I picked one letter up at random and examined its postmark—it had been mailed to a Marilyn Jones at this address, three years previously.

An electric wheelchair appeared along a corridor. The tiny creature driving it was about 30 years old and the size of a 6-year-old child. She had beautiful long golden curls and a doll-like face, with bright blue eyes and a painted red mouth.

"Hello," she squeaked. "I'm Daphne. What's happening?"

"I just brought Terry back."

"That was a stupid thing to do," Daphne said sweetly. "Why do you think Terry ran away?"

"Was she running away?"

"Sure she was! You'd run away too if you were cooped up in this dump."

Daphne manoeuvred her chair to a window and gazed longingly between the bars. "You're Indian, aren't you?" she asked. "Pisses you off though, being called Indian. What are we supposed to call you nowadays? Natives? First Nations? How about wagon burners?"

Before I could get a word in edgewise, Daphne went on, "Terry is Indian too, poor thing. We had other Indians stayed here, plenty of 'em; till they stepped out of line and nuns murdered 'em and chopped their bodies into small pieces and jammed 'em in the furnace. One Indian was a basket maker who made me a hat. Looks kinda goofy and scratches my head when I wear it though. Want to see it?"

"Another time, thanks. I'm waiting for Sister Mildred."

"Millie's the worst of the lot. They call themselves *nuns*. Nuns my ass. I call 'em ladybugs. The government pays 'em thousands of bucks a month for warehousing us. I heard that from a high-court judge so believe me, it's true. Pretend they're Christians but they're a bunch of perverts. Talk about orgies. I've seen 'em going at it. I know what I'm talking about."

I'd discovered a gossip, a policeman's greatest resource—when they tell the truth. I said, "Tell me more."

"If Millie's not a serial killer, I'm Queen Elizabeth and my wheelchair is the Royal Coach."

The inner door opened. Sister Mildred appeared again, her robes flowing behind her, and glided toward us on unseen feet. Daphne put a finger to her red lips, winked and scooted off in her little chariot along the corridors and out of sight.

Sister Mildred smiled. "Pay no attention to Daphne. She has peculiar obsessions."

"You're telling me," I replied, "How's Terry doing?"

"Terry gets these queer turns from time to time. I've given her a sedative," she said, her smile fading. "I'm sorry you have been put to this trouble, Sergeant."

"An hour ago, Terry fainted in my office after telling me that she'd lost her mother."

"That's a woman called Jane Colby. It is to be regretted, but I feel it my duty to tell you that, as a parent, Mrs. Colby is not quite what she ought to be. She drinks too much, and her parenting skills are limited. She neglected her daughter dreadfully. As a result, Terry started getting into trouble; that's why she's here, under my supervision."

"What kinds of trouble was Terry getting into, exactly?"

Sister Mildred's mouth twitched. "The usual kinds. What do you expect? Terry is a sexually mature adult with the mental age of an eight-year-old."

"An eight-year-old who managed to navigate herself downtown. Somebody capable of expressing feelings and wants."

"God must have guided Terry's footsteps to you, instead of to Rock Bay, or somewhere even worse. One can hardly blame Terry for trying, though. She misses her mother, at least some of the time. When Jane isn't drinking, she is delightful. We seldom see her like that, unfortunately, although Jane and I did have a lucid telephone conversation a few days ago."

Daphne's fluting laugh echoed down the corridor.

Jane Colby! When Sister Mildred mentioned the heavy drinking, it dawned on me where I'd heard that name. A couple of weeks earlier, Constable Denise Halvorsen had mentioned that she'd been dispatched to check out a bar fight, but by the time Denise arrived, everyone had dispersed, except for an injured man lying on the floor and a certain Jane Colby, who was too drunk to walk. Was she Terry's mother? The hairs on the back of my neck were tingling again.

Sister Mildred was staring at me expectantly. "Do you remember when, precisely, you last spoke to Terry's mother?" I asked.

"Monday, I spoke to her last Monday, or perhaps it was Tuesday. In this house, one day is pretty much like another. I lose track of the calendar sometimes. Our conversation was certainly less than a week back."

Sister Mildred pushed buttons on a keypad beside the door. "I don't wish to seem inhospitable, but we are rather busy at present. I think you can rest easy, officer. We'll take good care of Terry now." The automatic door opened and a blast of warm outside air entered, rustling her long skirts. "What a lovely day the Lord has made for us," she said. "It certainly is warm today."

"How do I get in touch with Jane Colby?"

"She lives on Welling Terrace. I don't recall the house number offhand."

"I want to nail something down precisely, sorry to ask again: When do you think Terry last spoke to her mother?"

"It was either Monday or Tuesday."

"You told me that was the last time *you'd* talked to her. Did Terry speak to her mother on that occasion?"

"Yes. That is, no," she said hesitantly. "Probably Monday, though I'm not quite sure any longer."

"This is a large house. Are you the only person on duty?"

She laughed outright. "It feels like that sometimes. We're supposed to have half a dozen people on staff during the day. At present we have to make do with four."

"How long has Terry been with you?"

"Years, off and on. Sometimes she stays with her maternal grandfather for short periods. Terry wears out her welcome, eventually, and the old gentleman needs a respite. She always comes back to us."

A buzzer sounded throughout the house; footsteps began to clack on wooden floors, and girlish laughter echoed along the hallways. Sister Mildred uttered a word seldom encountered in nunneries.

I pasted a grin on my face, thanked Sister Mildred and went out.

I was half-tempted to return to my office and file a Missing Person's report ... except that there was no real evidence that Jane Colby was actually missing, or that anything dire had happened to her. I felt foolish. Then I thought, "What the hell? It's a slow day anyway." And I *had* promised Terry I'd find her mother.

CHAPTER TWO

Welling Terrace was a short cul-de-sac on the Fairfield Slope. Faint sea breezes wafted along the tree-lined streets, and dry withered leaves lay like brown confetti underfoot. Half a mile away, downhill beyond the rooftops, sparkling surf whitened Victoria's beaches. Twenty miles farther away, half-visible in the heat haze, the snow-clad Olympics towered majestically on the U.S. side of Juan de Fuca Strait.

Jane Colby's residence turned out to be a modest '30s bungalow with a realtor's For Sale sign stuck in its front lawn. As I walked to the door, an Airedale dog appeared and snapped at me. I showed it the back of my hand. The dog and I were getting nicely acquainted when a wizened old man sporting a white linen suit and a blue silk shirt opened the front door. He lacked vigour but was still vain. Strands of dyed yellow hair dangled lankly below his Panama hat. His mouth was a thin red gash in a chalk-white face. Blinking watery blue eyes, he threw a tennis ball out onto the street. The Airedale chased it downhill.

"Sorry about the dog. The poor fellow's bored. Not enough exercise, I'm afraid," he said breathlessly. "If you're inquiring about the house, you'd better contact my realtor directly."

"I'm here to see Mrs. Jane Colby," I said, showing him my badge. "Is she home?"

"Is this about Terry?"

"Yes."

"I'm Fred Colby, Terry's grandfather," he said, his watery eyes narrowing. "Terry's all right, I hope?"

"She ran away from her care home this morning. Terry's worried about her mother, and I promised Terry I'd look into it."

"Where's Terry now?"

"I took her back to Crowe Street."

He appeared to forget me for a moment. Shaking his head unhappily, he backed into a vestibule and said, "I'm a little worried about Jane myself. You'd better come in."

We went into a wide living room that extended the full depth of the bungalow. It smelled of furniture polish and cigarettes. Curtains were closed to keep the sun out. Fred switched on a pedestal lamp; light fell on a sofa, easy chairs and an old-fashioned console TV. Flowers fresh from Mr. Colby's garden stood in a vase on a gleaming dining table. The room's predominant feature was a shiny black grand piano covered with photographs in silver frames. I glanced at the photographs briefly before he invited me to sit on the sofa.

He said, "Sorry. Every time I hear about Terry I expect the worst and forget my manners."

I wondered what he was apologizing for.

Moving carefully on arthritic legs, Mr. Colby lowered himself into an easy chair and asked, "Well, officer, how can I help you?"

"It would be best if I spoke to Terry's mother first."

He smiled thinly. "That might be difficult. My daughter has her own agenda. She comes and goes as she pleases. At the moment, I don't know where she is."

Mr. Colby might have been worried about his daughter, but he seemed slightly aggrieved, as well. I said, "I was given to understand that she lived here."

"She does, occasionally. Some time back, Jane moved in with Jack Owens. When that relationship ended, Jane didn't come back here. This place is really too big for one person, so I put it on the market." His gaze faltering, he added dolefully, "When it sells I shall move into an apartment, if I can find one that allows dogs. I won't need the piano—Jane's the only one who ever played it. She plays beautifully; it's her one real talent."

There was an element of insincerity in his words and manner. I asked, "Can you suggest where Jane might be now?"

"She might be anywhere," he replied in the same hollow tone. "It's a sad commentary on modern life, when a fellow has to confess he's lost track of his own child."

"When did you see her last?"

"A week, maybe 10 days ago. She popped around and I remember asking her for some mo—"

He was about to say money, but caught himself in time.

"Did your granddaughter telephone you today, or call around to the house?"

"Either is possible, I was out shopping for groceries earlier. That Thrifty store on Fairfield Road. I was gone for an hour, and I don't have an answering machine. Terry might have phoned me, or dropped by during my absence."

"Does she have a door key?"

"Goodness no. Poor Terry. She's not responsible, you see. I don't mean she's a bad girl, not at all, she's a sweetheart really."

"And she didn't leave you a note, obviously."

"Didn't, and couldn't. Terry can neither read nor write—not even her own name, poor thing."

"Do you have a picture of Jane? I'll see it's returned to you."

He nodded. Sitting on the chair had stiffened Mr. Colby's joints and it was a struggle for him to get to his feet and straighten out. He moved slowly across to the piano, pointed at a picture and said, "That's Jane. With Terry in Mexico when Terry was little."

He went out of the room.

The picture in question had been photographed on a tropical beach fringed with palm trees. Terry's mother was a slim handsome Caucasian woman wearing a flattering bikini. She had her father's pale colouring and yellow hair. Terry—a black-haired, copper-skinned child with a shy vulnerable face—stood beside her mother, one slender arm hooked around her leg.

I was brooding about the picture and what it signified, when Mr. Colby returned.

"I hope this photograph will do. It was taken about 10 years ago. Jane's changed somewhat, since then," he said, handing me a six-by-eight glossy. This one showed Jane posed on the deck of a large motor yacht, looking elegant in a blue blazer and white pleated skirt.

Mr. Colby cleared his throat and said, "I've been thinking. If you want to find Jane quickly, your best bet is to check at the Rainbow Motel. Failing that, you might call Jack Owens. I suppose you know Jack."

I shook my head.

"He's that chartered accountant fellow. I ought to warn you that Jack and Jane are—" Mr. Colby searched for an appropriate word "—*estranged*, at present. Jack Owens isn't the easiest fellow to get along with, in my opinion. I think she's well rid of him, frankly."

"Terry's part Native, so who was her father?"

My abrupt question unsettled him. His cheeks went red and he said huffily, "Terry's father was Neville Rollins, an aboriginal logger from Mowaht Bay. Neville was a peculiar character, a most unpleasant, sadistic individual. I must admit I wasn't too happy when, all those long years ago, Jane came home and announced their engagement." Frowning, he added, "You'll think me racist, but with all due respect, officer, there's more to it than that. I believed them unsuited. As it turned out, I was right."

That final platitude annoyed me, but I forced a grin and he went on, "Jane and Neville got married 20-odd years ago. In the Anglican church at Duncan," Mr. Colby said, speaking with his head cocked slightly to one side and frowning as if reliving unpleasant memories. "Jane used to come here covered in bruises. She'd make excuses. It was a while before I realized that Neville was battering her. Thank God, Neville suddenly disappeared when Terry was a year old. Some people think that he drowned, and it's possible, I suppose. Anyway, Jane's life's been difficult since, although she carried on as best she could, working at all sorts of things."

"What's this about a possible drowning?"

"As I believe I mentioned, Neville was in the logging business—in partnership with his brother, Harley."

Fred Colby stopped talking and gazed at me expectantly. If he had expected his words to provoke a strong reaction, he was not disappointed.

Born blind, Harley Rollins had lived in an almost catatonic state for the first six years of his life, cut off from the outside world and rarely speaking (or being spoken to). At the age of seven, Harley was taken to Vancouver where an ophthalmologist operated successfully upon his eyes. Since then, Harley Rollins had become a severe embarrassment to the Coast Salish Nation. Now a millionaire businessman referred to as Boss Rollins, he was widely suspected of being a witch.

A century and a half ago, Natives accused of witchcraft were shunned, even murdered, by relatives of people they allegedly harmed. Even today, for the most part, witches go about their affairs in secret. Just the same, many reports of witchcraft had come out of Mowaht Bay in recent years, some of which had been taken seriously. Boss Rollins and I hadn't met; I'd never in my life visited the Mowaht Bay reserve. Nevertheless, since I was one of the few Native policemen in these parts, Boss Rollins probably knew as much about my reputation as I knew about his.

Fred Colby was smiling. I said, "Tell me more."

"The Rollins brothers combined the letters of their first names, HA-rley and NE-ville, and called themselves HANE Logging. The day he went missing, Neville had been working one of those floating log rafts. It's been suggested that Neville fell into the water. Nobody else was there at the time so we'll never know. The thing is, he was never seen again. After seven years, the courts declared Neville legally dead."

"Jane never remarried?"

"No. Didn't choose to, though she had plenty of offers. With Neville gone, she stopped using the name Rollins and reverted to her maiden name. Things haven't been easy for Jane, especially since Terry turned out to be mentally challenged."

"What's wrong with Terry?"

"It's not genetic, if that's what you're thinking," Mr. Colby said defensively. "Terry was born normal. Shortly after her first birthday, Terry received brain injuries when the car in which she was a passenger hit a tree. My daughter was driving and it is possible that she had been drinking. Jane wasn't charged. All things considered, I suppose the authorities felt she had suffered enough. Neville hadn't been missing long. With all his faults, Jane loved her husband and she was upset, naturally."

All things considered, Fred Colby didn't know much and what he did know, or say, hadn't helped me much. Sudden moisture showed in his eyes. He cleared his throat, took a short stubby pipe from a side table and began to stuff it with tobacco from a humidor. I felt sorry for him and disappointed for myself.

I said, "You'll be hearing from the police again, if it turns out that Jane is actually missing. I'd have to notify Missing Persons. You'll be asked to make a formal statement, fill in forms etcetera. Is that all right with you?"

His voice trembling a little, Mr. Colby said, "Fine, Mr. Seaweed, I'll go along with whatever you think best. Let's just hope you find her instead."

I murmured some comforting platitude, shook hands with Mr. Colby and left him alone with his memories. The Airedale was waiting for me outside. Wagging his tail and panting, he dropped his ball at my feet. I threw it across the lawn into a clump of rhododendrons and looked at my wristwatch. It was eleven o'clock. The dog was still sniffing his ball out when I left.

CHAPTER THREE

Victoria's Rainbow Motel was located on the Inner Harbour's last remaining chunk of underdeveloped waterfront. It sat on a woodsy acre—originally a hunting lodge built in the days when most Vancouver Island residents were furry, four-legged and unaccustomed to the sound of firearms. Fred Colby hadn't mentioned it, but among the Coast Salish people, it was common knowledge that Boss Rollins owned the place. The motel's front door, made of iron-bound oak planks, was shut. I pushed it open and walked clear through the building without seeing anyone.

Ten yards of pebbled beach separated the back of the motel from tidewater. A small wooden boat shack stood on the west side of the property, along with a dozen upturned aluminum rental boats. A blue heron knee deep in water was keeping an eye on a mangy-looking dog loping toward it along the shore. When the dog got too close, the heron raised its wings, bent its spindly legs and heaved itself into the sky. The squawking bird's flight carried it over the *Mayan Girl*, a large motor yacht moored at the lodge's private jetty. In my mind's eye, I pictured a glamorous Jane Colby, posed on the yacht's wide deck.

A hundred yards or so to my left, a wilderness of tall masts rose above Fisherman's Wharf. Kayakers and small ferries criss-crossed the harbour between B.C.'s legislative buildings and the

Ocean Pointe Resort. A floating crane was lifting driftwood and other floating debris from the water and dumping it on a barge near the seaplane terminal.

I went back inside the motel. Once a destination for well-heeled sportsmen, it now possessed the sad ambience of shady inns catering to lonely misfits and drunks. To the left of the reception counter, glass-paneled doors opened onto a dining room. Similar doors led to a lounge. A hand-lettered cardboard sign informed me that the dining room was closed. The door opening onto a lounge/bar was closed, but it opened at my touch, and I entered.

The lounge was uncomfortably warm. Flames, leaping in a fireplace, threw flickering yellow patterns onto varnished walls and a cross-beamed ceiling. Somebody had been burning papers in there—half-burnt ash lay thickly on the hearth. Leather armchairs exuded the breath of ancient cigars. Apart from a stuffed cougar snarling up at the mounted head of an elk, the lounge was unoccupied.

I heard sirens and looked outside. Three prowlies appeared along Belleville Street, turned up Menzies Street and raced toward Dallas Road on what may or may not have been urgent police business. Some guys just like to put earmuffs on and make lots of noise. I felt cranky and didn't know why—James Bay affects me that way sometimes.

I was behind the reception counter, searching for the motel's guest register and fighting a vague feeling of irritation, when a tanned, handsome young body-builder showed up. Wide as a refrigerator, with halitosis and dirty fingernails, he was wearing a shirt that fitted him like a second skin, showing off mighty biceps and triceps. His torso had more bumps than an egg carton. The plastic nametag pinned to his shirt told me that he was Karl Berger, the manager. He might have been carved from wood, except for moist rubbery lips and moist blue eyes. He leaned across the reception counter until our noses almost touched and said, "There's a sign on the door saying the motel's closed, mister. What do you think you're doing here?"

"Making routine inquiries, sir," I answered politely. "I'm Sergeant Seaweed, Victoria PD."

Karl's eyes narrowed. "Seaweed? We got Siwash cops now?"

My irritation increased. "I'm not a Siwash. I'm Coast Salish."

Karl was one of those self-assured young people with little patience for those they assume to be lower down the intelligence ladder. He sneered. "Salish, smalish. I guess you're here about our missing speedboat."

"What missing boat is that?"

"Our *speedboat*," he repeated derisively. "The one got stolen a few days back. The one you're supposed to be looking for."

"I'm sure an active investigation is proceeding. I assume it's one of your rental boats."

"No, I just told you. It's a *speedboat*. Them rentals out there are just piddle-ass sport-fishing boats."

"So the motel is closed?"

"Don't you read?" he asked impatiently. "I told you, there's a sign on the front door."

"No there isn't."

Karl stormed across the front door, looked in vain for a sign that wasn't there and came slowly back.

"I understand that Jane Colby stays here. Which is her room?"

"Don't you listen? The place is closed. If it's closed it means nobody's staying here."

"May I see your guest registers?"

"There is no register."

"Operating a motel without guest registers is a criminal

offence. If convicted you can be sentenced to three years in prison," I told him untruthfully.

His irritating sneer faded a trifle. I said, "I demand to see the register. If you don't produce it immediately, you'll be charged with obstructing justice."

"Big deal," Karl snapped. "How come you're not chasing robbers?"

I produced a cell phone from my pocket and pointed to a button. "Listen, Karl," I said. "If I push this, you'll be inside a paddy wagon before you can pop another steroid."

After a moment of indecision, Karl grabbed a key from its hook behind the counter. Muttering to himself, he marched along a corridor and slammed the back door open. Pebbles crunched underfoot as we crossed the beach. Karl went into the boat shack and flipped a light switch, to no avail.

"Goddam fuse has blown again," Karl muttered angrily.

Fishhooks, lures and flashers lay half-visible inside a glass-topped display case. A poster advertising last year's King Coho Salmon Derby was tacked to a wall, along with Canada Fisheries Regulations and outdated *Sports Illustrated* calendars. Groping in semi-darkness, Karl brought out a pair of red, morocco-bound registers. One was for boat rentals. The other was the motel's guest register, according to which Jane Colby had booked into room 101 about a month previously. This didn't exactly square with the information I'd received from Fred Colby.

Karl took a package of du Maurier from his pants pocket, put a squashed cigarette in his mouth and lit it with a chromium-plated lighter.

I went outside. When Karl emerged from the boat shack I said, "Tell me about Jane."

Karl did not reply immediately. Gazing at the motor yacht, he said, "What's to know? Janey's a party girl, friend of the boss."

"A party girl?"

Karl's permanent sneer increased, but he didn't elaborate. I said, "Why do you keep those registers in a boat shack?"

"There any reason I shouldn't?" he shouted angrily. "There's laws saying where we gotta *store* books as well?"

Strongly tempted to strike Karl's head with a blunt instrument, I said at length, "Temper, temper! Let's have a look in room 101. You can lead the way."

Room 101 had a Do Not Disturb sign hanging from its doorknob. Karl used a master key, stepped aside and said, "Your move."

Room 101 was actually a hot and airless two-room suite scented with Airwick. I opened the blinds and a window. The suite's kitchen area was an ugly chaotic pigsty. Unwashed utensils lay on countertops, or soaked in a sink of cold greasy water. A three-burner hotplate, coated with baked-on grease, had last been used to heat a nameless substance that had boiled over and left black stains on the stove's white enamel surfaces. Empty wine bottles stood on coffee tables and a dresser. A Canadian Wildlife calendar pinned to the wall hadn't been changed since January. Women's clothing lay scattered on the floor and across an unmade bed.

Karl, standing in the doorway behind me, cleared his throat.

I turned to look at him. He wouldn't meet my eyes; his manner had changed.

I said, "Don't tell me that you didn't know about this mess."

"I mean, sometimes Janey was kind of noisy, but I never came in here," he said, without his usual swagger. "Janey has kind of a special deal with the boss. She just comes and goes. Don't pay no rent, so she don't get no service."

Karl went to the window and flicked his half-smoked cigarette onto the beach.

A hand-knitted sweater was draped across the back of a chair.

Tacked to a wall, directly above the same chair, was a copy of the photograph I'd first seen at the house on Welling Terrace—the one of a smiling yellow-haired mother, standing on a tropical beach with a little copper-skinned daughter. I went over for a closer look.

Karl said, "That's Janey, and I guess her kid. Only Janey don't look that way now. See her in the morning before her makeup's on, she's like death warmed over."

I heard footsteps moving around upstairs. "You told me the hotel was empty."

"It is, except for you and me."

"There's somebody downstairs."

Karl shrugged.

"This is a missing-person inquiry," I said. "Until I tell you differently, this room is off limits to everyone. That includes you, Karl."

"Janey is missing?"

"She may be." I looked Karl in the eye. "When was the last time you saw her?"

Karl shrugged. "She comes and goes."

"Can you be more specific?"

"The last time I definitely saw her was about three weeks ago. But there's no telling how many times she's been in or out since. I don't pay no attention to her."

"Fine, but remember. This room is off limits."

"That's okay with me."

Twin diesel engines revved up outside. We looked out of the window—the *Mayan Girl* was leaving the wharf. I asked, "That's not Harley Rollins' boat?"

Karl laughed. "No, it belongs to the boss's sister, Tess Rollins." He watched the yacht pull away and said wistfully, "I wish I had the money she paid for that tub."

"If wishes were horses."

"What's that supposed to mean?"

To provoke him into telling me something he might prefer I didn't know, I said brusquely, "That yacht's worth millions and you make what? Thirty grand a year, plus tips?"

"Screw you," Karl growled, jutting his chin. "Managing this motel is just a sideline."

"From what—delivering pizzas?"

Relaxing with a visible effort, Karl shrugged and said, "That's a dirty crack."

"No, I'm interested. Just what do you have going for you, apart from muscles?"

Karl was a piece of work, all right. He clenched his fists and for a second it looked as if he might swing at me, but he controlled himself and gazed stupidly out of the window. I opened the room's small refrigerator. It was empty, except for a carton of milk and a pound of cheddar cheese. Karl moved his weight from foot to foot, opened his mouth as if to speak, thought better of it and started to leave the room.

"Hold it," I said sharply.

Karl stood in the open doorway, his eyes narrowed.

"You told me initially that nobody was staying here. Why?"

"Nobody is staying here *regular*, that's why."

"You're a liar. If you want to save yourself unnecessary trouble, start telling me the truth." I pointed to the fridge. "There's fresh milk in there. Cheese. If Jane Colby didn't leave it, who did?"

"I told you already," he snarled. "She comes and goes, has her own key. How can I keep track of people who have their own keys?"

Karl was at the tipping point of exasperation. I gazed at him calmly and inclined my head toward the door. He went out, slamming it behind him.

The milk smelled fresh and the cheese had no mould. That

was a hopeful sign. Jane might have been here three, four days ago. Perhaps there was no cause for alarm, after all. I spent a few minutes checking closets, drawers, cupboards, boxes and pockets without finding anything interesting, except for evidence that Jane was living a squalid drunken life. I closed the blinds and the window, left the room and went down to the lounge. The fire in the hearth had burned itself out. I poked among the ashes without finding any legible scrap of paper.

After that, my nostrils needed an airing. I left the motel, found a conveniently placed Japanese cherry tree across the street and waited beneath it. It was hot, for Victoria, even in deep shade. It was hot like Tucson in August. Five minutes passed, 10, before a shadow moved inside the Rainbow Motel's front door, and it opened. A 60-year-old man hobbled outside, moving slowly and painfully with the aid of two walking sticks. He was tall and overweight, wearing a blue suit with an unbuttoned jacket that revealed his large belly. He had heavy fur-lined moccasins on his feet. Walking toward the motel parking lot, his face showed an agonized expression.

He was Henry Ferman, a private detective with an office on Fort Street.

Two cars stood in the lot: a 10-year-old blue Impala and a late-model black Viper. Henry got into the Impala. I deliberated about going over and speaking to him, decided the time wasn't right and watched him drive off toward the wax museum. The Viper, I reflected, had cost its owner $80,000 or more, and probably belonged to Karl Berger. If it were actually Karl's vehicle, he was either more affluent than appearances suggested or was living way beyond his means. I began to wonder what the profitable sidelines Karl had bragged about might possibly be.

After that, I took a walk, because sometimes I need reminding that Victoria is one of the world's most beautiful and picturesque waterfront cities. Mountainous high-rises shouldered skies of unsullied blue, partially obscuring my view of the Inner Harbour but providing welcome shade. I sat on the patio of a bar on Belleville Street, watching the passersby, some of whom were young women dressed in the flimsiest of garments, and for no reason at all I began to think about a woman called Felicity Exeter. A head waiter who looked like—and was dressed like—King Edward the Eighth when he gave up the crown to marry Mrs. Simpson gave me a menu and snapped open a linen napkin, and he didn't lose his smile when all I ordered was a lowly beer. Another catamaran ferry had just arrived from Seattle. Passengers were streaming ashore near B.C.'s Legislature. Green hills and snow-capped mountains rose majestically all around. I love it here. No wonder people come here from all over the world.

CHAPTER FOUR

I live in a two-room cabin on the Warrior Reserve just west of Victoria, B.C. I built it myself; it's fairly rustic, there's no piped hot water. I manage all right, with an airtight wood stove. A couple of years back I installed a 20-amp electrical system, enough to power a few lights and an apartment-sized fridge. My outhouse is a classic one-holer, half-concealed in a cedar grove.

When I returned home that night, I put the kettle on, stripped off the sweaty clothes I was wearing and had a good wash. I put on fresh underwear, cut-off jeans and a loose cotton shirt, and puttered around barefoot for a few minutes. I poured myself a cup of Earl Grey, carried it outside and was sitting on a log on the beach below my cabin, enjoying the evening, when Chief Alphonse came down from the band office to join me. The log was an ancient Douglas fir, big enough to accommodate 20 fat butts, but I shuffled a couple of inches to one side and said, "Welcome, Chief. It's good to see you."

"It's not good to see you looking so gloomy," the old chief replied, letting himself down onto the log stiffly, because of his lumbago. Gazing into my eyes he said, "Something's wrong. What is it?"

I told him about the odd feeling of irritability I'd experienced in James Bay.

"You were picking up vibrations. I feel 'em myself in James Bay," Chief Alphonse said. "Did you know there was a smallpox epidemic there in the 1850s?"

"I vaguely recall hearing something of the sort."

"Our ancestors tried to outrun it by moving to James Bay and hiding in the woods. It didn't do them any good. Missus Pox followed them over there and laid her hands on 'em. Nobody knows how many Indians died—thousands, most likely. Pox decimated the population, Indians *and* white folks. There's parts of James Bay that's one giant graveyard."

We watched the sun sink beneath the horizon. The chief moved restlessly. "Folks say that smallpox was introduced by white men, back in the 1700s. It may be true, only I have my doubts. I think there was smallpox here in ancient times."

Earlier that evening, the chief had been introducing Warrior children to Coast Salish Vision Quest mysteries. He was still wearing a traditional woven cedar bark cloak and a cedar bark steeple hat. He took his hat off and looked inside it. Perhaps he saw what he was looking for, because he said, "There's something else on your mind. What is it, Silas?"

"Boss Rollins," I answered. "He's mixed up in a case I'm working on."

"What do you know about Rollins?"

"Nothing much, rumours mostly."

"You got anything pressing to do right now?"

I shook my head.

"All right," the chief said, glancing sideways at the clothes I was wearing. "Give me a minute to change out of these fancy duds. And you'll need to put some shoes on. Then we'll take a little drive."

VICTORIA'S GORGE WATERWAY—A WIDE tidal river a couple of miles long—flows between the Inner Harbour and a tidal lake known as Portage Lagoon. At Tillicum Road, where there is nowadays a four-lane highway bridge, the river encounters Gorge Narrows, the site of Canada's only reversing waterfall. When the tide rises, there is a waterfall running from south to north. When the tide ebbs, the water reverses its direction. At certain spots along the Gorge, treacherous currents and whirlpools are strong enough to tip unwary boaters.

I parked my car on Gorge Road and followed the chief as he scrambled on foot down a narrow, bushy, little-used trail. After a bit, we reached a ledge of grass in the shadow of a high bank and sat down. When Chief Alphonse got his breath back, he pointed to the Gorge's swiftly flowing waters and said, "This is a tricky spot for canoeing, even now. It was worse in the old days. Before they dynamited some of them rocks under the water, there was a huge whirlpool four times a day. You couldn't take a boat through here. The whirlpool was ... enormous. There's one big rock left—you can see it at low tide. That's where Camossung lived. She was a young girl who got turned into a stone by Hayls, the Transformer. At Vision Quest time, Songhees youngsters who had been ritually prepared would dive into the whirlpool and try to gain spirit power."

Pointing to a chunk of smooth granite, about 20 feet above the water, Chief Alphonse continued, "That's the very rock our Vision Questers dived off, down and deep into the whirlpool. Some went down and never came up again—at least not in this lifetime. Some stayed underwater long enough that people thought they'd drowned, before they came back to the surface. There might have been a dry tunnel underwater; a refuge where people could breathe and find their power. Maybe that refuge still exists, I don't know. Maybe there's no refuge at all. Them Questers that survived the dive never talked about it. For them that got it, Camossung power was very big power. A lot of old shamans went in for Camossung power."

The chief stopped talking, reached inside his shirt and brought out a little cotton sack dangling from a cord around his neck. He produced a stubby soapstone pipe, stuffed it with kinni-kinnick and lit it with a match. To me, the smoke smelled foul—like smouldering grass—although the chief seemed to enjoy it. Grinning slyly, he offered the pipe to me. I declined.

The chief's smile faded as he wrestled heavy thoughts. By the time he had finished his smoke, the evening's shadows had length-ened. He put his pipe and tobacco away and said, "Camossung power was *wisdom* power. Them that got it were happy to have it, and the power was used wisely, for good purposes. However, as we know, there are other kinds of power. Power is sometimes used for evil.

"Now, you were talking about Boss Rollins, and here's what I have to tell you. The Rollins were members of the Mowaht Bay band. There's less than a hundred people belong to that band nowadays. Them Mowaht Bay folks have always been clannish; they don't have much to do with the rest of our nation. As young people, neither Boss Rollins, nor his sister, what's her name?—"

"Tess Rollins."

"—That's right, Tess. Neither Boss nor Tess were interested in Vision Quest as youngsters. They didn't spend any time in the Longhouse, because they were more interested in basketball and high-school dances. They did the bare minimum of ritual to keep themselves in good standing with their band, and no more. They say that along the years, Harley changed. Now he's Boss Rollins."

The chief looked at me inquiringly and asked, "He'd been a mechanic of some kind?"

"A welder. Harley took welding courses at Camosun College."

"So that's what he was, a welder. I don't think I knew that detail," the chief said, baring his teeth in a humourless grin. "At all events, a number of years ago Harley went through some kind of crisis. All of a sudden, after years of ignoring and even sneering at Coast Salish mythology and religion, he became obsessed with it. He developed a special interest in Earth Dwarfs. He came and pestered me a few times. I sent him away, because all Harley wanted was power. Harley talked to other local Coast Salish chiefs and shamans, but they all treated him the way I did. Didn't want no part of him. So Harley ended up going down to Washington State, where a witch called Unthame threw bones in the air and told Harley how to get the power he wanted."

Chief Alphonse pointed to the Gorge waters, where fallen leaves and twigs were floating in slow lazy circles. He said, "Unthame told Harley to look for power right here, deep in the Gorge. That's where Harley dived in."

"How do you know all this, Chief?"

"Because there were witnesses," the chief said. "Harley's sister Tess was one. The other witness was Billy Cheachlacht.

"It was years ago, night, in the middle of August, a thunder and lightning storm was raging when Harley and Tess got here. They didn't know it, but Billy Cheachlacht was here too. They thought they were alone. Billy Cheachlacht's dead now. Before he died, he told me that the air that night stank like rotten eggs. Spooky, hellish lightning strikes fell all around. Billy was right here at the Gorge, praying to Camossung, something he did every year. I was Billy Cheachlacht's chief. Billy came straight to me and told me what he'd seen."

There was a soft glitter in the chief's eyes as he said solemnly, "Billy saw *something*. Harley dived into the whirlpool and was underwater for a long time. When Harley came up from his dive, Billy Cheachlacht said a horrible little dwarf came out of the water with him. The dwarf came up, walked around, stayed talking with Harley and Tess for a while, then went back down into the water again." The chief added, "What Billy saw wasn't a dwarf, it was a ghost."

I thought about that. Coast Salish ghosts sometimes have human forms, but lack human souls and substance. I asked, "And you believe Billy Cheachlacht actually *saw* this thing, whatever it was, instead of just imagining that he saw it?"

"What I believe and what I don't believe doesn't matter. Maybe Billy Cheachlacht had been eating mushrooms, I don't know. I'm just telling you what Billy Cheachlacht told me."

"If Harley Rollins did get power, some of it must have rubbed off on Tess Rollins."

"And that's another weird thing," the chief added. "It's unusual for a woman to accompany her brother on any kind of quest, very unusual indeed." The night was now dark and moonless, but full of stars. There were no clouds at all.

The chief stood up and said, "It'll be pissing down in two days."

CFAX's weatherman was predicting a continued drought. The chief has second sight and many other queer ideas, but he's not always right about the weather.

Smiling, he spat on the ground and said, "Silas. It's time we went home."

IT WAS LATE WHEN I got back to my cabin. I put on a Gatemouth Brown record and opened a can of Foster's. It was still hot inside. I left my doors and windows wide open, wandered outside to the beach and sat on a log, listening to the Gatemouth's blues guitar. Red-necked grebes were hunkered down on the beach. A dozen of the birds showed me their yellow bills and ruffled their feathers before going back to sleep. The sea was ablaze with bioluminescent plankton; the lights of Victoria were strung like jewels across the dark horizon. Pebbles crunched toward me along the beach. It was a dream called Felicity Exeter, wearing a lavender pantsuit with an ivory silk scarf around her long white neck, and her hair, loose and flowing in a fall of golden moonlight. We'd known each other less than a year, and I still didn't understand what a rich, accomplished, beautiful and sexy woman like her saw in a Native only three generations removed from hunter-gatherers with bones through their noses.

She sat beside me and said, "I've been waiting for you. I saw you earlier, talking to Chief Alphonse, but I thought you'd come back. I'm glad you did."

"Feel like a beer?"

Felicity shook her head. Grebes entertained us by diving for fish in the shallows. After a while Felicity took my hand and kissed it without saying anything. I put the empty Fosters can down and said, "In the olden days, when the sea glowed like this and diving birds started feeding at night, my ancestors would put spotters on the roofs of their houses, sharpen their harpoons and watch out for the tuna that used to swim into this bay. Giant bluefins, you could see 'em gliding through the phosphorescence in the dark. The way we caught them, we carried fires aboard our canoes to lure them in. If that didn't work, we'd paddle our canoes quickly away from where they were feeding: our canoes created paths of light moving through the phosphorescence. Bluefins would follow us, come right up to our bows where we'd harpoon 'em. Big powerful fish. They'd tow us a mile, sometimes, before they went belly up. Once in a while they'd play possum. We'd drag 'em aboard before they were fully dead, and they'd thrash around, break a few legs."

"Halibut do the same," Felicity said. "My dad hooked a 100-pounder once, beat the hell out of it with a club. He told me that he would have sworn it was dead when we pulled it aboard, but it wasn't."

"Right, halibut are mighty fish. But there never was a halibut the size and strength of a bluefin tuna. The Salish name for bluefin tuna is *Silthkwa*. Silthkwa means *like the bow-wave made by a fast boat*. It's the way surface-feeding bluefins look."

"How big were they?"

"Full grown, they were seven or eight feet. Some of 'em were a bit longer. One fish was enough to feed the whole tribe."

"I never knew we had bluefins in these parts."

"We don't. Not any longer. Chief Alphonse reckons that in 50 years there'll be no fish left at all."

"I've been missing you, Silas, you don't call me any more," she said, standing up and looking down at me.

It was too dark to see her eyes. "I think about you all the time," I said.

She touched the top of my head with her fingers and was turning away when I took her in my arms. She undressed in my cabin with the window at her back. The curtains were open, and she looked beautiful in the moonlight.

CHAPTER FIVE

In Coast Salish mythology, the world's creation and its trans-figuration into modern form occurred long, long ago. In this mythology, the principal figure is Raven, who created living creatures from mud and other inanimate substances. Raven created more than men, snails and whales: Raven created truth and beauty. Sometimes known as The Trickster, Raven also created opposites, which is why we have disorder in the world. The next morning, after Felicity left, Raven disordered my mind with memories of Felicity taking her clothes off.

I drove into town on autopilot and made it all the way without killing anyone. After breakfast at Lou's, I took a walk. Douglas Street was thick with vehicles and pedestrians. I crossed Fisgard on a green light, thinking about Felicity Exeter but keeping a lookout for street hustlers. One then-popular swindle involved an "accidental" sidewalk collision, followed by a dropped and smashed valuable, such as expensive prescription eyeglasses and a demand for immediate cash reparations. Variants of this classic con have been practised for centuries.

On Fisgard Street, a young woman with a pierced nostril tried to sell me a subscription to a magazine published by victims of violence. She was from Calgary and lived in doorways. She had a grey, pinched, angry face and seemed on the verge of collapse. I took her over to the Good Samaritan Mission and got her fixed up with one of their counsellors. Afterwards I walked through Chinatown to my office. PC let herself out when I let myself in. I picked up the junk lying on the floor beneath the mail slot and threw most of it into the wastebasket. That reminded me of the fireplace ashes I'd found in the Rainbow Motel. Somebody had been burning papers—was that significant?

Back in the 1870s, when public hangings were still the rage, and this building was new, my room had been a harness maker's shop. Sometimes, if it's raining or humid, I detect nebulous odours of saddle soap and leather. I opened the curtains and looked across the street at Swans Pub. Swans looks as if it has been there forever. It hasn't. For the first century of its existence, it had been a grain and seed warehouse.

An elderly lady came out of Fantan Alley pushing a cream-coloured baby carriage inhabited by a cream-coloured toy poodle. The poodle had a red ribbon tied about its head and was wearing a red silk jacket. The lady, elegantly attired in a long dress of cream-coloured lace, had on a cream straw hat the size of a bicycle wheel. A couple of sweaty, sorry old bums in pee-stained khakis were sitting on the sidewalk, swigging from something concealed in a brown paper bag. They gallantly offered the lady a drink. She sailed past with her nose in the air.

The sun was rising above Swans' roof. In a few minutes, the area inside my window would be like a tanning salon, but that didn't worry me. What worried me was the raven, staring down from Swans' parapet. *Corvus corax* is a large bird. When our old people see one, they usually refer to him as Te Spokalwets (the same term we use for ghosts). In the best old stories, Raven is a mythological helper, who often steps in with a message when humans lose their way. I watched the raven for five minutes, before it flew off, leaving a message on the sidewalk that missed the bums by an inch.

It was definitely hot. If I hadn't been wearing a T-shirt, I'd have loosed my collar and rolled up my sleeves. I sat at my computer and checked e-mails. A message from headquarters announced that Detective Chief Inspector Bulloch was retiring. Detective Inspector Bernie the Tapp had been appointed acting Chief DCI. I sent Bernie a quick congratulatory e-mail, got up and stood looking out the window again, thinking about Detective Chief Inspector Bulloch.

Bulloch and I had gone a few rounds together over the years. Now, to my surprise, I found myself feeling sorry for him: 60 years old, facing an uncertain future, with fallen arches, a boozer's unlovely nose, hemorrhoids, divorced, and his son telling him to go fuck himself.

Beyond the window, the sun was climbing behind office buildings and microwave towers. Lowering my gaze, I noticed spots of black powder lying on the broad old-fashioned windowsill. It looked like soot. Something caused me to raise my eyes. A dark, mouse-size object was hanging from the curtains. It was a bat. I wondered how it had got inside the room. Maybe it had come down the chimney. More probably, it had flown in through the doorway, perhaps at night, while the janitor who cleaned the place had left a door open. When I checked, I saw fresh soot lying in the fireplace.

I left the bat alone and opened the door to let it go—if it wanted to go—before PC ate it.

What was going on? Bats in my office, ravens eyeing me from vantages, and all this on the same day? Unwilling to waste further time in the realm of the incomprehensible, I returned to my computer and ran a search on Neville Rollins.

Rollin's file officially confirmed some things I'd already heard. Twenty-odd years previously, Neville Rollins had married Jane Marie Colby. Two years later, Neville Rollins was reported missing. What Fred Colby had omitted to mention during our conversation, was that his daughter, Jane, had been charged with Neville's murder.

Bernie Tapp had been a rookie detective constable at the time. His superior, Bulloch, then a detective sergeant, had been on duty when Tess and Harley Rollins came in to report their brother missing. According to them, Neville had disappeared after a furious argument with his wife. The Rollins's then went on to accuse Jane Colby of murdering their brother and hiding his body.

When questioned by Bulloch, Jane Colby's testimony had been nervous and contradictory. She denied killing her husband and suggested that Neville had simply run away from their unhappy marriage. During the following week, Bulloch subjected Jane Colby to a relentless grilling. She stuck to her story. After reviewing the evidence against her, Crown prosecutors concluded that there was insufficient likelihood of a conviction. Against Bulloch's strenuous objections, Jane had been released. No trace of Neville had ever been discovered. After seven years, a judge declared Neville Rollins legally dead. Following which, for reasons best known to herself, Jane had reverted to using her maiden name.

The bat unhooked itself from the curtain and circled the room before flying out the door. I wished it luck. Next, I ran a search on Harley Rollins.

Harley's was a classic rags-to-riches story of a poor kid, born handicapped on an impoverished Indian reserve, who had re-created himself as a multi-millionaire businessperson. Along the way, Harley had been arrested and charged for tax evasion (two convictions), stealing Crown-owned timber (no convictions), Driving Under the Influence (one conviction) and intimidating Crown witnesses (one conviction). He had also been charged with causing grievous bodily harm to persons well known to police. He was also a dangerous witch.

I opened a drawer and got out my phone book. The listings told me that Rollins, Harley, had a rural-route address near the village of Mowaht Bay, a good hour's drive from Victoria. Just for the hell of it, I phoned Harley's number. A recorded voice asked me to leave a message, an invitation I declined. I was wiping soot from my windowsill when I saw Denise Halvorsen come out of Fantan Alley and head my way down Pandora Street.

Denise was a good-looking constable, about 25 years old. She had been with the VPD less than a year, during which time we'd established a strong platonic friendship. Her Scandinavian beauty was very appealing, and I loved her dry sense of humour. Occasionally, usually at Denise's instigation, we'd have lunch together.

I watched as the bums, still swigging what was left in their brown paper bag, offered it to Denise. She chose to ignore them and came inside my building. I heard her pass along a corridor to the washroom.

I sat back and put my feet on the desk, picked up the phone and called Henry Ferman. He didn't answer. Henry probably had call display, and a bad conscience.

Out in the corridor, a woman yelled, boots rattled across linoleum flooring, and Denise raced into my room, both hands folded across her head.

"A bat! A bat attacked me!" she yelled. "It flew into my hair!"

I gave her a reassuring hug (something she didn't resist), stroked her hair and murmured vague reassurances. Something soft and moist attached itself to my cheek. It wasn't a leech; it was Denise's lovely mouth. But before I knew it, she became her ordinary no-bullshit self. Lately, she's been acting nervous and strange when I'm around—swearing unnecessarily, for example, and pretending to be more case-hardened than she actually is.

"Christ, it's hot in here," she said. "No wonder I went crazy.

Why don't you keep those curtains closed?"

"It's against standing orders. I'm supposed to be visible and accessible when I'm working in here."

"Since when did you start working and obeying orders?"

I cleared my throat and said, "Feel like a trip to Mowaht Bay?"

She gave a faintly mocking laugh. "Me? Go to Mowaht Bay? No thanks. I watched *Deliverance* on TV once. That's the movie featuring Burt Reynolds, banjos and incest. It put me off places like Mowaht Bay for life."

"Did you know that Jane Colby used to live there?"

Denise stopped patting her curls and put her cap back on. Absently adjusting the Glock automatic belted to her shapely waist she added, "No, I didn't. Poor Janey, she used to have a lot of class, now she's pathetic. The last time I saw her she was drunk in Pinky's bar."

"You told me you'd gone there to check out an assault."

"That's right."

I asked, "And when was that, exactly?"

Looking at me with vague conjecture, Denise said, "About a week ago."

"Can you narrow it down a bit?"

"I can, as a matter of fact," she replied, taking a spiral-bound notebook from a pocket. After consulting notes she said, "I was on night patrol with Bob Fyles. But it wasn't a week ago, it was two weeks ago."

"Time flies."

"Yes, Silas, it does. That's a very profound observation."

"You were saying?"

"It was a Friday night. Exactly 14 days ago. Pinky's barman called 911 to report that somebody had bopped a patron with a beer bottle. A typical boozy TGIF punch up. We called an ambulance at 11:40 PM. Not for Janey, for the guy with a damaged skull. The ambulance carted him away at 12:05 AM. Fyles and I left Pinky's shortly afterwards."

"Who was the victim?"

"A man named Jack Owens."

I remembered Fred Colby telling me that Jane and Jack Owens had been an item, but had broken up. Was this some lovers' quarrel? "Did you recover the weapon?" I asked.

"Yeah. Fortunately the bottle didn't break. Bob took it to forensics. A nice set of prints."

"Jack Owens isn't an unusual name, I suppose. The one we're talking about is that accountant guy?"

"Yes, he is."

"So. Owens ended up in hospital. What happened to the perp?"

"I don't know; he was long gone. Some bodybuilder type, we heard. Nobody knew him of course. I can still picture Janey, flopped inside Pinky's when we left."

"Was she involved in the scrap?"

"I can't imagine how. When I saw her, she was too drunk to even stand up."

"Did she egg that bodybuilder type on?"

"Not according to the barman. It was a free-for-all and Owens just happened to be in the wrong place at the wrong time."

"How well do you know Jane?"

Denise shook her head. "Not particularly well, she's more of an acquaintance than a friend. We've known each other long enough to speak on a first-name basis if we meet."

"You called her Poor Janey."

"Ye-es. It's true, she's sliding downhill again."

"Again?"

"Yeah, well, you know, give a dog a bad name," Denise said,

moving uneasily. "She used to swing a little. One of those girls who asks guys to leave money under the pillow when they leave in the morning. That ended a while ago, I believe. Except that now she's drinking too much. If things go on the way they seem headed, she'll end up drooling on sidewalks."

Denise then went on to tell me of the many tragic cases she'd seen on the streets lately. Demented forlorn people, battered into despairing apathy, or obsessed with the junk piled up in their rusty shopping carts.

"Yeah, it's terrible," I agreed absently. "And by the way, did you know that Jane has a mentally handicapped daughter?"

"No. I didn't." As she said this, Denise got up from her seat and walked about the room. She said grumpily, "And by the way. We don't say mentally *handicapped* these days. We say *challenged*."

"Her name is Terry. She's about 20, lives in a care home on Crowe Street. Pretty girl."

"*Girl?*" Denise retorted, with a rising inflexion.

"Sorry, *woman*."

"Pretty, you said?"

"I think so."

Denise gazed at her fingernails; her expression softened. "I suppose Janey was pretty too, once."

"I'm trying to get a picture of her, but it's like looking at a kaleidoscope. Every time I think I've got a picture of the real Jane Colby, I meet somebody who shakes the kaleidoscope, and the pattern changes. She plays the piano. She's a mother. Sometimes she's a caring mother, and sometimes she's not. She's a drunk."

I was about to add possible murderer to the list. Denise interrupted me by saying, "The drunk bit is new. Janey's a good-time girl, at least since I've known her, but her drinking used to be moderate. The worst of it is, she's turning into an unhappy drunk."

"I'm not sure what that means. Do you mean she's an unhappy

woman who drinks? Or a woman made unhappy by drink?"

"Hell if I know, Silas. Too deep for me."

"Jack Owens and Jane Colby were an item. She lived in Owens' house for a while."

Denise seemed astonished. She hitched her heavy belt up and put her cap on.

Then I guessed out loud that the bodybuilder might be Jane's new boyfriend, and that she'd sicced him on Owens, her old boyfriend. When Denise said she doubted that, I told her about Jane being accused of murdering her first husband. That left Denise shaking her head in wonderment. I asked her to wait while I tried to reach Henry Ferman again. He still wasn't answering his phone. I decided to pay him a visit.

Denise and I left the office together. I locked up after closing the curtains. Across Pandora Street, a kid with studs in his nose and a Mohawk haircut with foot-long spikes started ogling Denise. Grinning and winking, he adjusted his crotch. Fortunately for Denise, the two fuckups who had offered her a drink previously got up and told the kid to beat it. It was a good thing that, though their brains were dead, their chivalry was not.

CHAPTER SIX

The Matbro Building on Fort Street was another heritage-brick holdover from Victoria's Gold Rush era. I entered it through a door located between a one-chair barber's shop and a bookstore. A wall directory in the Matbro's lobby listed astrologers, telemarketers, a hypnotherapist and a person who sucks wax from your ears using hollow candles. The building's ancient elevator was out of order, so I hiked up to the second floor. The office that I wanted was behind a pebbled-glass door marked HENRY FERMAN INVESTIGATIONS.

In 1974, Henry had been in Canada's far north, checking traplines, when he and his dog team went through the ice of a frozen lake. Henry lost his outfit but crawled ashore and got back to camp with nothing worse than frozen ears and feet. Nowadays, he hid what was left of his ears beneath a toupée. Indoors, and sometimes outdoors, he wore padded carpet slippers. His top speed wouldn't challenge a tortoise. What Henry lacked in speed, he made up in smarts.

His waiting room was larger than a domestic refrigerator but smaller than the back of a pickup truck. There was nothing inside it worth stealing, unless you count two rickety folding chairs and an Arborite coffee table with cigarette burns. Two long fluorescent tubes buzzed up on the ceiling. I was scanning the place for bugs when a chair scraped across the floor of an inner room. The inner door swung open. Henry Ferman grinned out at me and said, "I'll be blowed; it's the old dog catcher."

I asked, "All right, where is it?"

Henry pointed with one of his walking sticks.

After a long close look, I located a video camera's dark lens, about the size of a match head, buried in the scrolls of a cornice moulding. "Congratulations," I said. "You had me fooled."

"That's a nice little camera, made in Hong Kong. The whole unit is about the size of a thimble. I've been using a lot of them lately. Setting them up in convenience stores, gas stations."

"How about the Rainbow Motel? You got video cameras set up over there?"

Instead of replying, Henry hobbled back to his desk, propped his walking sticks against a wall and sat down.

Henry's place of business looked more like an electronics repair shop than a PI's office. There were a couple of filing cabinets, a Mac computer and a fax machine, although most of Henry's rented space was occupied by floor-to-ceiling shelves crammed with microphones, cameras, video monitors, long-distance listening devices and boxes of spare parts. A six-inch TV monitor, mounted on Henry's desktop, displayed a grainy image of his waiting room. Henry saw me looking at it and said, "The picture quality on those miniature cameras isn't perfect, but it's good enough for most purposes."

I sat down, crossed my legs because there wasn't enough space to stretch them out and said, "I saw you come out of the Rainbow Motel, Henry. This could be important so level with me. Were you installing cameras?"

Henry took his toupée off. Without it, he was as hairy as an apple. He scratched his scalp and said, "This damn rug. It itches like crazy."

"I guess it does," I said, not unkindly. "What's it made of, re-cycled scouring pads?"

Henry reached below his desk and produced a moulded-Styrofoam head with a happy face drawn on it with black felt marker. Henry placed the toupee on the foam head and said, "This is Mr. O'Haira."

"Hello, Mr. O'Haira."

"The first rug I bought was made of real hair. I asked the guy who sold it to me where the hair comes from. It seems there's an industry based in Mexico. Buyers go from village to village col-lecting women's hair. The women put the money toward their weddings." Grinning, he added, "Under NAFTA it's classified as slow-growth commerce."

"Fascinating as this all is, Henry, I'd still like you to answer my question."

"Which question was that?"

"I asked if you'd installed bugs in the Rainbow Motel."

"I admit nothing. Even if I did, so what? It's no crime to install closed circuit surveillance equipment on private property."

"That depends," I said reflectively. "It's probably not illegal to install them in a motel's public entrance. Not in bedrooms. Not in washrooms."

Henry's face composed itself to blandness. He looked at the yellow light streaming through his windows and said, "This sunny weather, I love it. It's why I came down from Whitehorse. They talk about planetary warming, but I don't know. It can't get too warm for me."

"Mr. O'Haira," I said. "Please ask your boss to turn round."

Henry swiveled his chair around to face me again. His eyes were wary.

I said, "Henry. Tell me about the Rainbow Motel, and Harley Rollins."

Henry laughed nervously. "Boss Rollins? He's a hard-ass logger."

"What else do you know about him?"

"Millionaire. Owns a sawmill, I believe. Maybe a bunch of other stuff, but it's all hearsay. I do business with that manager, Karl Berger, I've never actually met Rollins."

"Do you know his sister-in-law?"

"Who?"

"Jane Colby. She was married to Neville Rollins."

Henry took a deep breath and then blew air out of his narrowed lips while he chewed that over. He shrugged and said, "As a matter of fact, I do know her. Slightly."

I already knew the answer, but I asked anyway: "Jane goes by the name Colby, now. Did she and Neville divorce?"

"Hell if I know," Henry said.

"You seem to know quite a lot, though. How come?"

"Just business. I'm a detective, I know all kinds of mostly useless information," Henry said idly. "What's your interest in her?"

"Jane has been missing a few days, but perhaps you knew that too?"

Henry rubbed the crown of his head with a hand and said, "We're not that close, Silas. I don't keep tabs on her."

"Okay. But it might help my enquiries if you have videotapes of her comings and goings."

"Sorry."

"You don't have videotapes of her coming and going at the Rainbow Motel?"

"I just answered that question."

"Henry. I bow to no one in my admiration of your probity and veracity, but these denials have a ring of disingenuousness."

Henry leaned back in his chair and sighed deeply. His slippered feet poked beneath the desk like giant woolly caterpillars.

I said, "The circumstances surrounding Jane Colby's disappearance are beginning to look sinister."

The corners of Henry's mouth turned down as he reached into a desk drawer and brought out his office bottle and two plastic glasses. He splashed Montreal Scotch into them and shoved one toward me. It tasted like iodine, but I didn't say no when he offered me a refill. After he got settled again, Henry asked, "Okay. What do you want to know?"

"I want to know if you have installed closed circuit videotape cameras or other electronic bugging equipment in the Rainbow Motel."

"The answer is no."

Henry stared down his nose and made a blubbery sound by blowing more compressed air between his lips. I waited. Henry said, "All right. I'll tell you. I never installed any equipment in the Rainbow Motel. A while back, I *sold* them some video equipment, that's all."

"Who are *them?*"

"Karl Berger."

"You didn't help Karl to install it?"

"No. Next question."

"When is the last time you saw Jane Colby?"

"Can't remember, I haven't seen her for months. Probably ran into her on the street or something. Whenever it was, it was ages ago."

"Did you know she kept a room at the Rainbow Motel?"

"No," Henry said, with genuine surprise in his voice. "She has a house in Fairfield. What's she need a motel room for?"

"Good question," I said, getting up to leave. I added. "By the way, do you have call display on your telephone?"

"Yes. I get a lot of unwanted calls."

"You still haven't told me what you were doing in the motel earlier."

"You're a cop; your paycheque is paid by the government every month. You don't have to worry about paycheques bouncing, being late, being short," Henry said in a flat monotonous voice. "In the real world, things are different. Karl Berger is a slow payer. The sonuvabitch stiffed me out of nearly three grand. I was trying to collect."

"What will you do next? Sue him in small claims?"

"I don't know, I'm still thinking about it."

"So long Henry," I said, getting up and shaking his hand. "I'll be thinking things over too. If I come up with any bright ideas, I'll let you know."

"Yeah, fine, you do that, Silas," he said, although he didn't sound optimistic.

AT GOVERNMENT AND SUPERIOR, Raven was creating traffic jams. Two ambulances and a couple of prowlies were parked across the intersection with emergency lights flashing. Four uniforms directed traffic. Paramedics were tending an elderly woman splayed out lifelessly on the tarmac.

Two rubberneckers were discussing the mishap. "Hit and run," one man growled. "Some maniac ran a light and bowled her over."

"You saw it happen?"

"Sure, right in front of my eyes. A Camaro, I think. Maybe it was a Mustang. Skidded round that corner like a bat outta hell, burning rubber till it went out of sight."

"What colour car?"

"Dark. Maybe dark green."

"Let's hope they catch the bastard and dump him in a bath of cyanide."

That was enough Christian charity for me. I entered a nearby government building and rode an elevator to the fifth floor. Mr. Bonwit, the man I wanted to talk to, was behind a door guarded by a secretarial dragon. I'd arrived without an appointment so she gave me a grilling. I stated that I was a policeman on a routine enquiry. It didn't help. She interpreted my arrival as an immediate threat to herself, her boss, pension plan and working conditions.

Breathing down her short, cute, fire-throwing nose, she said, "You should have phoned first. Mr. Bonwit is in conference, you'll have to wait."

"Suits me. I'll just rest comfortably alongside your air conditioner for a few hours. Hustling poolroom bums in weather like this is no joke, believe me."

She scowled, pointed to a steel-and-leather contraption. I lowered myself into it and crossed my legs. After giving me a long, frightening glare, she addressed herself to a computer, finger-and-thumbed herself along Cyberspace Highway for a minute, then looked out the window and noted, "Traffic's moving again."

I extracted myself from the contraption. "Old woman accident fatality," I said, looking down on the street. "Now they're trucking her away in an ambulance. She was mowed down by a hit-and-runner in front of witnesses, but nobody saw anything useful. If you ask me, that's a metaphor for modern life."

The secretary sniffed. "That's a very dangerous corner. You take your life in your hands every time you try to cross, even when the light's green."

"Well, there you go," I said. "Nobody's got time for patience or courtesy these days."

"It's like I keep telling my friend. Slow down, I tell him. It doesn't do a blind bit of good."

"Courtesy's as dead as a stuffed alligator. Everybody's in a hurry, nobody's going anywhere."

Friendlier now, she glided across to Mr. Bonwit's door, knocked, opened it six inches, poked her head through the opening and exchanged words with the room's occupant. Next, she held the door wide open and said sweetly, "You may go in, sir. Mr. Bonwit can see you now."

I went in. The office was deserted, except for Mr. Bonwit, seated behind a massive glass-and-chromium desk. The room had only one door so the people with whom he had been in conference must have jumped out the windows. Bonwit was as sleek as a cat. Longish black hair lay flat against his head and curled slightly along his white collar. He had a narrow face, shrewd dark eyes, dark eyebrows, pale skin and pale lips. I showed him my badge and told him who I was.

Mr. Bonwit stood up, put his hand out and said, "I hope you haven't been kept waiting long, Sergeant. Please take a seat."

I sat down and said, "I'm making enquiries about a woman called Terry Colby. Terry is living in a care house on Crowe Street, where, I guess . . ."

"If she's a ward of the government, you might be wasting your time," Bonwit interrupted apologetically but firmly. "As you undoubtedly know, our files are confidential."

"Would it be against the rules for me to inquire if she's a ward of the government?"

"Strictly speaking, I need an order . . . but I assume the matter's important," he said. Smiling a little, he swiveled his chair to face a computer screen, shuffled a mouse, got what he wanted and studied it in silence.

"Yes," he said. "Keep it under your hat but Terry's one of ours."

I asked him why she was in care.

Spots of colour appeared on Bonwit's pale cheeks as he said, "I'm very sorry, but I can't tell you."

"Can't, or won't?"

"Both, sorry."

I stood up and glanced out of his window. Bonwit had one of the best views in Victoria. The provincial capital building was laid out before me in all its splendour. A statue of Queen Victoria stood on its green lawns, its regal bronze gaze directed toward an immense sailboat, the size of a cross-channel ferry, rounding Laurel Point. A Twin Otter float plane was taking off for Lake Washington in Seattle.

After pondering for a minute I sat down again and said, "Terry's mother is missing, Mr. Bonwit, and I'm starting to have a bad feeling about things. It probably doesn't appear on your files but 20 years ago Terry's father went missing as well. He hasn't been seen since. His body was never found and several highly experienced detectives think Terry's mother murdered him."

"So you're telling me what? That this is a murder inquiry?"

"It's too early to say. If she has been murdered, the sooner we get on top of things the better."

"You're a police sergeant. Murder cases are generally supervised by a more senior officer, are they not?"

"Ordinarily, but I'm a Native, as is Terry. I have a special interest."

Bonwit sighed. Leaning back in a chair he said, "Strictly off the record?"

"Strictly off the record."

"Terry's dull, mentally subnormal. Some time ago, we received information that she was prostituting herself. Terry was apprehended and assessed. Terry can be hard to manage and was being shuffled around between her mother and her grandfather, both of whom found her to be a major challenge. After hearing expert testimony, a family court judge ruled her incompetent. That's how she ended up with us."

"And that meant Crowe Street, or jail?"

"Crowe Street isn't perfect, but we had little choice in the matter. Few agencies accept violent clients. We count ourselves lucky that we got her into Crowe Street."

"Terry doesn't seem a violent type."

"She isn't. Not generally. Not until a trigger sets her off, and she explodes," Bonwit said, moving uneasily. He cleared his throat and muttered, "Actually, we received two separate complaints about Terry's behaviour. The calls were anonymous, so it's no use asking me who made them. Before we could act on the first call, another came in. Terry was a minor and apparently she had been prostituting herself. Anonymous or not, we take such calls seriously. A government worker investigated. Ms. Colby couldn't even manage Terry properly when she was little. Now Terry's grown. She needs 24/7 supervision and wasn't getting it."

"This prostituting allegation. Was it credible?"

"Of course. That goes without saying."

"Terry's family-court hearing. Was it her first court appearance?"

"It was, but Terry Colby has been on our files for years," he said, standing up and putting his hand out. "I can't say another thing and I sincerely hope that what I have said is kept strictly between you and me."

I thanked Bonwit, shook his hand, gave my card and said, "If you think of something later, something in the public domain that might help my inquiry, please call me at this number."

We parted friends. Bonwit was tapping his front incisors with my card when I went out.

Back on the street, a TV crew had set up a command post at the accident scene. Both ambulances had gone, but traffic squad uniforms were still running around with tape measures and cameras, and questioning witnesses. A man with a microphone was telling A-Channel viewers that the world would be a better place if hit-and-run killers were strung up to the lampposts and left dangling as a caution to the rest of us.

CHAPTER SEVEN

The next day when I woke, it was pouring. Clouds of mist were impaled on the totem poles near the longhouse. A yellow school bus, parked almost invisibly outside the reserve office, its emergency flashers blinking like giant red eyes, looked like a mythical beast. *What do you know?* I thought. *The chief was right about the weather.* I put a hat and rain slicker on over my T-shirt and shorts and made the short obligatory morning dash through the downpour to my outhouse. After the recent spell of tropical weather, it felt distinctly chilly; the temperature had dropped steeply overnight. When I left the outhouse, I stood under the cedars for a minute, watching the school bus, now fully loaded and driving out of sight along the reserve's unpaved roads.

Alfie Scow came by with a fishing rod over his shoulder. He said, "Hiya, Silas."

I asked Alfie what was going on.

"Chief Alphonse is taking the kids to Mystic Vale this morning," Alfie replied. "He thinks it's time they learned some ritual."

The kids had a long road ahead of them, I was thinking, as I returned to my house.

At nine o'clock it was still pouring. I'd already downed two cups of coffee, shaved, put on jeans and a wool tartan shirt and a pair of leather boots and driven myself to Lou's Café. It was

Saturday, nominally my day off. Lou's regular breakfast crowd was absent. The place was empty, except for parking meter attendants, girding themselves for another major offensive against Victoria's vehicular scofflaws.

Lou is a short, burly, angry man, born in a country that had then been called Yugoslavia. He spent his formative years as one of Marshal Tito's resistance fighters, battling Axis foes in conditions of appalling discomfort, cold and danger. You'd think—for a man who'd survived such experiences—that peacetime would be a piece of cake and he'd never waste another minute fretting about life's mundane trifles. *Au contraire*. Lou worries about everything.

I draped my slicker over a hat rack and sat at my usual table under a window. When Lou came over, I ordered coffee, bacon and eggs, pan fries and sourdough toast.

Lou folded his arms and said, "What are you guys doing about the oil deficit?"

"What oil deficit?" I asked. "Alberta's awash in oil. And gas."

"If that's the case, how come guys are buying my used cooking fat?" Lou countered. "A guy comes in yesterday, offers me 10 cents a gallon. Uses the stuff in his diesel truck engine."

"I reserve comment until after I get my breakfast."

A young couple came in, holding hands and laughing. Lou and I watched them sit in the far corner of the room, facing each other across a table. Still laughing, the man leant across and kissed his girl on the mouth.

Lou forgot about world oil shortages and went across to take their order.

I was thinking about Mystic Vale and young Vision-Questers, when somebody with a grip like a pipe wrench grabbed my elbow. It was Bernie Tapp. He said, "Yo, dickhead."

I replied, "And congratulations to you, Detective Chief Inspector."

"*Acting*," Bernie said. "Acting DCI. What are you doing here? It's your day off."

"Waiting for breakfast, but I'm a slave to duty, as you know."

Bernie crossed to the percolator, filled two cups, brought them back and gave me one.

"I'm fiddling around with a missing-woman case," I said. "A woman called Jane Colby."

"Did you report it to Missing Persons?"

"Sure."

"Clever of you, Silas, because Missing Persons is my business now. Better keep your nose out of it, if you know what's good for you. If I find you messing with my stuff I'll bust your balls."

He was smiling. I drank some coffee.

Bernie, who has a way of dominating whatever space he's in, went on seriously, "On the other hand, how about joining me on the detective squad? Keep your nose clean and maybe we'll bump you up. Sergeant to Inspector isn't impossible. Just think what it'll do for your pension."

"Not a chance, I'm happy with my present job."

"You call that dog and pony show a job? Give your head a shake. Helping little old ladies to cross the road isn't work. I'm offering you something you can get your teeth into."

Bernie raised the coffee cup to his mouth and eyed me quizzically over the rim.

It was a generous offer, so I mulled it over. In some ways, the prospect of joining Bernie's squad was not entirely unattractive, but, in my previous experience with the Serious Crimes Unit, I had disappointed friends and delighted enemies. Besides, I have a sort of blind stubbornness sometimes. I said, "I work better as a free agent."

"In this life, nobody's a free agent. One way or another, we're all slaves."

"I'd be free if I quit the force altogether."

Bernie's expression didn't change. "That'd just free you up for slavery of a different kind. Let's say you did quit, waved goodbye to a good pension and to lifetime security. What would you do instead?"

"Private inquiries? I was talking to Henry Ferman yesterday. I guess it put ideas in my head."

"Forget it. There's never been any money in that racket, there's less every day. The Internet's revolutionized the PI business. Any savvy guy with a laptop can solve most of his cases without leaving a desk."

I said feebly, "Money's not everything."

"Not till you run out of it."

It was time to change the subject. "I met this girl, Terry," I said. "She's half Native, Jane Colby's daughter. I'm starting to get a bad feeling about things. If Jane turns up dead, Terry will be an orphan. If nothing is done, Terry will probably spend the rest of her life in an institution."

"Why?"

I told him.

"Judging by what you say, an institution is probably the best place for her. Besides, there's nothing you can do about it."

"I think maybe there is."

"In that case, you're an idiot," Bernie said with sudden harshness. "This Jane Colby woman, is she Native?"

"No. She's the widow of a Native guy from Mowaht Bay."

With a sudden movement, Bernie sat back in his chair and his mouth tightened. He said, "This woman. Did she marry one of those Mowaht Bay Rollins?"

"Yes. She was married to Neville Rollins, before he disappeared."

"Before she murdered him, you mean."

A SUDDEN MUGGY DOWNPOUR DRENCHED the pavement. Raindrops pocked the Inner Harbour's murky green waters as I hurried along Wharf Street to Jack Owens' office.

Jack Owens, chartered accountant, also worked Saturdays. He laid my card down on his desk and waved me to a seat. He was a slim, middle-aged man with blue half circles under his eyes. His voice was polite and toneless. He had a tailor-made blue pinstripe suit and a Hathaway shirt and silver tie, but the white bandage encircling his head detracted from his professional appearance.

"So you want to talk about Jane Colby, eh?" he asked, looking at my card, instead of me.

"How would you describe your relationship?"

"I'd describe my relationship with Jane Colby as an illness," he replied in a level voice. "Fortunately, I seem to have got over it. I'll be quite happy never to set eyes on her again."

"Mind telling me why?"

"I don't see why I should. My business with Jane Colby is personal, nothing to do with the police."

"How's your head?"

Owens had been looking out his window. He turned toward me, eyes narrowing, and said, "It's all right, considering."

"I suppose it must be, considering. You were struck on the head with a bottle, were you not?"

"Precisely. I was unfortunate enough to be in the wrong place, at the wrong time."

"That time was two weeks ago, to be exact, inside Pinky's bar. Jane Colby was in the room with you. Your estrangement predates that occasion, I believe."

"You seem to know quite a lot about me. Or think you do."

"Perhaps I do, sir. If I get my facts wrong, feel free to correct me."

Owens stared into space, shrugged, leaned forward and

picked up my card again. After looking at it for the second time, he let it fall onto his desktop and said, "So you're a sergeant?"

"A lowly sergeant of police."

"I'd been in love with Jane Colby for years. She was on her own and I was married when we first met. I took my marriage vows seriously, so I didn't do anything about it. At first, that is. Jane was lovely, a talented pianist, fun to be around. I kept running into her at parties. One night I told her that she was very nice and that I spent a lot of time thinking about her. She told me she wasn't interested in married men. A week later, I asked my wife for a divorce. My wife was as shocked as I was. Our marriage had been no worse than most, but I was besotted with Janey. It's as I said—she was like an illness.

"When my divorce came through, Jane reneged on a promise to marry me. She consented to live with me, however. We bought a waterfront condominium apartment on the Songhees development. She moved in, everything seemed set, we were going to be together for the long haul—"

Owens suddenly stopped talking. His nostrils flared and his mouth tightened. He had been wearing glasses. Now he took them off and held an earpiece between his teeth while he reached into a drawer and brought out a silver cigarette case and a crystal ashtray, which he put on the desk. When he laid his glasses down, I noticed that the plastic earpiece was indented with tooth marks. Owens opened the silver box, took out a cigarette and lit it with a silver Ronson lighter.

By the time he'd finished doing all that, his composure had returned. He put his glasses back on, blinked his eyes and said, "Sorry, I don't smoke much any more, nasty habit. Anyway, as I was saying. I thought Janey and I were set. I was mistaken. We got along nicely for a few weeks. Janey drank too much. She woke up most mornings with terrific hangovers, and she had a wicked temper. Our relationship wasn't one of equals. Except in matters involving money, she was the dominant partner. Given a different age and a different chromosome, Janey would have been another Alexander the Great, Napoleon."

"But not another Warren Buffett, I take it?"

"No. Maybe another Anna Nicole Smith. Jane went through money like it was water."

Owens stubbed his cigarette out and immediately lit a second. After thinking for a moment he went on, "Our condo deal went sour. We'd paid too much for it, as it happens, and that didn't help matters between Janey and me. Janey's drinking got worse, her morning hangovers became more or less chronic. Even so, I still found her irresistible. What put the kibosh on everything, though, was that I advised her to invest in a company I was involved with—Manson Electronics. Fred Manson, the president, was a long-time client and friend. He had a great track record. Cut a long story short, Janey lost money on that deal too. Money she didn't have at the time. You may have heard about it. Manson Electronics went bankrupt in short order. We both lost—I'd poured my own money into it. After a screaming match, Janey moved out of my house and went straight to her lawyer. Sued me to recover her losses."

Owens touched the bandage around his skull. "Janey's total losses were about $100,000. Not a large sum."

"Barely enough to finance the Afghan war for two or three minutes."

"I planned to reimburse her. Trouble was, I was caught short. Divorce had set me back a packet and, as I said, I'd lost money on Manson. I asked Janey to be patient, but she was like a . . ." words temporarily failed him. "She was a . . . *termagant*, is that the word for an ill-tempered woman? She went completely crazy, nuts. I spoke to Janey's lawyer, explained my position. He was very decent, suggested I make one last try with Janey. Try to patch things up personally. I couldn't reach her. She wouldn't return my phone calls. This is a small town, though. I knew I was bound to run into her eventually, and I did. About two weeks ago, at Pinky's. She was drunk, but seemed in a good mood. She even smiled at me. The next thing I knew, I was in hospital with a fractured skull."

"You were in a fight?"

"I'm an accountant, for chrissake, not a longshoreman. A fight broke out and this bruiser came at me out of the blue, brained me with a bottle."

"And you've no idea who he was?"

"No idea. I wouldn't necessarily call it an attack on me personally. I was just an unlucky bystander. However, I have to assume he was a friend of Janey's. Lying in hospital with a non-stop migraine is no fun, but it had one benefit. When I came out, I was cured of Janey Colby."

"How long were you in hospital?"

"About a week. I had a minor skull fracture. The doc wouldn't let me go till my headaches eased up."

"When's the last time you visited the Rainbow Motel?"

"What's that got to do with anything?" he retorted, giving way to sudden anger.

"Just answer my question."

"Persistent, aren't you?"

"I'm a cop. We are as persistent as a dose of the clap."

"And as welcome," Jack Owens snarled.

I had been sitting with my legs crossed. I put both feet on the floor, put both hands on my knees, leaned forward and said, "What did you just say?"

Owens paled. In a lighter tone he said, "Sorry. I can't remember when I was last in the motel. Not lately."

"Try and be more exact."

"Sorry, but I can't. I seem to recall the Rainbow had a popular lounge, back in the good old days."

I thought about asking Owens' present opinion of Janey's loose morals, now that he was out of the relationship, but I enquired instead, "How would you describe affairs between you and Janey at this moment?"

Owens hesitated. Instead of replying, he picked my card up for the third time. He looked at it for a full minute before saying, "Actually, our business affairs have taken a turn for the better. I had a letter from Janey's lawyer yesterday. Apparently, Janey's coming into a little money, so they've stopped pressuring me."

"Coming into a little money? Could you be referring to the sale of her father's house?"

"No. And there's no guarantee Mr. Colby would give her anything. She's supposed to be coming into something big, actually."

The words were no sooner out of his mouth, than his face fell. He rose to his feet, crossed to the door and opened it, and said tersely, "That's it. I'm a busy man, sergeant. This interview is over."

"Wait a minute," I said.

I was wasting my time. That was that. Jack Owens had clammed up.

IT HAD STOPPED RAINING BY the time I left Owens' office. Steam rose from sidewalk; evaporating rainwater puddled along Wharf Street. I began to ask myself why I was so obsessed with this Colby affair. As Bernie Tapp had observed, it was really none of my business. Nevertheless, there was that raven to consider—the one I'd seen yesterday. Raven the Messenger?

Raven doesn't always show up in person. Sometimes he sends an emissary to deliver a garbled communication, the full meaning of which, oftener than not, becoming evident only after the passage of time. It had felt from the beginning that Terry Colby was just that kind of messenger. Then there's Raven the *Trickster*, that keeps us in stitches sometimes, but that is another story. I was so preoccupied with speculations about Raven and his many personas that my recollection of that walk from Owens' office to the Rainbow Motel is an almost complete blur. I vaguely recall collecting an evidence bag and a pair of latex gloves from my car. I must have walked past the Empress Hotel and the wax museum, and played dodgem with the usual Belleville Street tourist hordes, and yet, when I got to where I was going, I had a momentary feeling of dissociation, of being temporarily lost. Karl Berger's black Viper, parked at the sidewalk nearby, reoriented me.

Instead of the Rainbow Motel, I saw a new plywood fence, eight feet high, facing the street. The fence had an unlocked plywood door with *Danger Zone. Do not enter* stenciled across it. Upon opening the door, I discovered that the Rainbow Motel property was now a construction site encircled by chain-link fencing and the aforesaid fence. A yellow Cat dozer, operated by a man wearing a yellow hard hat, was levelling the property and uprooting trees. More building-razing machinery roared at the water's edge, where the vanished boathouse formed part of a growing pile of rubble. The motel was as yet unscathed. This time, there *was* a *Do Not Enter* sign on its front door. I went inside.

Karl Berger was up on a stepladder in the lounge, replacing an acoustic ceiling tile. Stretching too far, Karl lost balance and the ceiling tile upended, liberating a cloud of dust which enveloped Karl's hair and face like a grey velvet mask. Spluttering and blinking his eyes, Karl let go of the tile which fell to the floor and broke. Cursing, Karl descended the ladder and brushed himself off, too immersed in his predicament to notice my presence for a minute. When he did, he said less than graciously, "What do you want?"

I purchased a bottle of water from a vending machine in the lobby, put it into Karl's hand and said, "It's dirty work, Karl, but I guess somebody's got to do it."

Karl deliberated before taking a swig and said, again less than graciously, "Thanks. What do you want?"

"Nothing much," I lied. "I just happened to be passing, saw all the activity and decided to have a look."

"This is a hard-hat area," Karl said. "Dangerous to the public. You're not allowed in without permission."

Oozing phony charm, I said, "I suppose there'll be another high-rise building going up here, right?"

"Right. They're putting up a bunch of 10-storey condominiums, with fantastic views. They'll sell fast," Karl said, pouring what was left of the water over his face. Licking his lips and blinking his eyes, he heaved the empty bottle toward a wastebasket, but missed his aim.

The muck in Karl's eyes must have been painful, but he went on earnestly, "Real estate, you can't beat it. You should buy into these condos. Use a small down payment to get in on the ground floor, hold on for a bit. Unload when prices go up and make yourself a nice fat profit."

"Speculating? Is that what you're doing?"

"Me? I can't afford it; those units start at 500 grand. The penthouses will go for two million apiece, and up."

"You could afford a down payment if you unloaded your Viper," I said. "It's worth what, about 20 grand?"

"Fuck off!" Karl said hotly. "That baby's worth a hundred grand."

I stared up to where the missing tile had left a gap in the dark open ceiling.

"Jesus," Karl said. "This crap in my eyes, I'm going blind."

"Do you have a room here?"

"What's it to you?"

"You'll hurt your eyes if you rub them like that. Go to your room and lie down. I'll rinse them out."

"I don't have a room here. I got my own place in town."

"Your office, a broom closet, whatever."

Karl looked at his feet. He was wearing dirty runners. "Okay," he said.

I bought another bottle of water from the vending machine in the lobby and followed Karl along a corridor. He unlocked a small windowless storage room and we went in. He switched the light on, revealing a single-faucet sink. Paint cans, cleaning supplies, rolls of toilet paper and the like rested on wooden shelving. The room's only chair was a battered recliner upholstered with stained tapestry fabric. When Karl sat down on it and stretched out, he ended up facing a wall-mounted TV.

I said, "Put your arms to your side, Karl, and stretch out flat. Try to keep one eye open. I'll hold that same eye open with my fingers while I pour water onto the eyeball. Got it?"

"I got it."

"Good. This won't hurt a bit."

He made a good patient. I sluiced most of the crap out. Afterwards, I handed him a damp cloth.

"Now what?" he said, ungraciously.

"Just rest for a few minutes. Try to keep your hands away from your face. The cloth will help take the sting away." I handed him the water bottle. "Here. You might as well finish this."

He poured the remaining water over his eye, then handed the bottle back to me. "Maybe I should go see a doc. Have him take a proper look."

"You do that, Karl. The closest clinic's on Menzies Street."

He grunted.

"I'm outta here," I said. "See you later."

"Yeah, I'll be seeing you." After brooding for a minute he said, "Thanks, I owe you one."

"Tell me something," I said, remembering the bodybuilder who had smashed a bottle over Owens' head. "Ever go to Pinky's?"

"Where's Pinky's?"

"Pinky's is a bar, on View Street."

"Don't know the place."

He's lying, I told myself.

I said, "You should try it. Drive that Viper over there some night. Have yourself a few beers, hustle some chicks and take 'em for a spin."

Karl shook his head. Before leaving the room, I had a final look around. What drew my attention was the DVDs stacked on a shelf. Movies with titles like *Deeper Throat. Gertrude's Night In. Tight Fit.*

I ruminated myself back to the lounge and climbed the step-ladder to see what Karl had been trying to cover up with the ceiling tile. Somebody, presumably Karl, had used pliers to cut and remove bundles of coloured electrical wires. The device to which the wires had been connected had been removed. I got down from the ladder, dropped Karl's used water bottle into my evidence bag and left the building.

Seeing me emerge from the motel into sunlight, the dozer operator gave me a cheerful wave. I waved back. That mound of piled-up rubble had grown considerably. Tons of loose gravel had been scraped from the surface of the lot, exposing a broad shelf of dry blue clay. Clay which—to judge by the dozer's labouring engine—was almost as hard as limestone.

I was about to leave the property when a voice said, "Excuse me, sir."

A bushy-haired man with bright blue eyes and fat cheeks was addressing me.

"What can I do for you?" I asked.

"Are you with the construction gang?"

"I'm a city cop. Silas Seaweed."

"Bernard Cole. Cole Adjusters."

Cole gave me his card. He said, "I'm investigating a speedboat theft. It went missing from this place a couple of weeks ago."

Two weeks ago! I felt a little frisson of excitement—maybe Te Spokalwets had sent this man to me.

I said, "Karl Berger mentioned there was a missing boat. Making any progress?"

"Sort of. I know when the boat went missing. Helluva thing. What happened was, a big black-hulled fishboat went through the Johnson Street Narrows at exactly 3 AM two weeks ago last Friday. We know that, because the bridge operator logged it. What happened next is, the fishboat's generator broke down and it lost all its lights for a few minutes. It would have been virtually invisible in the darkness, because there was no moon and it was slightly overcast. The fishboat was more or less drifting for a bit, before the crew got the emergency generator running. In the meantime, a speedboat rammed it. It's practically certain to be the speedboat I'm looking for."

"Let's hope you're right."

"What I'm looking for now is a blue and white Starcraft aluminum boat, 22 feet long, with damaged bows."

"Has Karl Berger been cooperative?"

"Yes. I can't say the same for Harley Rollins, the guy who actually owns the boat. Why do you ask?"

"Karl plays things pretty close to the chest, Mr. Cole. It would take years of psychoanalysis to determine why," I said, giving him my own card. "Give me a call if you make any progress, will you?"

"No problem. I suppose I can rely on a *quid pro quo?*"

"Sure. You scratch my back, Mr. Cole, I'll scratch yours."

CHAPTER EIGHT

I picked up the MG from outside Lou's Café and drove over to police headquarters on Caledonia Street. The duty sergeant was behind a counter, doing two-finger exercises on a keyboard. Focused on his task, he didn't look up when I entered. A middle-aged couple huddled on a bench in the waiting area, holding hands. I took the elevator up to Forensics. Victoria's police headquarters was only a few years old, but faint institutional odours already permeated the place. The Forensics office was unoccupied. I left the evidence bag containing the plastic water bottle in "Killer" Miller's in-tray, along with a note asking Killer to see if the fingerprints on the water bottle matched the prints found on the beer bottle that felled Jack Owens.

I went back to my MG, gazed sightlessly across the street and did some thinking. I started the motor, drove down to Blanshard Street and headed north.

It was turning into a brilliant day. The air was hot now. Along West Saanich Road the scent of pine resin was heavy in the air. Fifteen minutes afterwards, I was driving along a washboarded back road filled with ruts and potholes, running alternately between brilliant sunlight and dark evergreen shade. Forest Service signs advised me that the fire hazard was extreme. Snowmelt trickled down mountain creeks. The woods and the road were bone dry.

Thin clouds of dust hung suspended in mid-air.

As I was crossing over a one-way bridge, a tailgater honked at me. I ignored him. The road was too narrow for passing and besides, loose gravel, ruts, sharp turns, fallen rocks and avalanche-warning signs spoke louder than honks. After a slow descent, I reached the bluffs overlooking the sea. The jackass stopped banging his horn when I pulled two wheels onto the shoulder of the road and stopped. The tailgater was a young guy driving a four-by-four Chev. He gave me the finger and roared past.

It was low tide. Fifty yards away on the rocky shore, a Vietnamese family was digging clams. Barefoot and stooped over, wearing wide conical straw hats and rolled-up pants, they looked like rice harvesters. Dall's porpoises, leaping in the waves, demonstrated the joys of unfettered existence. Harlequin ducks—males and females in pairs—paddled among beds of kelp. I eased the MG back onto the road.

The little beach town of Mowaht Bay opened up as the road widened and levelled out. About 30 more or less identical frame houses lay strung along the road, like washing on a line. I pulled up outside a '60s-style Texaco station and got out of the car. From where I stood, I could see most of the town. Little Leaguers in baseball uniforms were straggling in twos and threes out of the houses and onto the sun-baked road. Throwing balls back and forth, trailed by barking dogs, they dawdled toward the playing fields of a distant school.

A sign in a window informed me that the Texaco Station was closed for 15 minutes.

The Bee Hive Diner, directly across the street, looked like and turned out to be a former E & N railroad caboose, painted a garish blue instead of the traditional red. The front of the diner stood on the street, its back on pilings. The tide rose and fell beneath it.

A big man wearing a plaid shirt, heavy-duty black cords and

yellow suspenders came out. After giving me a long, hard stare, he put a toothpick into his mouth and walked toward me. At almost the last moment he detoured toward the town's government wharf, paused at the head of a ramp and gave me another long, hard stare, just as scary as the first one, before walking away and out of view among fishboats and other vessels. Maybe I reminded him of somebody he disliked; it happens to me a lot.

I lost interest in him when I noticed the *Mayan Girl*, tied up alongside a tugboat. The last time I had seen *that* yacht, it had been moored outside the Rainbow Motel.

I crossed to the diner, pushed the screen door open and stepped into the fuggy atmosphere of hamburgers and coffee. A counter ran along one side of the diner's narrow room, upholstered booths along the other. Racks filled with magazines and paperbacks covered part of one wall. Windows looked out on the government wharf and spectacular views of Mowaht Sound. I sat at the counter. The diner's short-order cook was lean and small, and looked to be in his late forties or early fifties. He fixed me up with flatware, a paper napkin and a glass of iced water then handed me a menu that probably hadn't changed one iota since the diner had been created.

The cook's identical twin brother, wearing a ball cap and blue coveralls with *Texaco* embroidered on it, was sitting with his elbows on the counter, battling the *Times Colonist* crossword. The sea surged among the pilings beneath the diner's wooden floor.

An overweight kid with dye-streaked hair hanging down over his collar was sitting alone in a booth, drinking Coca-Cola and scanning *Playboy*. When I entered, the kid looked up. It was the tailgater. He hid his face among Hugh Hefner's bunnies.

I ordered coffee and checked the menu. When the cook brought my coffee, he tilted his head and raised his eyebrows. I ordered a hamburger and fries.

"You want onion rings with that?"

"Sure. Give 'em a good singe."

The Bee Hive didn't have a Wurlitzer, but it had AM radio. Little Anthony and the Imperials were singing "Tears On My Pillow."

Texaco man's lips moved as he silently sang along. After a while, he pushed his ball cap back with a grimy finger and scratched his forehead. More time passed before he looked across the road to where my MG was parked and asked, "In a hurry for gas?"

"After I've eaten will be soon enough."

Texaco man tasted his coffee, made a face and said, "I'm Tommy Slapp. That guy shuffling his skinny ass behind the counter is my brother, Ronnie. He calls himself a chef. Been making coffee here for 30 years, Ronnie has, and still hasn't got the hang of it."

The chef polished his grill with a rag soaked in cooking oil before starting my hamburger and onions and fries. He said good-naturedly, "Pay him no mind. You're sitting next to Tommy motor mouth. Pity it don't have a muffler."

The kid got up and put the bunnies to bed in the magazine rack. Ronnie had eyes in the back of his head. Without turning he said loudly, "Don't even *think* about it."

Looking aggrieved, the kid put money beside the till and took the bunnies home.

"Jerk," Ronnie said, without acrimony. "Comes in here, spills Coke all over my magazines then wants to sneak off without paying."

The coffee was almost strong enough to hold a spoon upright. "Coffee all right?" Ronnie enquired.

"Perfect," I lied. "Just the way I like it."

Now Little Anthony was singing "Goin' Out of My Head"— his all-time great.

Distant rumblings announced the approach of an immense

logging truck. Massively loaded with giant cedar logs, it created minor earth tremors going past the diner. One log was at least four feet across at the butt.

Tommy said idly, "That's one log Boss Rollins won't be stealing."

"I wish them drivers would learn to slow down," Ronnie grumbled. "One of these days they'll shake this diner off its footings. It'll slide down this goddam bank and end up in the Sound."

I said, "I didn't know we had commercial trees that size left on lower Vancouver Island."

Texaco Tommy and diner Ronnie exchanged meaningful glances.

I added, "You men have been around this country for a while. A woman called Jane Colby used to live here. Maybe you'd know her?"

Texaco Tommy jerked as if somebody had just prodded him with a sharp stick. He said, "Who wants to know?"

"Me, I'm a cop."

"What's Janey done now?"

"She'll tell you herself, next time you meet her."

Tommy took my reproof in his stride. "I ain't seen Janey for ages," he stated, shaking his head. "How about you, Ronnie? You seen Janey lately?"

Shrugging his shoulders, Ronnie used a shiny metal spatula to scoop my lunch onto a plate, added a sprig of parsley, slid it in front of me and refilled my coffee cup before I could stop him.

I asked for another glass of water and said to Tommy, "Tell me about Boss Rollins."

"Boss is another famous character, but what the hell and who the hell he's bossing nowadays is a good question," Tommy said sarcastically. "Me and my brother's been around this country since Boss Rollins was a ragged-ass punk, stealing logs to buy his first chainsaw."

"Anything Tommy says, officer, take it with a pinch of salt," the chef said. "We were all ragged-ass punks, back in them days. Tommy bad-mouths the Boss because the Boss got tired of paying too much for Tommy's gas. Boss made a deal with Esso, bought his own fuel tanks and saved himself a mint."

"Keep quiet and stick to slinging hash, Ronnie," Tommy said. Leaning toward me he added in a stage whisper, "Be warned. This joint is ptomaine city. Only reason anybody eats here is because the next café is across the Sound."

"Pity you can't sell the gas that comes outta your mouth, Tommy, 'cause you'd never be poor," the chef joked.

The hamburger was surprisingly good; the fries and onions crisp, the way I like 'em. I asked, "Jane Colby grew up here, I understand?"

"Miss Popularity, that's Jane," the chef replied, adding with a broad wink, "Just ask my brother."

Suddenly deaf, Tommy bent his leathery neck and gazed at his crossword.

The chef went on, "Tommy and Janey was high-school sweethearts, or might have been, if either one of them had ever went to high school. Then Janey up and married Neville Rollins. Tommy, he was heartsick. Aren't that right, little brother?"

Tommy's lips twitched, but he didn't rise to the bait.

The chef went on, "At age 16, Janey was the sweetest bit of pussy on Vancouver Island. Talk about Miss Popularity. Tommy wasn't the only one fancied her."

Tommy suddenly got up from his seat and slammed out of the diner.

Ronnie grinned and said, "Tommy's pissed, but he'll get over it."

I speared a fork full of chips and, to encourage further musings, said lightly, "I'm told that Jane's marriage didn't last."

"To be fair, that weren't Janey's fault. Neville went missing. Got fed up with her and just took off, some think, but I don't know. It was a big mystery, Neville just disappearing like that. Some folks say he got depressed and ate a shotgun, but folks will say anything. Start rumours out of pure wickedness."

"Somebody told me Neville was hard on Jane. That right?"

Ronnie seemed to realize that he'd said too much. Instead of answering, he shrugged his shoulders.

I finished my meal, declined more coffee and said, "How do I find Boss Rollins' place?"

"On the reserve. He'd be an idiot to live anywhere else. On Native land, he doesn't have to pay no taxes. His house is up Sawmill Road, the second turning to the right after you leave town. There's a Forest Service notice board just this side of the turnoff. That'll be nine dollars."

The chef looked down at Tommy's unfinished crossword and said, "What's a six-letter word, beginning with L, which means 'Appropriate to fare without meat'?"

I shook my head.

"Lenten," the chef remarked complacently, adding, "Pay no attention to what my brother said about the Boss. Tommy's a bit wooden headed, sometimes. Maybe a bit of jealousy there too."

I pondered Ronnie's words for a minute and said, "Listen, all joking aside, was your brother Tommy a serious contender for Jane Colby's affections?"

"Hell no," Ronnie answered with a laugh. "He'd have liked to be, but so would I, so would anybody. She didn't take Tommy seriously; he never got to first base. Janey was fucking the reserve instead. One time, she had the hots for the Boss, but I guess all along it was Neville she really wanted."

CHAPTER NINE

Outside, Tommy was lying on a creeper beneath my MG. He scooted out from under and said affably, "Nice little motor. Bodyworks' great, no rust. Ever think of selling it?"

"Not seriously. I wouldn't mind trading it for a '39 SS Jag or a Riley Pathfinder."

"A '39 SS, Jesus," Tommy said, his eyes glazing over with the kind of look you encounter in strip clubs. He added, "Forget what Ronnie said about Janey. My first love was an Austin A90. I still haven't got over her."

As I was pulling away from the station, Tommy said, "Drive carefully, pal. If you wander into the woods, watch out for Sasquatches."

Sawmill Road hadn't been graded in years and it was another winding, washboarded, rutted, potholed disaster. Mowaht Bay Road had been bad—this was worse. Second- or third-growth forest grew thickly on either side, rising toward the crests of distant ridges to hide the sun. For the most part, the road fell steeply away to the right. Occasionally, I caught distant glimpses of the Sound. Ramshackle cabins and house trailers began to appear. Half-hidden among the trees, they were surrounded by gutted cars, cast-off appliances and neglected vegetable gardens. After a while, it became apparent that Sawmill Road was looping around the slope of a mountain and back downhill toward the Mowaht Bay Road. I went past a 30-foot wooden gillnetter, propped upright on blocks. Years earlier, somebody had removed most of the boat's hull planking. Standing high and dry, its white oak ribs were like the bones of a gutted whale.

Billy's Smokes was a modular home situated at a fork in the road. A rusted Fargo pickup was parked outside, along with beater Studebakers, Dodges and Chevs. Billy used his front parlour as a duty-free tobacco outlet and cafe, and lived in the back. He was locking the glass doors of a cigar and cigarette display case when I entered. Half a dozen men were lounging about the place, smoking, coughing and drinking beer. Billy was short and wiry. The skin of his face and neck was deeply wrinkled; his fingers were like sausages from years of handling cold-water fishing lines. I introduced myself.

Billy slipped a bunch of keys into his pockets and said, "Silas Seaweed, eh? I've heard about you."

"How about a bottle of Blue?"

Billy took one from his cooler, snapped its cap off and put it on the bar. "That'll be two bucks," he said.

I gave him a toony and asked directions to Boss Rollins' house. Billy pointed to the road's left-hand fork and said, "It's another half mile. You'll see a culvert with water underneath; next thing you'll see is the HANE sawmill. Just keep going; Boss's house is the yellow bungalow at the end."

I was going out of the store when somebody said, "He the money guy?"

Everyone laughed. I paused in the doorway and turned. The man who had spoken could have been anything between 30 and 50 years old. Stooped and wiry, wearing cheap shades, missing most of his teeth, he looked at me and said, "Check it out. He's no banker."

Billy said, "Shut your mouth, Knot-head."

It was an interesting moment. Billy followed me out to the MG. He took a can of chewing tobacco from his pocket, put a pinch between his cheek and gum and said, "Pay no attention. Knot-head is only one step up from retardation. As for the rest of these boys, they put up a good front except, since HANE closed, front is all they've got left."

"Who's the money guy?"

"Nobody, it's just a rumour," said Billy, spitting a line of juice onto the dirt. "Some guy's supposed to be interested in buying the mill, giving these guys their jobs back. It'll never happen."

Billy went back inside.

I resumed my journey, crossed the culvert and plunged deeper into more regions of sad shanties and trailers. The long-defunct HANE sawmill was locked up tight behind chain-link fencing. Half a dozen logging trucks stood among the weeds of a 10-acre clearing, along with pickups, front-end loaders and Caterpillar earth-moving equipment. The sawmill buildings were a group of architecturally dissimilar timber and corrugated-iron structures that had obviously been added one at a time during the mill's expansion phase. A pit bull, crouched on a mountain of sawdust, pointed its nose at the sky and howled as I drove past.

Boss Rollins' house stood on the slope of a hill. It had a roofed porch, stucco walls the colour of dried mustard and a red-tiled roof. A detached two-car garage with a dusty black Lincoln inside stood next to it. A few acres of the surrounding woods had been logged, graded and fenced. Apart from a section of carefully tended lawn around the house, the ground was littered with rocks left behind when the glaciers withdrew from here 10,000 years back. Goats and sheep, nose down in sparse grass, ignored me when I stopped in front of the house. The MG's water temperature gauge was registering in the upper range, I noticed, before I got out of the car.

This was black bear and cougar country. Waiting for somebody to answer my knock on the door I wondered idly how much livestock Boss Rollins lost to predators in an average year.

Nobody answered the door. I assumed that someone was about the place, because curtains fluttered in an open window. I went back to the MG and raised the hood. The fan belt was loose. I collected tools from the kit in the back of the car, selected an appropriate wrench and leaned inside the hood.

Somebody shouted, "Hey, you!"

A pot-bellied Native man with a round puffy face and thick black hair was eyeing me from the house. He looked angry, like an infant whose pacifier has just fallen out. A foot shorter than myself, he was sweaty and dishevelled and carrying a long-handled shovel. He was dressed in a white shirt, black pants and black, pierced leather cowboy boots with three-inch heels. Give him a steer's-head belt buckle and a tall black hat with feathers in it and he'd be a dead ringer for the guys who hawk turquoise souvenirs in the Mojave. So this was the witch. He didn't look dangerous; he looked furtive and ridiculous.

"What the hell do you want?" he yelled.

I smiled. He edged closer. I said, "Mr. Rollins? I'm Sergeant Seaweed, Victoria City Police."

Boss Rollins tilted his face upwards to look me in the eye, heavy black brows pulled down, holding that shovel across one shoulder as if it were a rifle. His eyes were thick and oily—the eyes of an unstable man veering toward rage. I held his gaze and waited for him to speak.

"I asked you," he said aggressively. "What do you want?"

"I'm a cop," I said mildly, showing my badge.

He waved it away and said thickly, "A stranger drives on my property and works on his car like it's his fucking garage, how do I know he's a cop?"

"This isn't a joke, Mr. Rollins. I'm here to ask questions about your sister-in-law."

My question startled him. Visibly agitated, Rollins drew his chin in toward his neck and a nervous reflex twitched his mouth slightly off centre. "Wait here," he said, and strode to his house.

Tightening the fan belt, I began to think about witches and shamans—religious polar opposites. Rollins fiddled around with black magic. If stories about him were true, he was adept, capable of summoning malignant spirits from the world of the dead.

Shamans on the other hand commune with beneficent spirits conjured up in sacred places—caves high in the mountains or on lonely promontories overlooking remote lakes. There the shamans wait, fasting for days in conditions of appalling discomfort and pain, until possessed by enchantment. The intensity of such visitations temporarily endowed shamans with second sight and the power to heal.

A good 10 minutes passed before Rollins came down the lawn from his house. I had no idea whether he'd been making a phone call or had been conjuring up evil spirits, and tried not to worry about it. I had tightened the belt but still had my head under the hood when I heard approaching footsteps.

"I'm here," he said, speaking to my back.

I lowered the hood and said, "Loose belt. Engine was over-heating a bit."

"What's this about Janey?"

I gave him a brief nod of acknowledgement. Without hurrying myself, I put my tool kit away and wiped my hands on a rag. When they were clean enough to suit me, I folded my arms, drew myself up to my full height and said, "You own the Rainbow Motel, correct?"

He said belligerently, "What is this, a cross examination?"

"Take it easy. Cops *do* talk to people. It's nothing personal." I said in a pleasant conversational tone. "I should remind you that hampering police in the performance of their duties is a serious offence. Anybody rash enough to try it can be arrested for obstruction. After that, nosy policemen can come back here with search warrants; seize files, search hard drives. If you've ever visited a dodgy website they'll find out about it. You'll become enmeshed in a nightmare. Your life will be a living hell for years."

Rollins' mouth fell open but no words came out.

I added, "On the other hand, you can cooperate. Then we'll leave you alone."

He asked me what I wanted to know.

"I'm looking for Janey Colby. Maybe you can help me find her."

His confidence returning, he said with a snicker, "Shouldn't be too hard. Try the East End of Vancouver. She'll be tits up in a gutter someplace."

"Alright, I'll try just once more. To repeat: do you own the Rainbow Motel?"

"What do you think?"

"I don't *think*, I'm a cop. Do you have a particular reason for being unhelpful?"

"That's it," he said, taking a step backwards. "I'm calling my lawyer, right now."

"You're not phoning anybody. You're going nowhere till I'm through with you."

"Who d'you think you're talking to? Nobody tells me what to do," he snarled, taking another step backwards and turning on his heel.

I tapped his shoulder to get his attention, whereupon he whirled around and threw a clumsy, ineffectual punch. He was slightly off-balance. I brought up my right arm up and hit him in the face with the point of my elbow. There was a hollow crunching sound. Rollins fell to his knees, holding his bloody nose.

I'd made a big mistake and knew it immediately.

Rollins got up, yanked his shirt off and used it to staunch the bleeding. "I'll break you for this," he said, speaking in a blubbery nasal whine that made his bombast ludicrous.

I felt hot, tired and disgusted with the way I'd handled myself. Nevertheless I said sternly, "I asked you when you last saw your sister-in-law and I want an answer. Savvy?"

Blood dripped down Rollins' bare chest and onto his fat belly. Tenderly fingering his nose he said, "You're dead meat, mister."

"Answer my question."

"I haven't seen Janey for weeks," he said, his voice shaking. "How do I know when I saw her last? Maybe it was a month ago. I'm too busy to keep a diary."

"Were you in the Rainbow Motel, two weeks ago?"

"Again, I don't know. Maybe I was, maybe I wasn't. I don't remember."

"Let me refresh your memory. Two weeks ago last Friday is when somebody stole your speedboat."

Surprise made him blink. "That fixes it. I was nowhere near the motel that day. I was here. The reason I know is because Karl Berger phoned me, told me the boat was gone."

"All right, we've established something. Now, if you didn't see Janey two weeks ago, when did you last see her?"

Rollins had calmed. He said, "What's the big deal? Janey goes where she wants, when she wants. Am I supposed to be Janey's keeper?"

"Do you live here alone?"

"Mostly. A woman comes in to shove a vacuum cleaner around. She makes supper when I'm home."

"Does she live on the premises?"

"She goes home every night."

"What time?"

"It varies. Usually she's gone by six."

I said, "Can anyone confirm that you were on the reserve when your speedboat went missing?"

"Probably, I'd have to think about it. I was probably at the sawmill all day. I'll ask my timekeeper, next time I see him."

"The sawmill's closed, everybody's laid off. What's this about a timekeeper?"

"He's a timekeeper/watchman/dog-handler. If I didn't keep somebody at the mill they'd strip it clean in a month."

I took out my cell phone and said, "What's your timekeeper's number?"

"Waste of time calling because it's Saturday. Weekends he comes and goes. Everybody's off fishing, or playing ball, or something."

Rollins was lying. "Okay," I said. "That's all, for now. You'll be hearing from me again."

He stalked back to the house without another word, that bloodstained shirt dangling from his hand like a freshly killed game bird.

I started the MG and let it run while I wrote up some notes. By the time I'd finished, the engine's water-temperature gauge was registering in the high normal range. I shut the engine off and rechecked the belt. The tension wasn't great, but it was better than it had been. I figured I could make it back to the Texaco station okay. That assumption proved wrong.

I drove back to the main highway, turned left toward Mowaht Bay, and I was still accelerating when a deer bounded out of the woods into my path. One moment I was doing 50 kilometres an hour, the next moment I'd come to a full stop. The seat belt saved me. The deer bounced off the front bumper, picked itself up and limped into the bush. The MG's front end was concertina'd, and the headlights were bits of broken glass. Steam, gushing from a busted radiator, condensed in oily dribbles down the windshield. The steering wheel was jammed.

I called 411 to get Texaco Tommy's number. His line was busy.

A Toyota Land Cruiser appeared from behind a bend in the road. I put my thumb out. The Toyota skidded to a halt. A bearded man aged about 30, wearing brown cord pants, a red flannel shirt, caulk boots and an aluminum hard hat got out and surveyed the wreckage. He lit a cigarette with a match and carefully broke the match into two pieces before dropping it onto the roadway.

"Deer?" he asked.

"Right. It went thataway."

"Yeah, they're tough, but it won't get very far. A cougar will be having it for dinner soon."

"Lucky cougar," I said. "I'm Silas Seaweed."

"Urban Kramer," he said. "Can I give you a tow? I've got a chain."

"Thanks, but the steering is jammed. If you're heading into town maybe you could ask the Texaco guy to tow me in."

"Sure, no problem," Kramer said amiably. "You okay? Not hurt or anything?"

"I'm fine," I replied, and gave him my card. "Here's my cell phone number. Ask the Texaco guy to call, confirm he can tow me in today, instead of next week."

Kramer put my card into his shirt pocket and drove off.

It was late afternoon, still blistering hot. A rickety five-wire fence blocked entry to the adjacent forest. I noticed—in a place where a section of fence had fallen down—a well-used game trail. The injured animal's tracks wound faintly uphill through dense bush. Altogether, it was a sombre, shady backwoods. Shafts of diffused orange-coloured light filtered through the canopy creating grotesque shapes and shadows. On an impulse, I set out along the trail and in less than 10 minutes, I reached a spot from which Boss Rollins' house was visible. Rollins was digging a hole at the foot of his lawn. Odd. What was he doing? I watched from the trees for a couple of minutes before resuming my search for the deer.

I found it lying along a trail. It appeared uninjured, but it was dead. I stood beside it, bowed my head and said a Coast Salish prayer. When I looked up, the sun was shining directly into my eyes through a break in the trees. Squinting myopically, I noticed a large unnatural shape in a dark patch of bush. It turned out to be a steam-powered logging donkey.

A hundred years previously, that chunk of obsolete hardware had been the last word in hi-tech logging. Outmoded for decades, nowadays rarely seen outside forestry museums, it consisted of a steam-powered winch and a vertical boiler. The whole rusty contraption was built on a steel platform supported on long wooden skids instead of wheels.

My cell phone rang. Texaco Tommy said, "Urban Kramer just gave me the bad news. I'll be with you in about an hour."

I sat down on the donkey's raised platform. My thoughts wandered aimlessly, until I focused on an interesting fact: Earlier, I had noticed Boss Rollins' Lincoln. Now I remembered Rollins' DUI conviction; he'd had his licence suspended for six months.

It was very hot, and my eyes closed; perhaps I dozed for a few minutes. I stood up, stretched and took a final look at the steam donkey. It had been built long ago by the Victoria Machine Depot and, given its antiquity, was reasonably well preserved. Why hadn't Rollins sold the donkey for scrap, or donated it to a museum? Then I noticed something peculiar. The boiler's furnace door was welded shut. Why? Perhaps, I thought, to prevent kids from climbing inside the furnace and latching themselves in.

Earlier in my career, I'd been called to investigate the death of a small boy who had suffocated inside one of those old-fashioned fridges with self-locking doors. Once inside, the poor lad had been doomed.

Something moved in a patch of shrubbery. I became aware of bad-smelling air, and of a low unearthly wailing. *Kids!* I thought. *Kids throwing stink bombs.*

I ran into the shrubbery and began to look around. I saw nobody, although a circle of flattened grass showed where a dog or a wolf had been lying. The ground felt cool to my touch—no animal had lain there recently. That foul sulphurous odour increased, trees began to creak, branches rustled, the earth moved beneath me. I didn't imagine this. The ground definitely shook, I felt it distinctly. Some weird force was at work and whatever it was, that force, or agency, meant to harm me. I was remembering Tommy's remark about Sasquatches when there was a crash as something massive fell over. The earth trembled again, and a humanoid face appeared—or something like a face; it was a parchment-coloured oval with eyes, partially concealed by green leaves.

Like a man in a nightmare, trying not to panic, I backed away. There *are* secret places in Coast Salish territory where ghostly creatures linger—or can be summoned. As I moved, the ground sloped precipitously. I lost my footing and began to slide. Seconds later I was dangling face down over the edge of a bluff. The only thing separating me from permanent oblivion was a slender young arbutus. I grabbed its smooth trunk and dragged myself to safety. When my heart stopped hammering I moved to a place where I could see down without danger. In a steep valley below, a narrow trickle of snowmelt widened out into a large circular pool.

By the time I reached my wrecked car, my jitters had faded. All the same, I was very relieved when Texaco Tommy showed up in his wrecker and I put that spooky place behind.

CHAPTER TEN

Two hours later, I was at the Bee Hive's counter, digesting one of Ronnie's mushroom, sardine and olive omelettes. Four rambunctious teenagers were bingeing on ice cream sundaes in a booth behind me. Ronnie, leaning against a cooler, filled his lungs with what passed for air in there and used enough of it to say, "How you enjoying Mowaht Bay so far?"

"As compared to what? Afghanistan?"

"Tommy gave you bad news, did he?" Ronnie said glancing out the window across the street, where his brother's legs were visible beneath the wrecked MG.

"It could be worse. Your brother thinks it'll be driveable by tomorrow afternoon. I'll have it fixed properly in Victoria, after the insurance adjuster sees it."

"Does that mean you're staying the night here?"

"Stay where? All due respect, Ronnie, but Mowaht Bay reminds me of a girl I used to know: she was nice on our first acquaintance but soon got tired of me."

"Chrissie has a room above her beauty parlour that she rents out sometimes. Maybe it's available. Want me to phone her and find out?"

I was turning the idea over when Ronnie added, "It's across from the Legion Hall. Nothing fancy, just a bachelor pad."

Amusement writ large on his face, Ronnie added, "I hope you're not a light sleeper. The Legion gets noisy on weekends."

"Okay, but tell Chrissie it's only a one-night stand."

The teenagers were ready to leave. After they paid and went out, Ronnie lifted his phone off its wall-mounted cradle, dialed a number and spoke a few words. He put a hand over the mouthpiece and said to me, "Chrissie says the room's yours if you want it. It'll set you back 40 bucks."

"Tell Chrissie I'll be right over."

I paid for my dinner. Ronnie put a CLOSED sign in his window, locked up and followed me out.

"That's it," Ronnie said, pointing to a wood frame commercial building, adjacent to the government wharf. "Chrissie's in her parlour, waiting for you."

It was Saturday night and getting dark. Texaco Tommy had stopped work and was in his office, taking off his coveralls. Loggers and mill workers were cruising back and forth in hot rods, SUVs and four-by-four pickups—raising dust and hollering at the girls congregated near the Legion Hall. Couples strolled arm in arm, enjoying the cool of the evening.

Ronnie joined his brother inside the gas station. I unlocked my car, and I was reaching inside for the overnight bag I carry for emergencies when a series of minor explosions disturbed the night—people were setting off fireworks over by the school. The twins hurried off to witness the excitement as rockets began lighting up the sky.

Just then, two masked men appeared from behind the Legion Hall. They came toward me carrying baseball bats and wearing generic plaid shirts, dark jeans and caulk boots. "That's him," one of them said, raising his bat. Only it wasn't a bat. Oily metal glinted as he aimed a shotgun, fired and missed. The sound of exploding fireworks cloaked the Sound. A third masked man emerged from the shadows.

Boxed in, I ran across the street onto the government wharf. The wharf's plank deck was slippery underfoot as I raced out along a float between fishboats and pleasure boats. When I reached the end of the float, I was jammed. Instead of diving into the icy water I jumped aboard a troller and tried to open its cabin door. It was locked. Looking around for a weapon of some sort I noticed a box, full of fish-line sinkers. Made of cast lead, they were the size of tennis balls and weighed a good 20 pounds each.

The goons had followed me onto the wharf but in the darkness had lost sight of me. Now they were getting their bearings. I heard them talking before they moved toward me, so I picked up a lead sinker. A man with a baseball bat reached me first. When he leapt aboard swinging, I hit him with the sinker. He collapsed at my feet with a broken jaw, but his bat struck my left arm first. The man with the shotgun showed up next and skidded to a stop. He was taking aim when I threw another sinker at him with the full strength of my right arm then dived into the water.

It was freezing water, delivered straight from the Arctic to B.C., but I knew that if I dived deep enough, shotgun pellets would lose their killing velocity. I heard, or sensed, another explosive blast. My left arm was useless. I kept diving—down and out into deeper, blacker water, until I ran out of air and had to come up. Numb with cold and shock, my danglers fully retracted, I refilled my lungs and dived again. This time I surfaced in the air space beneath a float, where I was safe for the moment, and could breathe. Footsteps pounded back and forth on the deck above my head. Fireworks were still making plenty of noise.

I heard somebody say, "We musta got him. Let's go."

Ice was licking my bones. I had to get out of that water before hypothermia set in and I drowned. I submerged again and swam out from beneath the float. When I surfaced, I was too weak to lift myself one-handed onto a float. I was floundering hopelessly toward the shore when a woman said, "Here, catch!"

A rope fell across my shoulders. I wrapped it around my wrists and held on. Hydraulic motors whirred. The rope tightened as I was hoisted clear of the water and swung aboard a large boat. I flopped around on a wide wooden deck while somebody untangled the rope then led me across the threshold of a cabin into warmth.

My breathing was shallow and fast, my teeth were chattering. I couldn't speak and my left arm was useless. The woman said, "You have to get out of those wet clothes, fast," but my fingers were numb. I couldn't help myself. The woman pawed at my buttons and zippers and ripped at me until I was naked. Feeling less than human, I was helped down a companionway and shoved into a shower stall. The woman opened faucets and got thoroughly soaked herself before she had the temperature adjusted properly and left me to it. I stayed in the shower long enough to empty the boat's hot water tank. Mentally, things were still pretty much a blur.

Monogrammed bath towels told me that I was aboard the *Mayan Girl*. As I was drying myself, the woman returned and opened the bathroom door partially. A hand appeared holding a white terrycloth bathrobe.

My saviour said, "Here, put this on. When you're ready, come on through to the main stateroom. I'll have hot drinks waiting."

I reached for the bathrobe and managed to say, "Thanks," in a tone that sounded reasonably human, but I was still disoriented. When I moved, it felt as if I were immersed in a thick viscous substance that resisted motion. I put the bathrobe on and sat on the floor shivering uncontrollably. Somehow, I had ended up in a laundry room. The clothes that I had been wearing were in a basket beside a washer-dryer unit. It was probably very warm in there, but my skin was covered with goose pimples. My shivers were getting worse, and my left arm hurt like hell. I couldn't think.

The woman returned and said something. I didn't reply. She came right into the laundry room, dragged me to my feet and we went together into a stateroom with a king-sized bed in it. I fell into the bed, still wearing that bathrobe. The last thing I remember she was climbing in beside me. I felt her animal warmth as she encircled me in her arms before I passed out.

CHAPTER ELEVEN

I woke with a violent start. In that uncertain moment between sleep and waking I didn't know where I was. Reality asserted itself—I was in a large, luxurious stateroom. The room was dark when I got out of bed, except for grey portholes. I tested my left arm; it hurt when I tried to raise it, but no bones were broken. I drew a curtain and peered out through a porthole.

A bearded fisherman was on the wharf staring glumly at the troller I'd tried to hide aboard last night. Shotgun pellets had punched holes through its deckhouse, wrecked the radar and smashed windows.

My overnight bag was at the bottom of the Sound but a Lady Gillette razor, soap, fresh towels and a new toothbrush were laid out in the bathroom for me. I was finishing a one-handed shave when my rescuer knocked on the door. I put the bathrobe on and opened the door. She handed me my freshly laundered clothing and said, "Breakfast's ready when you are. Grapefruit to start. Coffee. Bacon and eggs. Okay?"

"I'll say. Believe it or not, it's my birthday. But for you, I wouldn't have made it."

"Your hundredth?"

"Fortieth. And thanks. Thanks for everything."

"Congratulations, many happy returns. I'm Tess Rollins. I

checked your wallet when I emptied your pockets before washing your clothes so I know who *you* are."

She moved all the way into the room and leaned back against the wall with both hands in her pockets; one knee bent and the sole of a bare foot pressed against the wall. She was a West Coast Native woman, wearing a short, low-cut summer dress that revealed expanses of flawless bronzed skin and the beginning of a cleft between her breasts. She looked about 40. Her face wasn't beautiful. In fact, it was downright plain, even ugly, but her figure was lovely. I remembered that those strong shapely legs had wrapped me to her hips last night. She had a certain indescribable appeal—hard to explain, an allure that stirred my heart immediately. Perhaps it was the way Tess looked at me, her grace, her way of moving. Her voice was low and nicely modulated. A long time later I found out she'd taken elocution lessons.

My spine tingled. *She* was Harley's sister? Did she know I'd scuffled with Harley yesterday? Did she know about the goons, no doubt sent by Harley, who'd tried to murder me? I said slowly, "You're Harley Rollins' sister?"

She smiled. "That's right. Do you know him?"

I dodged the question by saying, "Who doesn't? The man's famous."

"This is RCMP territory, so what brings a Victoria cop out this way?"

"I'm off duty," I replied. "Just looking around for something."

Tess smiled flirtatiously. "*Me*, maybe."

I smiled back and began to relax. But, still cautious, I decided to probe. "So how *is* your brother?"

Tess frowned. "I dunno."

"You don't know?"

She shrugged. "We're not speaking at the moment. Me and Mr. Temper had a fight."

That was good news.

It was her turn to probe. "So how'd you end up in the water last night?"

I held up both hands. "I wasn't drunk, if that's what you're thinking."

Tess laughed. "Oh no, of *course not!*" Then we both laughed.

"Seriously, though, a lot of people around here don't like cops very much," she said meditatively. "Maybe that explains why you ended up in the water."

"Maybe. I've got a bad habit of leading with my chin."

"I don't know how you survived. You were in the water for ages before I dragged you out."

"I'm no lightweight. How did you manage it?"

"I used the Zodiac winch. Welcome to Mowaht Bay."

I grinned at her. She smiled and went out.

TESS ROLLINS AND I BREAKFASTED together on the upper sundeck. The area covered by its laced-canvas roof was no bigger than a squash court. I stopped digging a silver spoon into my beautifully sliced and segmented grapefruit and looked out. A lumber carrier was steaming into Mowaht Sound. The vessel was in ballast and its propeller, half-exposed, churned water to foam at its stern. Its passing wake set the *Mayan Girl* rocking.

I said, "The *Mayan Girl* was moored at the Rainbow Motel's dock a few days ago. Karl Berger mentioned the boat was yours."

"What else did Karl tell you?"

"About you? Nothing."

"Karl's a world-class phony. Don't believe everything he tells you," she said caustically. After a pause, she went on, "Mowaht Bay can be a tough town. Saturday nights, it's full of dull, bored rednecks throwing their weight around because they can't think of anything better to do. But shooting people and trying to kill them is rare, even here. What's going on?"

"Funny you should ask. I came here because I'm trying to locate your sister-in-law."

She looked blank for a moment. "You mean Jane Colby?"

"Do you have other sisters-in-law?"

"No, but it's funny. I don't think of Janey as being related to me. Not anymore. I mean, she was widowed ages ago. We've nothing much in common. She moved on, we both moved on."

She looked at me seductively, her eyes half closed, with the trace of a smile on her luscious lips. It was a very nice smile. I was feeling better every minute.

Tess sipped a little coffee, leant back in her chair and crossed her legs. Her Mona Lisa smile became less enigmatic. She said, "What's Janey been up to lately?"

"She hasn't been seen for a while. Your niece is worried about her, which is why we're on the lookout."

"Poor Terry. Sorry if I don't take this very seriously, because Janey was never exactly Miss Normal. She was always kind of a flake."

"So I'm finding out. A tracer job which at the outset looked fairly straightforward has turned out to be anything but."

Tess kept smiling.

I went on. "Yesterday I visited your brother, Harley. I thought maybe he could help me track Janey down."

"And?"

"Harley wasn't much use. Maybe *you* might have some suggestions?"

"Have you talked to Janey's dad?"

"Yes. And to Jack Owens."

"Who's he?"

"For a short while he was Jane's significant other. Neither he, nor Janey's dad, have seen her for a couple of weeks."

"So, basically, Janey's been missing for a couple of weeks," Tess said with a laugh. "That's what all this fuss is about?"

Tess's brown eyes were flecked with gold, the skin around them completely smooth and too unwrinkled. I wondered if she'd had Botox injections or plastic surgery. Unexpectedly, she reached forward and touched my hand. "Sorry Silas, but don't you think maybe you're taking this matter too seriously? I mean, two weeks? If I go out on my yacht I lose touch with the whole world for months at a time."

"To be precise, how would you describe your present relationship to Janey?"

"I thought I already had. Our present relationship is nonexistent. We were friends once, when we were going to school and growing up." Tess added wistfully, "People change, you know. Janey's not the girl she used to be."

"How is she different?"

Instead of replying immediately, she slowly sipped more coffee. I thought she was going to ignore my question until she finally said, almost apologetically, "It's very sad, but people tell me that Jane is drinking too much."

A couple of tugboats were nudging that cargo ship in toward a distant wharf, where three immense cranes bestrode mountains of raw logs, ready to load another cargo for Asia.

Tess said, "We've all changed. Our dad was a longshoreman, one of the few guys on the reserve with a real job. When I was a kid all I wanted was to get out of Mowaht Bay. Escape. I set my heart on becoming a hairdresser; it was the height of my aspiration. Harley wanted to be a welder. He took a vocational course at Camosun College in Victoria. The fees wiped him out so he had to sleep in a car, live on Ritz crackers and bottles of ketchup filched from the school cafeteria. After getting his diploma, Harley worked at the Esquimalt dockyard, honing his skills."

I said carefully, "Now some people say he's a witch."

"If so, they're idiots, and I hope you're not one of them," she said heatedly. She seemed to realize she'd been too vehement, because she laughed then explained, "Some lazy people would rather believe he had help from the supernatural to reach his success. They should drag their idle butts off the mattress before dawn every morning. Go to work early and keep at it till dark— which is what Harley did for years."

I grinned at her.

"I'm sorry, I shouldn't be venting like this. Where Harley's concerned I get carried away, tend to run off at the mouth. Besides, this black arts crap people talk about, it's all fraud and bullshit."

"Maybe so, but there are places around these mountains where I prefer to have company after dark. I'm not the only one. If it's all fraud and bullshit, why do people feel this way?"

"Because we've been brainwashed for hundreds of years?" she replied, laughing.

"Assuming it wasn't all witchcraft, how *did* Harley parlay a welding diploma into the HANE logging empire?"

"A big part of the credit goes to brother Neville. Neville inherited the brains in our family. He was the youngest. Two years younger than me, seven years younger than Harley."

She seemed to run out of things to say. To prompt her I said idly, "Did you fulfill your life's ambition?"

She eyed me quizzically.

"What I meant was, did you become a hairdresser?"

"Actually I did. Got a job as an apprentice beautician in Vancouver. As it turned out, the hairdressing life wasn't as fabulous as I'd expected. I was ready to quit and relieved when Harley offered me a job. The minute he did, I handed in my curling tongs, moved into Harley's front office. General secretary and gofer. I couldn't even type, initially. I learned as I went along. We all did."

She stopped talking and gazed at the Sound, but perhaps she was peering down memory lane.

"As I was saying, Neville had all the brains. He won a Harold Macmillan scholarship. Neville was the first guy on the reserve to finish high school. He went to UBC and came out with honours in forest management. Harley always made good money, welding, and he idolized his little brother. Harley subsidized Neville through the four years he was away studying."

She stopped talking and said suddenly, "Gee, it's nearly noon. Talking is thirsty work. You fancy a beer?"

"No thanks, I wouldn't mind more coffee."

"Help yourself," she said, going to a small refrigerator set up behind a counter in the yacht's dining salon.

From the way she looked, walking away, I stopped thinking of her as plain and was beginning to realize she was one of the sexiest women I'd ever met. She was something, all right. She came back with a bottle of beer, said, "Cheers," and drank straight from the bottle.

She rambled on, "After a couple of years at the dockyard, Harley went into business for himself. He bolted a portable welding outfit to the back of a junky old pickup truck. Harley's motto was, 'Have stinger, will travel.'" She laughed. "It was corny, but it worked. Harley travelled around, doing emergency and maintenance welding in back-country logging camps and sawmills, every sort of job that came his way. Harley soon built up a good reputation. If fancy, difficult welding was needed, he was the guy they called for."

She stopped talking and leaned forward to pick up the bottle. That low-cut dress cooperated. She took another drink and sat back, a faraway look in her eyes.

I asked, "How did Jane Colby fit into this picture?"

Tess stroked the side of her face with the cold bottle. "She was right in the middle of it, from the beginning. Harley was like me; an ugly little squirt. Janey was beautiful. Harley, believe it or not, was Janey's first boyfriend. Harley was just nuts about her. People never understood what Janey saw in him. A pretty white girl running around with a ragged-ass reserve Injun. But they had a helluva lot of fun together, while it lasted."

"Then what?"

"Then Janey took up with Neville. The sneaky cow was two-timing both of my brothers. Virtually the whole time Neville was away at UBC, Janey was seeing him, sleeping with him. Harley didn't know. He never suspected a thing until the day Janey told him it was over, she was going to marry Neville. I'm getting ahead of myself though. Neville had graduated with his forestry degree by that time. Harley and he were in business together."

"Partners?"

"Not exactly," she said, hesitantly, adding, "You know Harley has a police record."

I nodded.

Tess grinned. "Harley soon realized that the profits he made fixing other peoples' sawmills were peanuts, compared to the profits his customers raked in by cutting timber. Harley wanted a piece of the main action himself. So he set to work and built his own little sawmill from scratch, hired first-class sawyers to run it for him. Harley's main trouble was finding enough logs to keep his mill running. A lot of the time, Harley had orders he couldn't fill. The big forest companies had a lock on most of the available timber and kept squeezing him out."

Tess drained the bottle, put it back on the table and showed a bit more anatomy crossing her legs. Maybe she didn't even realize it. She went on, "Harley couldn't buy all the logs he needed legitimately, so he stole them. He drove a logging truck into the bush on weekends when the big camps were shut down. Helped himself to all the lumber that was lying around loose. He was a thief himself, and he bought stolen lumber from truckers. Harley paid top dollar and got caught more than once. Caught, convicted and fined. Harley just laughed. The fines he paid were penny ante compared to what he was making. And don't kid yourself; Harley wasn't the only cowboy roping timber out there."

"True. Harley was just the boldest, and the biggest."

"Rubbish. The biggest log thieves of all time are those guys granted tree farm licences by the government. They were given virtual monopolies to limitless quantities of B.C.'s Crown timber and became billionaires, every single one of them. Guess who got screwed?"

"British Columbia's taxpayers?"

"Goddam right. B.C.'s taxpayers and B.C.'s Indians. Till 150 years ago, we had all the trees we wanted. Next thing we know, there's all these white Europeans in our midst. They're pissing on our heads, telling us where to live and what to do. However, all that's beside the point. If we ever settle our land-claims issues, we'll get our forests back. The point is that Neville came home from UBC."

"And?"

"Harley's *modus operandi* had been crude. He was a clumsy old-style thief and fixer. Harley bribed people. He paid goons to strong-arm uncooperative logging-camp guards. Neville changed all that. He was a modern fixer. Neville wore expensive suits, joined golf clubs and developed winning cocktail-party manners. Instead of bribing camp guards, he gave mid-level government bureaucrats season tickets to Canucks games. He schmoozed with B.C. cabinet ministers. He didn't give people boxes of chocolates at Christmas. Hell no. Neville gave people holidays in Fiji. It was no great surprise, after Neville laid the groundwork, that when HANE Logging applied for B.C. timber licences, they started to get 'em."

"It sounds terrific."

"It was terrific. Till Harley found out that Neville had been banging his girlfriend, and was going to marry her."

Tess's beer bottle was empty again. I padded across to the fridge, took out two fresh cold ones, screwed the caps off and gave one to her. We touched bottles. I said, "Cheers."

Tess's eyes were clear and brilliant; in them, I perceived a hint of anger. She went on, "Harley and Neville were never partners in anything but name. It was Harley's company, 100 percent. They did everything on the basis of a handshake, if that. Maybe they never even shook hands. After Neville and Janey got married, though, things changed.

"HANE Logging was becoming a huge success. People with MBAs from Harvard and Queens were being hired to manage the head office in Victoria. Harley branched out into other businesses, property investments, who knows what all. After Harley started making all this money, he deliberately set out to break the brother who'd made it possible. Harley took his time. First, he demoted Neville from chief sales manager to office manager. A few months later, he busted him even further, to assistant manager of woods operations. When Neville went missing, he was working as a foreman on the booming grounds. God only knows why he put up with it. Maybe Neville kept remembering that his big brother had put him through college. Maybe he had a guilty conscience about Janey.

"I didn't like what Harley was doing to Neville. Still, Neville had brought misfortune on his own head. Besides, Neville was a big boy. He didn't have to put up with anything he didn't want to. He was young, and he was very, very smart. He could have worked for somebody else, started his own outfit. He could have just walked away from Harley at any time, there was nothing stopping him."

Tess's face was grim. "I'm not nearly as smart as Neville, but I have other qualities. When I saw how Neville was being treated, I got anxious. Walked into Harley's office one day and demanded a piece of the company. He asked me why I thought I deserved it. I told him I deserved it because I was his sister.

"Harley didn't even hesitate. He made me a 33 percenter, then and there. That's how come I'm living on a yacht, instead of giving blue rinses to bitchy dowagers. The only stipulation Harley set on our deal, I had to promise never to give one dime to our brother Neville, or to Neville's wife. If I did, the deal was off. That was hard on me, but the arrangement I have with Harley is cast iron; my own lawyer drew it up. Then Neville went missing, never came back. For a while, I kept expecting him to show up. In a way, I'm still waiting."

Tess stopped talking and looked at me expectantly.

I said, "Harley must have changed his mind about Janey, since."

"It's news to me, if he did," she said. "Harley hates and detests Janey Colby."

"Why?"

"Because he thinks that Jane murdered his brother."

"I heard you and Harley *both* believed that—and said so to the police."

Tess sighed. "Sure, but I've had years to think about it since, and I don't think Janey had it in her to kill my brother. I don't. Harley still believes it though, and he still hates her."

"In spite of which, Janey has the use of a free room at the Rainbow Motel."

Tess nodded thoughtfully, "You're right, she does. I stand corrected. I was surprised, when I found that out. That's recent, though, it only happened these last few months. Love is very akin to hate, right? Maybe Harley's starting to feel sorry for Janey."

"Maybe Tiger is changing his spots. I wouldn't count on it, though. I think there's still a bit of goon left in your big brother."

Tess rejected that suggestion by shaking her head.

"How do you feel about Janey?" I asked.

"She's a bitch, how do you expect me to feel?"

"I looked at Harley's sawmill yesterday. It's shut down, been shut down for a while. I've heard rumours he's bankrupt."

"He *is* bankrupt. Not yet officially, but near enough. I guess he'll salvage something from the wreckage. He won't end up with nothing."

"And you? How will you come out of it?"

"I think I'll manage," she said, still a bit heated because Jane Colby's name had come up. A moment later, her face was in complete repose, she looked sleek and satisfied, like a cat that had just devoured a saucer of cream and was ready for something even better. Tess appeared to size me up; her smile wasn't quite static as she finished her third bottle of beer. Her eyes were very bright, their pupils too small.

There was a lifesaving equipment locker on the starboard side of the deck. It was about the size of a camp cot, covered with a long leather cushion. She rose languidly from her chair, stretched, kicked off her shoes, said, "I'm tired of talking," and lay down full length on that leather cushion, watching me with lazy eyes. She looked completely irresistible so I went and stood over her. She smiled, enjoying my unmistakable admiration. Her eyes closed. She opened her eyes and asked me if I'd ever been married.

"Once," I said. "Her name was Nancy."

"Any kids?"

"No."

She began to tell me about the difficulties women like her faced—avoiding gold-diggers, for example. The world was full of con artists and gigolos looking for a meal ticket. Sometimes she went on cruises, package tours—tried to pass herself off as a working girl, but that hadn't worked either.

A slight breeze ruffled her hair. A few thin high clouds drifted in the turquoise-coloured sky. Mowaht Mountain rose in the distance. The heat was creating silvery water mirages—that Japanese freighter appeared to be floating on a thin strip of mercury. I was suddenly aware of an acrid odour, something unpleasant, like burning rubber.

She said, "Last night, when I crawled into bed with you. I hoped you liked it as much as I did."

Her words didn't have the results she perhaps intended because I felt a sudden deflation of spirits, an unpleasant blow of depression that came out of nowhere. My trip to Mowaht Bay had turned into a disaster. Embarking with her on an exercise of trivial indulgence would make things worse. I had been avoiding looking directly into her eyes, but now I did so, and saw something dark and malignant.

"This is funny, right?" she said in a low voice. "Funny ha-ha *and* funny peculiar."

"What's funny about it?"

"For a minute there, I thought I had a handle on you. Maybe I was wrong."

I mumbled something about being tired and went to my cabin. Tess stayed away.

CHAPTER TWELVE

I woke after a long doze. I cleaned myself up, brushed my teeth and got dressed. Passing along a companionway, I came across a large cabin that turned out to be Tess Rollins' office. The door was open, so I poked my head inside. She wasn't there. As an office, it was first class, with a Mac computer, executive recliner, built-in cabinets, the works. The walls were decorated with framed black and white photographs.

Tess was up on deck, wearing a monogrammed white terry-cloth robe with nothing underneath it. Every time she moved, she showed plenty of beautiful bronzed leg. She was moving around a lot I noticed, making strawberry waffles from scratch with an old-fashioned electric waffle iron that looked incongruous amid the yacht's modern hi-tech gadgetry. I sat down at a table set with monogrammed silver cutlery and linen napkins. The table's centrepiece was a cut-glass vase full of fresh yellow chrysanthemums.

The day was now quite beautiful. The mountains, which last night had been black and forbidding, appeared now as variegated strips of green between folds of blue-grey water and unsullied blue skies. Tess's carefree manner suggested a return to our former footing; now she couldn't do enough for me. She smiled winningly and asked, "What'll it be, Silas? Champagne or Chardonnay?"

It occurred to me then that life is sometimes a matter of comparison between having stress and not having stress. I looked at her, composed, smiling and coming on. "Chardonnay," I said.

Tess pushed an intercom button and spoke a few words. Seconds later, a man dressed in a steward's uniform, looking to be around 60, arrived on deck with a bottle of Chardonnay in a silver ice bucket. I'd never seen him before, although I should have suspected his existence—the *Mayan Girl* was obviously too much work for a single-handed owner.

The steward uncorked the bottle, doled a finger's worth into a glass and indicated that I was to taste it. The bottle had a French label, the contents tasted okay. He filled two glasses and departed. I handed Tess a glass. We drank, looking into each other's eyes. Hers were sparkling. We ate a great many strawberry waffles, washed down with cold white wine. When the first bottle ran dry, the steward reappeared as if by magic with a new one. Tess laughed a lot and we both had a pleasant buzz. She looked smooth, sleek and contented, like PC after a can of tuna.

I said, "About Jane Colby. There's something bothering me, maybe you can explain it."

"What's that?"

"It strikes me as very peculiar that Jane abandoned Terry. Terry must be very difficult to live with and control. Jane drank too much, but women who abandon older children must be rare."

"Women who murder their husbands are rare too, but they exist."

I held my wine glass up to the light and smiled at it.

"Janey has a lot of character flaws," Tess continued. "As I told you, my dad was a longshoreman. Fred Colby was an accountant. Mowaht Bay is blue-collar and Janey had a very irritating habit of reminding us that she belonged—or thought she belonged—to a superior class. When she and Neville got married and the HANE empire started making big money, she became practically unbearable, an insufferable snob who even insulted members of her own family. My mom and dad couldn't stand her.

"Janey doted on Terry when she was a baby, treated her like she was a Christ-child. That all changed after Terry's accident. After that, Terry was brought up by babysitters and maids. See, a less-than-perfect child didn't fit into Janey's value system."

In the ensuing long silence, I became aware of the subdued whine, emanating from the distant dock, where cranes were transferring Vancouver Island's timber to a Japanese freighter.

Something bumped the side of the yacht, and a male voice yelled: "*Mayan Girl*, ahoy!"

Tess and I looked down over the railing. Urban Kramer had arrived in a Boston Whaler and was tying up at the wharf. With a muttered, "Oh hell," Tess threw her napkin down on the table and disappeared below. I went to the head of the boarding gangway. When Kramer saw me standing there his smile vanished and the look of astonishment which replaced it was almost comical. He walked aboard and said, "Good Christ, it's you, Seaweed. What are *you* doing here?"

"Just finishing brunch," I said, backing away from the nimbus of Old Spice.

He stared around for Tess, didn't see her and said doubtfully, "Somebody said you'd been hurt."

"Who said?"

"Everybody. It's all over town that a Victoria cop was roughed up last night."

"But who exactly told you?"

"Gee, what's the difference?" he said nervously. "I was in the Bee Hive earlier, people were talking. You look pretty good for a guy was beaten up and ran into a deer."

"I've been lying down, recuperating."

"Best thing for you, probably. Where's Tess?"

"She's around here somewhere."

"Is Ralph here too?"

"Ralph?"

"Tess's steward."

"That his name? Yeah, Ralph's aboard. Fancy a glass of cold white wine?"

"Damned right. It's hot again, today."

Kramer had shed his logger persona and morphed like a butterfly. Today he was ridiculously overdressed in a Harris tweed suit, yellow vest, a white shirt with a starched collar and a knitted wool tie that matched his tweeds—totally unsuitable garb for a summer's day in B.C.

He sat down at the table and yanked off a pair of rubber overshoes to reveal maroon brogues. That morning his face was the colour of hammered liver. There were purple crescents beneath his eyes. But if he wasn't the best-dressed logger on the coast, Prince Charles doesn't play polo.

"You managing to stay warm enough, Urban?"

He looked down at the clothes he was wearing and laughed, "I am now. But I've been out in the whaler. It's cold on the water."

I took another look at Urban's whaler. It didn't match the description of the boat missing from the Rainbow Motel. I poured him a glass of wine, refilled my own glass and waited for him to say something interesting. He obliged by asking, "Known Tess long?"

"Not long."

"I thought you were staying at Chrissie's place, over the beauty parlour."

Kramer seemed to know all about my movements. "I was supposed to. But, one thing led to another and I ended up here."

"You spent the night with Tess?"

"I spent the night *aboard*. There's a difference," I said sharply. "Let's not start any rumours."

The rebuke threw him for a minute. Instead of pursuing the topic he said, "Hear that ruckus last night? I suppose you must have. Drunken lunatics were setting fireworks off," he said self-righteously. "Them rockets are still red hot when they land, create a fire hazard. Next thing you know, the forests are ablaze from here to Port Renfrew, sawmills and other logging-operations are all shut down."

"You're a logger yourself?"

"Not me. I'm a government scaler," he replied complacently.

I asked, "Did you know Neville Rollins?"

"Yeah, sort of. I used to see him around, I guess."

"How would you describe him?"

"How about a short, runty little wagon-burner?"

"I'm more interested in your impressions of him as an individual."

"He was the most vindictive little bastard I've ever met," Kramer began. Then footsteps sounded, and he turned away to admire Tess Rollins, looking splendid in a white shirt and shorts and white kidskin deck shoes.

Kramer lost all interest in me. He bustled to his feet, clasped Tess by her upper arms and tried to kiss her on the mouth. Tess turned her head away and Kramer's lips brushed along her cheek. She seized his hand, shook it awkwardly and said, "Urban, meet Silas Seaweed."

Kramer was like a football player who'd just caught a grenade instead of a ball. "We've already met," he mumbled.

She was tense; we all were. That day, two men and a single woman definitely made a crowd. To spare everybody further embarrassment I said rather formally, "The Texaco guy's probably got my MG ready to roll by now. So, thanks for your hospitality, Tess. It's time I was getting along."

"No no, you can't go yet, let's have more wine," she said with an attempt at vivacity, but her smile was thin. She grabbed my arm and whispered, "Don't leave me alone with him, *please*."

Turning to Urban she asked, "Had breakfast yet, Urban?"

"Of course not," he said, flushed with anger. "I had coffee at the Bee Hive, that's all. We had a breakfast date. Did you forget?"

She clenched a fist and put it to her forehead, as if suddenly remembering, but the gesture was contrived. She said, "I'm sorry, Urban. You two get acquainted; I'll put my apron on, make some waffles."

"Don't trouble yourself," Kramer said stiffly.

They were conscious of me but I wasn't a participant in what was going on there. I was an object to talk across, like a garden wall. I didn't mind. I no longer wanted to leave. I wanted to see where this sparring would lead. It led downhill. Looking angry and perplexed, he muttered a terse goodbye and hurried ashore down the gangplank.

Tess's expression was unreadable. "Sorry about Urban. He acts like that, sometimes. The poor guy tries too hard. Notice his ridiculous clothes? It's all this snow and rain. Twenty feet of the stuff falls on us every year. It gets to some people in the end and rusts their brains."

"He keeps himself well informed though."

"He can't help being well informed. In company towns the size of this one it's hard to keep secrets." She laughed and shook her head, adding impishly, "Urban probably spent all night in the Legion hall. Playing pool and drinking too much. He plays badly, loses money and puts himself into a bad temper. Why does every man who goes in a pool hall think he's Minnesota Fats?"

"It beats me. I play poker myself, and I think I'm the Cincinnati Kid."

"Yeah, but you probably win more than you lose." She looked enquiringly at me. "I hope you don't make too much of this, Silas. Urban and me, we're not going anywhere. He's had the hots for me for years. My money might influence the way he feels. Too bad, because I don't find him attractive. Maybe I should send *him* on a cruise."

I laughed. Tess ran her tongue over her lips, leant back against a railing, grabbed my hand and said mischievously, "Do you find me too assertive?"

I considered her question seriously for a moment. She looked at me closely and said, "You told me you'd been married. Nancy, wasn't it?"

I nodded.

"Anybody taking her place right now?"

My mind switched to Felicity Exeter. "There's a woman I met last year. I was working on a case and we hit it off. I see her sometimes."

"Is she white?"

I nodded.

"Forget her then, because it won't work; she'll never understand you," Tess said earnestly. "I've been wanting to fuck you since last night. There, I've said it. Don't tell me you don't feel the same way."

"What's this? You trying to make me feel sorry for you?"

She reacted like I'd slapped her face.

"Call it what you like," she snapped. "Half-honest guys, they're the only ones I get. When I *do* meet somebody genuine he's not interested."

"Who do you think I am, Marcel Proust?"

Her face hardened and her voice became husky. "Who?"

"Proust. A guy who did all his best work in bed," I said, grinning. "He was a writer, not a lover."

"Just who the hell are you, anyway?"

"Silas Seaweed. I'm a cop, with the Victoria Police Department."

"I wish you weren't," she said, looking across the railing. "I wish you were just simple and uncomplicated."

"Like you?"

A fleeting smiled curved her lips. "I tell you this much, Silas. If you ever do get interested in me I'll never bore you."

CHAPTER THIRTEEN

Driving away from Mowaht Bay, the MG's speedometer registered an unsteady 40 kilometres per hour. When I pushed it faster, it skittered sickeningly from side to side—reminding me of the time I fell off a mechanical horse at Monty's pub. When not actively wresting to keep my car on the long and winding road, I thought about Harley Rollins—putting together the things I knew, the things I suspected. As for Tess Rollins, I tried, difficult as it was, not to think of her at all for fear of losing track, driving off the road and ending up in the saltchuck, where my sex life, my supernatural life and all my other lives would reach a sad, sordid, inglorious finale.

I made it back to Victoria about 8 PM and dropped the MG off at Ted Rushton's Brit Car shop. After looking over the damage, Rushton's service manager told me the car would be off the road for the better part of a month. He gave me a full-size Chev loaner, a car that, compared to my sprightly British coupe, drove like a tank.

Back at my cabin on the Warrior Reserve, I had a couple of short drinks, showered Mowaht Bay's dusty road off my sweaty body, put on a terry robe and uncapped a bottle of Foster's. My spine felt stiff and my tongue tasted like a roofing shingle. I ate a carton of chicken and potato salad, cleaned my teeth, drank two glasses of water then went to bed and slept dreamlessly. A jangling telephone woke me up. I was gargling mouthwash when my answering machine clicked in. Detective Inspector Bernie Tapp's voice said, "Silas. Put your feet on deck and pick up the goddam phone. We need to talk."

I reached for the phone and asked, "What time is it?"

"It's nearly 7:30. That's *ante meridian*, in case you were wondering."

"What's up?"

"I need you at headquarters, right now," Tapp said, banging the phone down hard.

I had a cold shower, put on my sergeant's uniform, pocketed my electric razor and went outside, Chief Alphonse was herding another bunch of chattering kids into the yellow school bus. The chief waved. I walked over to him and said, "Chief, we need to talk."

He nodded and said, "That'd be good. I'd enjoy that."

"How about after lunch, today or tomorrow?"

"Fine, meet me at the band office, say four o'clock. Me and the kids are always back home by then."

I GOT INTO THE CHEV and started driving. The car had a 383 V-eight under its hood. Before I knew it, I was doing 70 and still accelerating. The Chev wasn't as much fun to drive as the MG, but it was a lot faster. I slowed down, plugged my razor into the lighter socket and started mowing. A red light brought me to a stop in Vic. West, where the Johnson Street Bridge had been raised to let a freighter move through to Point Ellice. Glancing in my rear-view mirror, I noticed a shiny Ford Mustang, parked two cars behind me.

The bridge came down. I drove on and parked in the police lot on Caledonia Street. Walking upstairs to Bernie Tapp's new office, I thought back through the years, resuscitated in memory some of the cases that Bernie and I had worked on together: murders, blackmails, rapes. After 10 years, many of those cases remained unsolved.

Mrs. Nairn, the sad-eyed brunette who was the acting DCI's private secretary, was typing in an anteroom. She waved me right on through. I tapped on Bernie's door and went in, a malicious satisfaction stirring within me because DCI Bulloch now belonged to police history.

Tapp's office overlooked the Memorial Arena. I found him standing with his back to the door, spreading birdseed on a window ledge. Without turning around he said, "Shut the door, Silas. You're causing a draft."

"How did you know it was me?"

"I saw your reflection in this window, but I'm psychic as well."

Bernie Tapp is a little less than six feet tall. He has an 18-inch neck. If men were measured like automobiles, he would be a big-block V-eight running on high-octane. He is 50 years old. He has strong, blunt hands and he can bench-press hundreds of pounds. That day, he was wearing a red lumberjacket with burn marks on the pockets, a blue sweatshirt, faded jeans and leather boots with cleated rubber soles.

I said, "What's a matter? They didn't issue your DCI's uniform yet?"

Bernie closed the window, placed the can of birdseed on a filing cabinet and sat behind his desk. A couple of pigeons landed on the windowsill and began to peck.

"The harbourmaster called us three days ago," Bernie said. "They'd found a body, floating in the Inner Harbour. We picked it up, put it in the morgue."

"Three days ago? That's very interesting. But why ruin my beauty sleep and drag me over here to tell me about it?"

"I thought you'd want to know. Guess whose body it was?"

"Jane Colby's," I said, without even thinking.

"That's right. How did you know?"

"Maybe I'm psychic too, but it was actually a guess. Also, somebody probably told you I've been making inquiries about Jane Colby."

"That's correct. We had a phone call from a lady on Crowe Street. She's accusing you of unprofessional conduct."

"Sister Mildred?"

"No, her name's Daphne-something."

I shrugged my shoulders, and at the same time, my hand moved reflexively toward the pocket where I used to keep cigarettes and matches. I'd quit smoking more than 10 years previously, so the reflex was a bit odd. This case was getting to me.

"I talked to Sister Mildred, Terry Colby's guardian. I called on Terry's grandfather as well, but that was *two* days ago," I said. "I'll swear they knew nothing about Jane Colby's death at that time."

"Perhaps not, but *we* knew. Mr. Colby should have been notified. Somebody screwed up, time was wasted, although there's a reason," Bernie said. "When Inspector Manners looked into it, he discovered that Jane Colby's next-of-kin is a mentally handicapped child."

"We say mentally *challenged*, nowadays. Incidentally, Denise Halvorsen saw Jane Colby in Pinky's, two weeks last Friday."

Tapp's eyebrows came together. He said, "Okay, open up. Tell me everything."

I told him everything. I told him about meeting Terry Colby, visiting her Crowe Street care home, visiting Fred Colby, and about my trip to the Rainbow Motel. I told him about my stay in Mowaht Bay, and about my punch-up with Harley Rollins.

Bernie said incredulously, "You came to blows with Harley Rollins?"

"I merely defended myself. Later on I met Harley's sister, Tess."

"Did you beat her up, too?"

"No, but we came close to committing a biblical sin. When I went back to Mowaht Bay, three of Harley's goons showed up. They tried to kill me and damn near succeeded."

"How do you know they were Harley's goons?"

"How do I know it'll get dark tonight?"

"Serves you right," Bernie snapped. "Harley Rollins is too big to fool with. You should have been more tactful."

"Maybe. I gave one of his goons a broken jaw. Afterwards, I spent the night on Tess Rollins' boat."

"There's more; tell me the rest of it."

I told him about the goons who attacked me, and how I'd ended up on Tess's boat. I told him about the logging donkey, and my ghostly encounter. Bernie took the whole thing in stride. Grinning cynically he noted, "If one of these guys does have a broken jaw, identifying him will be a cinch."

Bernie was making a move to stand up when I said, "There's more."

He sat down again, his face lengthening as I recounted Denise Halvorsen's story about seeing Jane Colby in Pinky's bar.

"That's all very useful. You've been a busy boy, Silas."

Bernie got up, put a tweed cap on his head and said, "Okay, let's go."

"Where to?"

"The morgue. En route, you can tell me a bit more about this ghost you think you saw."

"En route, you can tell me what 'Nice' Manners is doing on this case."

"Detective *Inspector* Manners, if you don't mind. He's been promoted to the job that could have been yours, if you'd played your cards right."

CHAPTER FOURTEEN

The forensic pathologist had grown old at his trade. Age and experience had carved deep grooves down his long, bony face. He led Bernie and me into a cold, antiseptic chamber that smelled of formaldehyde. A minute later, we were staring down at the naked remains of a thin, middle-aged alcoholic. We'd already inspected the white shirt, jeans and runners Jane Colby had been wearing when they plucked her out of the water. Five dollars in loose change, a VISA card and a B.C. driver's licence had been recovered from the leather billfold found in her pockets. The pathologist was gazing intently at the corpse's ghastly neck wound. She appeared to have been garroted, almost beheaded. The pathologist nodded to a female assistant. Between them, they flipped the body face down on its marble slab. The pathologist pointed wordlessly, so Bernie Tapp and I leaned forward for closer looks. The dead woman's back, shoulders and legs were covered with numerous deep parallel bruises, contusions and cuts. Pebbles were deeply embedded in the white pulpy flesh of her body. When Bernie and I had seen enough, the pathologist and his assistant turned the body back over.

Bernie Tapp said, "It looks like a hit and drag, to me."

"Indeed," the pathologist said, "Those abrasions suggest that a vehicle knocked her down on an unpaved road. It appears that the driver then hooked a line around the woman's neck and dragged her behind his vehicle."

"Why *road?*" I asked.

The pathologist pursed his lips.

I went on, "She might have been knocked down in an unpaved parking lot. She might also have been knocked down on a glacial moraine, or in a gravel pit. Then she was towed. But not necessarily along a road."

The pathologist stated, "She had sexual intercourse before death. It is an interesting case because, despite all appearances, her death was probably caused by drowning."

Tapp's brow knotted. "How long do you figure she'd been in the harbour?"

"I don't know. Long enough for deposited spermatozoa to die in situ. Two, maybe three weeks, but that's just a guess at present. We'll narrow it down after more tests."

Bernie cleared his throat. I looked at him. He raised his eyebrows and said skeptically, "Doctor. You just told us she's been in water for weeks, yet you still found sperm in her vagina?"

The pathologist gave him a pinched smile. "You are surprised, Chief Inspector?"

"Acting Chief Inspector," Tapp said, adding uncertainly, "Sperm is a liquid, right? You'd think it'd wash out."

"Not at all," the pathologist said. "We'd expect to find traces of ejaculated sperm in a woman's vagina as much as 10 weeks after intercourse. We've sent a sample of the sperm to the DNA lab."

Bernie and I took turns borrowing the pathologist's magnifying glass and examining the dead woman's neck injury. It looked as if a steel cable the diameter of a finger had been wrapped around her neck then tightened. Tiny flakes of rust were discernible in the wound. I said as much to Bernie, who had reached the same conclusion. I pointed out, "Technically, I guess, she wasn't strangled. She was garroted."

"Quite right," the pathologist returned. "The garrote appears to have been a multi-strand steel cable. It's hard to believe, but a garrote was not the primary cause of death. She died by drowning, unquestionably."

Tapp and I had seen enough. We went out of the room and along a corridor to an inner office with windows instead of walls. The clerk working at a desk inside the office was a tired-looking older woman wearing a white lab coat. Dark liver spots discoloured the skin of her hands. A tin of breath mints lay on her desk. Bernie asked her when it would be convenient to bring Jane Colby's father in to view the body.

The clerk popped a mint into her mouth before making a telephone call. We heard it ring along the corridor. After a short conversation the clerk put her hand over the mouthpiece and said to us, "To identify it officially, right?"

Bernie nodded impatiently.

She put the telephone to her ear again. After listening she grunted, put the phone down and informed us, "They'll clean it up a bit first, do cosmetics and that. Her father will have hysterics otherwise. Let's say, three hours?"

"Fine, three hours," Bernie said tersely.

Bernie and I left the building and stood on the sidewalk beside his unmarked Interceptor. He said, "According to you, Denise Halvorsen saw Jane Colby in Pinky's two weeks ago last Friday." I made a mental calculation. Bernie had made the same calculation. He went on, "That's 17 days ago. Correct?"

"Correct. It's Janey's last reliably reported sighting."

Tapp's cell phone rang. He listened to the phone for a moment, returned it to its pouch and said, "I gotta go. B and E on Dallas Road," Bernie said. "By the way, remind me: what's Jane Colby's dad called?"

"Fred Colby."

Bernie got into his Interceptor and fastened the seat belt. I tapped on his window, and he opened it. I said, "I've got a special interest in this case. I'd like to stay involved, if that's okay with you."

"A special interest," Bernie repeated, smiling grimly. "You horny bastard. I'll lay odds you're humping witnesses. Again. Who is it this time?"

"*Again?* What do you mean, again?"

"You want me to give you a list?"

"Pillow talk breaks plenty of cases."

"Plenty of careers get broken the same way."

"I'm concerned because Terry Colby's a Native."

"Native? I've just seen Terry's mother. I'll lay you odds she's white, 100 percent. That means Terry's half Native, at most. And bollocks to the rest of it. Don't tell me, because I can guess. You spent the night on Tess Rollins' yacht. So that's it, right?" he said, shaking his head in disbelief. "I can't believe it, you're screwing the dead woman's sister-in-law, and this is a murder case. Will you never learn?"

"Bernie, I am not fucking and have never fucked Harley Rollins' sister."

Bernie gave me a grin as tight as a fisherman's knot. "Do you have a suspect in mind?"

"Several, nothing definite."

"Okay. Go ahead, just don't mess with evidence, is all," he said, tapping the steering wheel with two fingers. "This woman, Tess. Good looking, is she?"

"Attractive, not good looking."

"She must have something going for her."

"Let's put it this way. I'd rather look at Tess Rollins, naked, than look at you in a detective chief inspector's uniform."

Bernie drove away.

I STROLLED BACK TO POLICE headquarters, deep in thought. Bernie had been right to suspect me, even though, this time, he was wrong. Having carnal knowledge of witnesses, although not expressly prohibited by Victoria's police code, certainly is a high-risk activity.

Back at Caledonia Street, I got into the Chev, drove it to the parking lot behind Swans Pub on Pandora Street, locked the car and walked across the street to my office. I let myself in, picked up the mail lying on the floor beneath the slot and threw it on my desk. PC, taking her ease on my blotter, leapt to the floor and bolted into the bottom drawer of a filing cabinet, where she'd been shredding valuable papers. Then the penny dropped. PC was getting rounder by the day; the bottom drawer of my filing cabinet had become the designated maternity area.

I opened the curtains wide and smiled at passersby for a minute before switching on my answering machine. There were two intriguing messages for me. The first, from "Killer" Miller, in forensics, informed me that fingerprints found on the plastic water bottle I'd left with him had been run through the computer. They did not match the prints found on the beer bottle that felled Jack Owens in Pinky's Bar, nor those of any known felon.

The second phone message was from Bernard Cole—the insurance adjuster I'd met at the Rainbow Motel construction site: Mr. Cole had an update on that missing speedboat. I rang him right away.

Cole said, "We've located the boat. It had been driven onto a beach near the Cadboro Bay village. Its bows were damaged, and it's undoubtedly the boat that rammed that seiner."

"So we know, within minutes, exactly when the speedboat was stolen?"

"Correct," Cole replied. "It rammed that fishboat 17 days ago."

"*Sixteen*," I said. "It would have been 17 days if the fishboat had been rammed before Friday midnight. The actual ramming occurred at 3 AM, Saturday morning, according to what you told me."

Cole laughed and said, "You're exactly right. That was sharp. I don't suppose you know who the thief is."

"Not yet, but I'm working on it. Where's the boat now?"

"It's parked outside the repair shop at the Oak Bay Marina."

"Sorry, I know this sounds elementary, Mr. Cole. But there is no doubt that this is Harley Rollin's boat?"

"No doubt whatsoever; the serial numbers on the boat match those on Rollins' policy."

"Good. I believe I'll just pop around to the Marina, take a look for myself."

"Mind telling me why you're taking such an interest? I mean, it's only a missing boat."

"It's part of an ongoing inquiry, and I owe you one, thanks."

I examined my facts: Seventeen nights earlier, Constable Denise Halvorsen had seen Janey Colby at Pinky's. Present on that occasion also was Jack Owens, Janey's former boyfriend. During the course of the evening, a blow delivered by an unidentified assailant had felled Jack Owens. A few hours later, Harley Rollins' boat had been stolen from the Rainbow Motel. Were these items related in any way, or was it just simple coincidence that Janey went missing, that her boyfriend was attacked, and that Harley Rollins' speedboat went AWOL at more or less the same time? My brain stopped working. I felt stale, listless and, to a certain extent, frustrated. I was overdue for a workout session at Moran's Gymnasium. Punching a bag clears my mind wonderfully, sometimes.

PC was standing outside the filing cabinet, her back arched, claws extended and purring ecstatically as she shredded another folder. I checked her litter box, filled her saucer with milk, closed the curtains and went out.

First, I drove over to the Oak Bay Marina and parked near the Orca statue. Sunlight, glinting off the waves, was hard on my eyes, so I put my shades on. Sailboats were tacking around Jimmy Chicken Island in a light breeze. The island, I noticed, had been partially denuded of vegetation by recent grass fires. A couple of women were launching a two-person kayak at the Beach Drive launching slip.

A shiny black Lincoln turned onto Beach Drive from Windsor Road. The car's tinted windows prevented me from seeing the driver as it came into the marina parking lot. I ducked out of sight behind a Hummer stretch limo. Moving slowly, the Lincoln went past and parked near the coffee shop. The driver got out, locked the car then strolled down a flight of stairs out of sight. It was Tess Rollins' steward. I'd seen that Lincoln before—in Harley Rollins' garage.

Coming out from behind the Hummer, I could see that Harley Rollins' speedboat was up on blocks outside the boat-repair shop. It was a modest open Starcraft aluminum 22-footer—a basic mass-produced aluminum day-boat fitted with an adjustable canvas bimini and a Plexiglas windshield. The boat appeared to be about five years old, and the only thing special about it was two massive Evinrude outboard motors. Their propeller blades were bent like pretzels, with one blade broken off completely. Bits of pulverized wood lay deeply embedded in the boat's crumpled aluminum bows. I peered over the gunwales. Four damp flotation cushions and a couple of damp orange life jackets lay untidily in the bilges, along with plastic buckets, dirty foam coffee cups, rubber fenders and several fathoms of galvanized-iron anchor chain. The boat's Danforth anchor (disconnected from its chain) was stowed in a rack in the bows. One end of the anchor chain was shackled to the after bulkhead. The other end of the chain wasn't connected to anything.

I was pondering some mechanical damage to the boat's after

bulkhead, when a workman wearing blue dungarees emerged from the repair shop. He lit a cigarette and sighed. "Quite a mess, eh?"

"Yes, although I suppose it can be fixed."

"Sure, we can fix anything, only this job won't be cheap. Them Evinrudes will need new legs, for a start. What makes me so mad is, it's all so bloody unnecessary. I mean, some hooligan steals the boat and takes it for a joyride, right? That's bad enough. Only, what does he try to wreck the boat for?"

"Beats me," I answered truthfully.

"Bloody maniacs. Speed demons, thieves, they're all cut from the same cloth," the mechanic said, with rising anger. "Tell me something. How many outboard motors do you think get stolen from this marina every year?"

"I haven't the foggiest."

"Last year, we lost 19. Nineteen outboard motors were pinched from this very marina. This year, we've already lost 10."

"What about security?"

"The marina's locked at night, on the land side. That doesn't stop engine thieves though. They come by water, after dark. In and out in two minutes. Some of these outboards are worth thousands."

"Do you ever catch 'em?"

"The odd one. Kids, mostly," the mechanic said, tapping ash from his cigarette. "Generally, they're too young to prosecute. The Oak Bay police take 'em to the station, give 'em a good talking to, call their parents, and that's the end of it. Professionals never get caught."

"What happens to the stolen motors?"

"Your guess is as good as mine. They move 'em across the province; sell 'em through the classifieds maybe. People are always looking for reliable used outboards. There must be good money in it, because the thieves are so brazen."

The mechanic threw his half-smoked cigarette to the ground,

trampled it underfoot and returned to his repair shop.

I checked the rivets securing the Starcraft's serial number plate to the hull—the rivets were original, had not been tampered with. I would have been highly surprised to find things otherwise. I took another, closer look at the mechanical damage on the rear bulkhead. It appeared as if somebody had been raising and lowering an anchor chain across the stern. I knew enough about boats to recognize this as unusual. It is customary to swing anchors over the bows. It is also customary, and wise, to keep anchors securely shackled to their chains. I was still wondering about all that when I went across to the Marina Coffee Shop.

Ralph, Tess's steward, was drinking coffee and eating Danish pastries at a table beside a window. I picked up a tray, bought myself coffee and smoked-salmon quiche at the lunch counter.

I needed information, and the steward might be able to provide it. I wondered how to go about obtaining the information without setting off alarms that might reach Boss Rollins' ear.

I carried my tray over and said, "Remember me? I'm Silas Seaweed. Mind if I join you?"

"Mr. Seaweed," he said, surprised but apparently not discomfited by my arrival. "I'm Rhenquist. Ralph Rhenquist. Sure, sit down, how are you sir?"

"Fine," I said, smiling to let him think that nothing serious was intended. "You're a long way from home, Ralph."

"Please just call me Rhenquist. It makes life so much easier if I maintain a certain distance from my employer's friends. I hope you understand." I grinned at him.

He pointed across the blue sparkling waters of the bay to a headland, a mile from where we were seated. He said, "In one sense, sir, I'm not far from home, because I was born over there, on Ten Mile Point. My grandparents lived on Tudor Road in the '20s. I was born and grew up in their house, actually."

"I hope you still own it, Rhenquist. A house on Ten Mile Point is worth a bundle today."

"Alas sir, I do not. The house went out of the hands of my family in the '60s."

Rhenquist was small and wiry. His face was as brown as a walnut and as wrinkled as a dried apple. He had the modest, self-effacing manner of the perfect gentleman's gentleman, along with the appropriate diction and vocabulary. He was wearing a neat blue suit, a white shirt and a black tie. His black shoes gleamed like wet olives.

Rhenquist went on, "Practically speaking, nowadays I have *no* home. I have my own cabin on Miss Rollins' boat, and a room in Miss Rollins' house here in Victoria, and that's that."

"What brings you here from Mowaht Bay?"

"It's my day off, actually. Mr. Rollins knew I was coming into town, so he asked me to take some things in to the drycleaners."

"Didn't I see you drive up in a Lincoln?"

"I suppose you did, sir. That is Mr. Harley's car, although he hasn't driven it for a while. It appears that he wants to start driving again soon, so he asked me to give the Lincoln a run. Make sure everything's all right."

"And is it?"

"Oh, perfectly, sir. All it needed was a good polishing and an oil change."

I remembered reading the police report that Harley Rollins had temporarily lost his licence over a DUI charge. "It must have been a bit awkward for Mr. Rollins, not being able to drive."

"Indeed it was, sir."

"So how did he get about?"

"I'm sure I don't know, sir. Does most of his business by telephone, I suppose. If he absolutely had to go somewhere in a hurry, he'd use a taxi, I suppose, or get a lift from one of his many friends."

"Or he could use a boat?" I asked innocently. "Using a good fast boat, he could get from Mowaht Bay to Victoria in what, a couple of hours?"

"In good weather, perhaps," Rhenquist said, adding apologetically, "Technically, his driving ban extended to boats, I believe. Besides, a boat isn't very practical, is it? Not as a usual thing. I mean, the water's quite often rough in Mowaht Bay and along the Straits. Especially in winter."

Rhenquist rose from his seat, wiped his mouth with a paper napkin and said, "Goodbye, sir. I must be getting along."

I nodded. He went out.

Two commercial fishermen wearing paint-smeared coveralls came in to get take-out coffee. I was going to ask them something, when my cell phone rang. It was Bernie Tapp.

Bernie informed me, "I'm calling from headquarters. They're taking Fred Colby and Terry Colby to the morgue right now."

"You think that's wise? Terry's got the mind of a 1. Seeing what's left of her mother will terrify her."

"Maybe. We'll soon know," Bernie replied. "Anyway, it's up to you, you said you have an interest. If you want to witness the proceedings, better get over there."

"I'm at the Oak Bay Marina. Be right over."

"What are you doing in Oak Bay?"

"Tell you when I see you."

Bernie gave an affirmative grunt and hung up. He had sounded a bit terse with me, which was unusual. I wondered why. I paid for my meal and went out of the café.

CHAPTER FIFTEEN

Bernie was waiting for me on the street outside the morgue; we entered together. A clerk directed us to a small, dimly lit room with curtain-draped walls where the dead woman lay on a gurney beneath a yellow plastic sheet. The room was hot and it smelled powerfully and unpleasantly—a heavy, cloying, almost sickening jungle scent. It was like being in an alligator swamp.

Bernie and I waited for five minutes before Fred Colby came in. He walked slowly, using a walking stick, and appeared calm. Constable Denise Halvorsen and Sister Mildred escorted Terry Colby in a moment later. I wondered if Sister Mildred had sedated Terry, who appeared peaceful and composed.

A male attendant flicked a wall switch and a small spotlight shone down on the gurney.

Bernie murmured something to the attendant, who drew aside the yellow sheet to reveal Jane Colby's face.

Death had exiled Jane Colby to the Unknown World. This was probably the first dead person Terry had ever seen in her young life, and I half expected her to faint, or to become agitated. She didn't, because Jane Colby did not look dead. It was as if she were alive, peacefully sleeping. By some wizardry, a cosmetician had transformed the ghastly object dredged from the Inner Harbour into a lovely temporary work of art.

Jane Colby's long yellow hair—thinking back, I suppose it must have been a wig—flowed down her face in lovely soft shiny waves, covering her ears and resting on the upper part of her shoulders. Jane's eyes were closed; her unwrinkled unblemished skin was pale, flawless. Her red lips were full, moist-looking.

When Fred Colby, visibly moved, leaned forward to kiss his daughter, the morgue attendant restrained him gently and whispered something in his ear. Tears welled up in Mr. Colby's eyes. Denise Halvorsen handed Mr. Colby a tissue, and he blew his nose.

As for Terry, she let out a small gasp and asked her mother to open her eyes.

Speaking in her normal voice, Sister Mildred said, "Terry, dear. Your mommy can't open her eyes, because she is sleeping. Your mommy is in heaven with Jesus."

"When can I talk to her?" Terry asked, in a baby-like voice.

"We don't know that yet, do we?" Sister Mildred replied. "That all depends upon when Jesus *wants* you to meet your mommy, doesn't it?"

"Does it?"

"Yes, it does, so you be a good girl and remember to say your prayers," Sister Mildred said, putting an arm around Terry's shoulder.

Bernie cleared his throat. Denise didn't say anything. She didn't have to. The dead woman, until now *officially* anonymous, was anonymous no longer. This was Jane Colby, for sure.

Sister Mildred took Terry's hand and led her from the room.

Bernie Tapp, Fred Colby and I went into the morgue office, where Colby signed a few necessary forms. When these formalities were completed, the three of us went outside onto the street. Earlier, Mr. Colby had mentioned that he had come to the morgue in a cab, so Bernie offered to drive him home. Mr. Colby accepted.

Bernie said to me, "Listen, Silas, You and me, we've got a few things to talk about. Meet me in Mom's Café?"

"See you in half an hour," I said.

Bernie and Frederick Colby went off.

I GOT INTO THE LOANER AND let the engine run for a minute while I switched on the radio and scanned the horizon for Interceptors. There weren't any, so I put the loaner into gear and headed for James Bay. My car radio was tuned to a rock station, playing Pink Floyd's *The Dark Side of the Moon*. Then the disc jockey reminded us that Syd Barrett, Pink Floyd's co-founder, had died prematurely, at the age of 60. The jockey then went on to say that Barrett had left the band in 1968 because of mental instability, exacerbated by his use of LSD. I seemed to recall that Barrett had died of diabetes, which we used to call sugar diabetes, which is the disease ravaging North American Indians, which ... I tried to concentrate on my driving. It wasn't easy. Sometimes I get these loops playing endlessly inside my mind. I finally deleted the diabetes loop, whereupon I became conscious of my geographical surroundings. I was in James Bay.

Again, I got that odd feeling I sometimes get when going along James Bay's quiet, tree-lined streets, the feeling that sends shivers down my back. It starts between my shoulder blades and works south. That day, I felt it rather powerfully. Maybe it was because I couldn't entirely banish the memory of Jane Colby, lying dead in the morgue. Maybe it was because another Ford Interceptor was following me. And maybe it was something else entirely. I made a mental note to consult Chief Alphonse about all this the next time I saw him.

I stopped the loaner in the dusty unpaved parking lot outside Mom's Café. Within shouting distance of Victoria's Fisherman's Marina, the café is a rusty corrugated-iron building, mainly patronized, until recently, by fishermen and blue-collar work-ers who know good hamburgers when they taste them. Mom's had recently been discovered by the local smart set. Today there were BMWs and Audis in the lot, in addition to pickup trucks. I noticed a shiny Ford Mustang parked outside the café's rear entrance, where, atop a garbage can, a Siamese cat was grooming itself. I glanced at my wristwatch and saw that it was nearly 3 PM. Where had the day gone?

I went in and sat at a vinyl and duct-tape upholstered booth near a window. The girl behind the lunch counter picked up a cof-fee pot and a menu, and came over to see what I wanted. I ordered coffee and apple pie à la mode. She filled my cup and went back to propping up the counter.

The same two fishermen that I'd seen in the Oak Bay Marina's coffee shop were standing together beside Mom's Wurlitzer, pon-dering the music selections, which have changed little since Jim Morrison was laid to rest in Paris's Père Lachaise cemetery. They fed the Wurlitzer some coins and listened in respectful silence to "Shine On You Crazy Diamond," the song that members of the Pink Floyd band had recorded as a tribute to their troubled former bandmate.

I was eating pie and ice cream, brooding about the imperma-nence of life, when Bernie Tapp came in. Bernie signalled for cof-fee en route to my table.

I stated, quite loudly, "I'm being followed."

Bernie's features sharpened. Three young women seated across the room turned to glower.

Deliberately strident, I went on, "Everywhere I go I see unmarked Ford cars. The guys driving 'em pretend they're fishermen, but they can't kid me. I know what they really are. They're gumshoes."

Speaking in the usual casual tone he uses when he's lying, Bernie said, "You're paranoid, pal. Better rein yourself in. If you don't, the next thing you know you'll be hearing strange voices. You'll be buttonholing strangers on the street, end up tranked to the eyeballs in a psych ward, a mere shadow of your former self."

"Hogwash," I said. "If those guys by the Wurlitzer aren't working for Internal Affairs, that spider crawling through your hair is a vampire bat."

Brushing a hand across his hairy scalp, Bernie scowled at the men lounging by the Wurlitzer. They went out without a word. "Assholes," Bernie snarled. "Bunch of buffoons and nitwits."

I said, "Better come clean, Bernie, and tell me who they are and what they want. We know each other too well. You ought to know better'n try to flannel me."

"I don't know anything about it. Your pal Bulloch probably borrowed them from the Mounties," Bernie said, as he stared into space. I followed his glance. The two "fishermen" were getting into their Ford Mustang. When they drove off, dust rose from beneath their wheels, until they reached blacktop, on Superior Street.

"Remember telling me about the first time you ran into Terry Colby?" Bernie asked.

"I remember."

"How did she know *then* that her mother was in trouble?"

"Terry didn't tell me that her mother was in *trouble*. Terry told me that she'd *lost* her mother."

"Okay, but how did Terry know that? I mean, there she is, isolated in that care home, not talking to anybody. It was only a week or so since she'd seen her mother."

"Sorry, Bernie, I don't see the relevance, and besides, you're stalling. It's time you came clean."

Bernie picked up his coffee cup, drank and then set the cup down on the table in the exact centre of a paper napkin. "As far as you are concerned, buddy, the late great Detective Chief Inspector Bulloch has reached the end of his rope. Complaints about you keep rolling into headquarters, and Bulloch has had it up to here with you. When he leaves the force and sinks out of sight forever, he'd like to take you under with him."

"I thought he'd already left."

"Technically. He's still on the payroll a few more weeks."

"I'm not entirely surprised. You did tell me that a very reliable sex-obsessed woman called Daphne had reported me."

"She's not the only one. I don't suppose Harley Rollins likes your manners either."

"Did he file an official complaint?"

"No, but I should think he's considering it."

"Boss Rollins attempted to have me murdered, he's not entirely unbiased."

"In your opinion, that is."

"You don't believe me?"

"Actually, I do believe you. Except I'm your friend, Bulloch isn't. He's hated you since the days you were a detective constable under his direct command. He hates you because you deliberately get up his nose. Bulloch was Victoria's chief detective. You interfered in the Calvert Hunt murder inquiry, solved the case yourself and made Bulloch look bad. You did the same thing with the Ellen Lemieux case. You're a neighbourhood cop, one step up from a Boy Scout. Let me remind you: nowadays, your job is to help little old ladies across the road."

I felt a growing irritation and opened my mouth to tell Bernie that I'd never sought credit for solving either of those cases. He went on, "Forget Internal Affairs. Bulloch would have bled you white, but he's on the way out. I'll close the operation down. It was his last desperate attempt to ruin you."

"Old cops and old cons are the same," I mused. "They keep going back to the spot where their skids were greased."

"Some old cops, maybe. Police detection works best when

there's cooperation. The force works because it has an established hierarchy, established leadership, set rules and regulations.
Bureaucracy is a necessary component of our business."

He was right. I said, "Let's meet for breakfast, tomorrow?
Eight o'clock, Lou's Café?"

"Okay, I'll see you there. Maybe you'll see sense, take me up
on my offer. You'd look good in an inspector's uniform."

"Gotta go," I said, getting up from my seat. "I've another
appointment at four o'clock.

But when I got back to the reserve, Chief Alphonse was
absent. Maureen, the band secretary, told me he'd be away for a
day or two; our scheduled conversation would have to wait.

THAT NIGHT, I HAD TROUBLE sleeping. About three o'clock, I got
out of bed. Crazy ideas flapped around in my head like deranged
birds. I tried to wash them away with a slug of rye. I drank it
quickly, poured myself another and sat down in an armchair, trying to evolve theories that would explain recent events without
recourse to the supernatural.

Chief Alphonse believed that, in his quest for power, Harley
Rollins had stayed underwater for a long time. But had he? In
the minds of Coast Salish and other First Nations peoples, the
natural and supernatural worlds are inseparable. Each is intrin-
sically joined to the other. Religious knowledge, and practical
knowledge, both are necessary for survival. Many Coast Salish
Vision Quests involve swimming and diving in deep cold water
where—in states of breathless trance—Questers encounter the
supernatural overseers that afterwards govern their lives. People
prepare to receive spirit power after rigorous cleansing rituals
involving fasts and bathing. Only individuals socially and physi-
cally cleansed are thought ready to engage in Vision Quests, and
to receive the knowledge and strength necessary for survival.

In the Coast Salish religious pantheon, there is an entity known as Hayls, the Transformer. Hayls came down from the north with his friends Mink and Raven. Hayls taught the first people how to live and speak, how to make houses and fishnets. Hayls is powerful, although our chief supernatural entity is the Sun. Sun, ruler of men and birds—everything that creeps, walks and flies, including creatures from the Unknown World, such as earth dwarfs and water dwarfs.

My whisky glass was empty. I poured another three fingers.

If Billy Cheachlacht did see Harley Rollins dive into the Gorge that night, and did not see him surface for a long time, then one might assume that he'd been under water for that whole time. Not necessarily. Perhaps Harley had swum under water for a while, before surfacing in a spot where Billy Cheachlacht couldn't see him. On the other hand, if Harley had actually been under water for all of that time, was there a rational explanation? Perhaps an under water tunnel or air pockets? Influenced no doubt by the rye I was drinking, many unlikely scenarios presented themselves to scrutiny, some more absurd than others.

My thoughts turned to Detective Chief Inspector Bulloch.

I thought Bulloch was a very tough nut. I wondered what he'd really had in mind when he'd turned his dogs onto me. Pure vindictiveness, just because I'd stepped on his toes? Bulloch was an unsavoury, constipated bureaucrat, but he had risen to DCI rank. I had to admit, he wasn't a complete fool. Turning tracking dogs loose against his officers was an expensive proposition, however, not something to be lightly done. The object of his exercise, undoubtedly, was to get me chucked off the force. Would I be a fool and oblige him?

I gargled with salt water, cleaned my teeth and lay down on my bed for an hour.

CHAPTER SIXTEEN

Pinky's Bar and Grill was a redneck dive on View Street. When I got there, about eleven o'clock that night, big chopped Harleys with long chromed forks, handlebars as high as your head and high-gloss paint jobs were parked outside. Inside, a band was playing deafening rock on a small stage. Overweight bikers with the usual tattoos and earrings were quaffing ale, eating half-raw steaks, or lurching around the dance floor with puffy-faced blondes wearing minis and spike heels.

I was drinking house rye and ginger at the bar. Doyle, Pinky's red-haired bartender, was wearing a Foster's apron, black pants and a starched white shirt with rolled up sleeves. He had the red complexion, watery eyes and slightly fuzzy voice of a man who drank all day long. Doyle noticed my empty glass and gave me an interrogative look. I said okay and told him to have one himself. Doyle mixed another rye and ginger, placed it on a fresh bar mat and moved a dish of peanuts closer to my elbow. A mirror behind the bar reflected the bald spot on the back of Doyle's head.

I said, "I don't see any bouncer here tonight."

Doyle—who learned his trade in Belfast—said, "Would you be referring to Warren Harris, sorr?"

"Yes I would, unless Pinky has more than one bouncer on his payroll."

"I wouldn't call Warren a bouncer, sorr," said Doyle. "Warren's just a waiter, so he is. Only time we need real muscle is when there's expensive name bands playing. That's when Pinky puts a cover charge on. He hires a couple of bikers to stand outside, so he does, to keep out the filth and check IDs. The kind of fellers we let inside, we wouldn't generally be needing any muscle at all. At all, at all."

Doyle pulled himself a glass of draft, threw back his head and poured it down his throat. He brushed foam from his lips with the back of a hand and directed a grateful smile at me.

"So tell me, who ejected Jack Owens a few nights ago?"

"Ejected, sorr? Harris carried the poor helpless soul outside, is all. What it was, was this. Somebody brained your man Owens with a bottle."

"Where's Harris tonight?"

Doyle pointed his finger at a large, 30-year-old, heavyset man with a broad spread nose. "That's him. Serving drinks to that four-some over there."

I finished my drink, set the glass down on the bar, wandered casually across the room and sat at a table near the band. When Warren Harris came over I said, "Bring me a double rye and ginger, and have one yourself."

Harris carried his tray across to the bar and spoke a few words to Doyle. Harris returned with my drink and said, "You were asking questions about me?"

"Not about you personally. I asked Doyle if there was a bouncer on duty. My name's Seaweed."

"Doyle says you're a cop."

"That's right. I am. I am an off-duty cop. Sit down a minute."

A thin woman came out of the ladies room, looked around and ended up at a table adjacent to mine. She was 30 or so, garbed in a dark, long-sleeved dress made of some soft, silky material.

When she rested her elbows on her table, the sleeves slid down from her wrists, exposing the scabs and needle tracks on her thin white arms.

Harris did not appear to be the kind of man who'd take any crap. He was wearing wraparound shades, a purple polo shirt and red pants. With an air of cultivated amusement, he sat next to me and said, "You're off duty tonight, are you?"

"That's what I said."

"In that case, what I'm thinking is, maybe you want to score some crystal? Nail some pussy?"

"Like the lady sitting at the next table, for instance."

Harris laughed. "If I tried, I might be able to arrange someone better for you."

Harris thought he had my number, which suited me. I said, "There was a punch-up in here a few nights back. A man called Jack Owens was involved in a disturbance. Correct?"

"More or less. Jack Owens ended up on the floor, bleeding, but Jack didn't cause the disturbance. Somebody else did."

"Who was that?"

"One of our regulars, a skank called Jane Colby."

I wondered if it were possible that Harris didn't know she was dead. I let that pass and said, "Tell me what happened that night."

Harris sighed; it was as if I'd placed a burden on his patience. He said, "Jack Owens and Jane Colby used to be a couple. I think they met each other right here in Pinky's one night. Then they had a falling-out. That night you're talking about; it was busy in here. Janey was drinking by herself, half in the bag. Owens was minding his own business at the bar, sitting with his back to the room. I guess neither of them knew the other one was here." Harris shrugged his beefy shoulders. "Then, just about closing time, Janey flips out of her gourd, starts screaming her fool head off. Owens turns around and sees it's her. Jack went over to see what's the trouble. Janey went nuts, tried to scratch his eyes out. I dragged 'em apart. The next thing I knew, a war had broken out. A regular headbanger, with half-cut assholes punching each other out, bottles flying, the works. Owens went down.

"Doyle called 911, cops and meat wagons showed up. I went looking for Janey, planning to chuck her out too, but she saved me the trouble. Pulled herself together and asked Doyle to call her a taxi. When the taxi came, I put her in it. She told the driver to take her home, and that was that."

"You said *home*. Do you remember the address she gave the driver?"

"No-o, sorry."

"I don't suppose you noticed which cab company it was, either."

Harris put his head to one side as he thought that question over. He said without conviction, "It might have been a Blackbird cab."

Across the room, a biker was trying to lift an ATM from its foundations. Harris asked, "Can I get you anything? The sky's the limit, in here."

I shook my head. Harris went over to the ATM, put both arms around the biker's stomach, squeezed, and manhandled him off the premises.

The band had hiked its decibel level several notches higher than I found comfortable. I moved back to the bar for the benefit of my ears.

Two minutes later, the woman in the black silky dress was sitting next to me. Her name, she said, was Candace. She brushed my leg with a smooth bare thigh and said, "There was a time, mister, when they wouldn't let Siwashes into this place."

I had nowhere to go with that one so I let it ride. She was bad news, although her long beautiful legs reminded me of Felicity Exeter. I asked Candace what she was drinking.

"Mint juleps," she said.

"You a southern girl?"

"I'm a girl who likes the north, east, west and, if you'd like to try it, the south too. Just as long as you pay the freight," she said, and ran her tongue over her lips.

When she finished her drink, I asked her if she'd like another.

"Sure," she said. "Ain't you the nice little gentleman."

Doyle poured another rye and ginger for me, and mixed a julep for my delightful companion. Doyle made his juleps with real mint. Candace picked the mint leaves out of her glass and chewed them before drinking. She leaned toward me and her black dress opened at the neck, revealing quite lovely breasts. She shifted her pelvis and said, "If you've finished admiring my titties, how about we finish these drinks and go to my place?"

"Thanks, but I'm okay here."

"I'm not good enough for you?"

I thought about those scabs and tracks, now hidden by her long sleeves. Smiling, I lifted my glass to my lips and drained it.

"Fine, so I slam a little junk. Does that make me dog meat?" she snapped.

Doyle said, "Will it be another couple for the road now, sorr?"

I shook my head. I'd been drinking for quite a while and was feeling the weight of it. The band belonged in a garage, not a public bar. Candace squeezed my knee and said, "I heard you talking to Harris, earlier. If you want to know about Jane Colby, I'm the one you should be talking to."

Doyle had overheard. He made an impatient gesture and said sharply, "Off you go, Candy. Be a good girl and leave the gentleman alone."

Candace didn't say anything, but, fast as snake, her hand snaked across the bar and her long red fingernails scratched the air an inch from Doyle's face.

Grinning, Doyle shoved my tab toward me across the bar.

I was reaching for my wallet when Candace grabbed my elbow. "Come on, it's still early," she said, moving restlessly on her stool. "Let's sit together at that table over there. We'll have one more drink and I'll tell you all about the Back Room. What do you say?"

"You watch your bloody mouth, now, Candy," Doyle said menacingly.

"Fuck you and the goat you rode in on," Candace retorted.

The band packed up their instruments. There was a merciful pause in the noise, until Doyle hit a switch. Wall-mounted speakers the size of coffins piped Led Zeppelin into the room.

I owed Doyle $56. I peeled three 20s from my wallet and dropped them on the bar. There were a couple of fifties in my wallet. When Candace saw them, her smile widened.

I stood up and told Doyle to keep the change.

"Don't you be going and paying any notice of any malarkey she might tell you about the Back Room, sorr," Doyle said in his thick brogue. "The Back Room is private, members only. You have to be a member, sorr, to get in the Back Room. Costs $100 a year. And you have to come recommended, sorr."

"And you can go play with yourself, Doyle," Candace retorted. "*I'm* a member, see? A Back Room Club Member in good standing. I've got my own fucking key."

Candace stood up. Moving unsteadily on those spike heels, she tottered away from the bar and between the drunken bikers gyrating around the floor with their mommas. After a moment, I followed her.

There was one more room in Pinky's. Candace used her key

to open a door hidden behind the bandstand, and I followed her into a small airless rectangular facsimile of the club we'd just left. It was unoccupied and dark, until Candace flicked a light switch, whereupon strings of tear-shaped Christmas tree lights, looped around the walls, bathed the room in a dim purple haze.

"Janey Colby's been picked up and laid down in here more times than the Queen of Clubs," Candace said, gazing wickedly at the room's collection of cheap mismatched chairs and tables— some of which lay upturned—and at a huge plasma screen television set angled against a corner, from whose blank opaque glass my own dim image was reflected. The room's miniature bar was securely locked behind a sliding metal screen.

Candace said, "Shut the door, Siwash. I need a smoke."

I closed the door. Candace opened her purse, took out a joint and lit it with a match. The smell of marijuana was soon blending with the Back Room Club's residual odours of booze, hot sweaty flesh, urine and yesterday's deodorant.

She righted one of the room's upturned chairs and sat on it backwards, her legs wide, one arm draped across the chair's backrest. She said, "Can I trust you to do the right thing by me, big boy?"

"Can you suggest any reason why I'd want to?"

"You're interested in Janey Colby and I'm going to tell you a story, maybe it'll be worth something," she said. She took a few greedy drags and then offered the joint to me.

I shook my head.

"You're not exactly Mr. Conviviality, are you?"

"I suppose you know I'm a cop."

"Sure I know. So what's next? Are you going to bust me for possession?"

"No."

"The last I heard, cops paid for information."

"Only if it's worth something."

She took a clip from her bag and smoked the joint right down, before grinding it under the sole of her high heels. "The thing you don't know about Janey Colby is, she was no angel. After that husband of hers died, she needed to earn a living, and the way she earned it, she fucked the whole coast. For years. Janey fucked her way from Vancouver to Puerto Vallarta and back. I don't mean she was a street hooker; Jane was always high class. Whatever you call it, it sure beats pounding a typewriter, and it pays better too.

"Janey's on the game?"

"She *was*, for years, till she polished her resumé and latched up with Jack Owens. What I'm saying is she was no angel. Back to that night in here, the night Janey went bananas. It was blue movie night; there were only a handful of us."

"You were watching blue movies?"

"Explicit. Doyle was running the show and pouring drinks. Things were more or less normal, till Doyle slides in a fresh cassette. A cheap little homemade video it was, shot by some amateur with a minicam. It started off slow, no soundtrack—just a fat little aboriginal in a bedroom with a young girl. At first, they're just talking to each other, their lips are moving anyway. She's drinking coke from a can. He's smoking a joint. Then the Indian guy jumps up, grabs the girl and flips her onto ass. Next thing is, she's got both legs open, and he's going down on her. It's nothing special, right? But when Janey Colby looked up and saw what was showing on the screen, she just completely lost it, started screaming at Doyle to turn the TV off.

"The trouble was Doyle didn't move fast enough to suit her. So Janey ups and throws a beer jug at the TV set. It's a miracle the screen didn't break; the jug just bounced off of it. Now the Indian's got the girl on her knees, he's reaming her, still no sound track. Just Janey, screaming and carrying on. Everybody else in here is pissing themselves, laughing."

Candace looked at me expectantly. I didn't say anything, because I was running the blue movie through my mind, and guessing whom its participants might be.

"But the best was yet to come," Candace said. "That girl was Janey's daughter and the man was her uncle, Harley. Does that blow your mind, or what?"

I gave Candy $100 and returned to Doyle's bar. He was polishing the bar with a cloth, and whistling. I said, "Tell me about the blue movie that set Janey off."

Doyle appeared to give my question some thought. "You'll have to remind me, sorr. Which movie would that be, now?"

Careful to look him right in the eye, I grabbed his wrist, squeezed it hard and warned, "Don't mess with me, Doyle."

Doyle's air of amusement vanished; suddenly he looked worn and tired. His glance fell. When I let go of his wrist he massaged it absently and said, "There's people bring movies into the Back Room now and then. That's how some of these eejits get their kicks. You can rent 'em anywhere. That movie you're thinking about? I don't know where it came from or who brought it. Could have been one of the members, I don't know one more thing about it, and that's a fact."

"You're a liar, Doyle. I want that movie, so let's be having it."

"I'm sorry to say you can't have it, sorr, because here's a funny thing. When Pinky found out about it, he pulled the tape out of the cassette and set it afire, so he did."

Doyle smiled a little, but he was lying through his teeth.

WHEN I LEFT PINKY'S, stars were out and the moon was casting its cold light over the sleeping city. There was a bad taste in my mouth and my ears were ringing. I wished I were with Felicity Exeter. I needed to be with somebody sweet and honest for a change. But our relationship was at the complicated stage where neither of us fully understood the other. I remembered Tess Rollins' words: Felicity was white, we were of different cultures. She was rich, polished, sophisticated. Were our cultural differences too wide? When I was with her, it never seemed so, but . . .

The Blackbird Cab Company operates out of an office in the basement of the Blanshard Hotel. I began to stroll that way. I was going down Store Street (an area inhabited after dark by drifters and winos), when a familiar voice said, "What's up, Silas?"

The voice belonged to Constable Bradley Sunderland. Sunderland had been pounding a beat the best part of 30 years, and he was the VPD's unofficial Santa Claus. Every Christmas he toured rest homes, handing out candy bars and playing tin-eared accordion music to captive pensioners. One year, in recognition of such meritorious services, Victoria City Council awarded him a silver plaque. Apart from that plaque, and citations for assault, drunkenness, dereliction of duty and persistent tardiness, Sunderland would have nothing but a boiler-plated pension to show for his years on the force.

Sunderland was standing in the dark, on the top step of an unlit office building, smoking a cigarette. He said, "Come up here for a minute, unless you'd rather get wet."

I joined him. "Is it supposed to rain?"

"You just wait and see," Sunderland replied, chuckling, as a street-cleaning vehicle appeared on the street, spouting water and scooping up trash. Water splashed the sidewalks, dousing the bums sleeping in doorways.

Still chuckling, he said, "I get the driver to adjust his nozzles when he comes along here. Roust these idlers out of it, and wash the smell of them and their piss away."

Men and women rolled out of their dripping sleeping bags, cursing. Sunderland was enjoying himself, but I was tired. Fed up and half drunk—the whole episode just struck me the wrong way.

I said good night, was going back down the steps, when Bradley said, "What do you think about Bulloch retiring, eh?"

"About time he went," I snapped. "The era of bent witnesses and rubber hoses is over and done with, thank Christ."

"What do you mean, over and done with? Bulloch got results, didn't he?" Sunderland asked angrily. "Me and Bulloch joined the same year. We're both on the sunny side of 60."

I forced a laugh, tapped Sunderland's arm and said, "Forget it, I was only kidding. Besides, you don't look a day over 80."

Stiff with rage, Sunderland stormed down the steps and walked out of sight. I rubbed my neck and resumed my walk, following my nose toward the Blanshard Hotel's neon sign, revolving slowly in the black sky above.

The Blackbird Cab Company's duty dispatcher was a heavy woman of 65, wearing a yellow muumuu. I'd phoned; she was expecting me. Her office was the size of a handicapped-washroom and when I entered she had her feet under a tin desk and was speaking into a mouthpiece held in place by a metal band clipped around her dark hair. Smoke curled up from a cigarette, resting in an overflowing ashtray in front of her. She smiled at me. Still talking, she waved me to a flimsy folding metal chair. I sat down on it gingerly and looked at the paperback with which she had been whiling away the graveyard shift. It was a *Flying Saucer Manual.* Its lurid cover depicted a naked maiden with very large breasts being pursued across an unearthly plain by bug-eyed monsters.

Her name was Mrs. Scargill. When she finished talking, she scribbled notes into a logbook, put a smouldering cigarette into the exact centre of her lips and took a deep drag. "You interested in space aliens?" she enquired, breathing smoke in my face.

I couldn't back up, there was no room, and my chair was already jammed against the wall. "Interested in space aliens? Who isn't?" I replied. "How else can you explain television? Don't tell me human beings invented TV. Alien invaders have been monitoring the earth for 50,000 years. It's just hard to make people believe, that's all."

She looked at me intently, trying to decide if I were serious, and guessed wrongly. "Believing isn't hard for me, I'm a convert. I've done my homework. I was at a convention in California last year. That's all they were talking about—invaders and alien sperm thefts. I went to a sperm-donor seminar. Had to pay extra, but it was worth it."

"I'm sure it was," I said. "Now, what about the cab that picked up a woman outside Pinky's?"

Mrs. Scargill asked me to tell her the exact date and probable hour the cab had been dispatched. I did so. After flipping back through the pages of her logbook she said, "Alf Gzowski picked up a fare at Pinky's about that time. I wasn't on duty, myself, but it says here that Alf drove a woman to the Rainbow Motel."

Mrs. Scargill's phone crackled. She shoved the logbook toward me and pointed to the relevant entry with nicotine-stained fingers. The information had been written in a kind of shorthand, but it was plain enough. Alf Gzowski had taken Jane Colby to the Rainbow Motel on what was probably the last night of her life.

While speaking into her mouthpiece, Mrs. Scargill stubbed out one cigarette, took another from a pack of Player's and lit it with a disposable lighter. She reached out across the desk, retrieved her logbook and made another entry. Over the next five minutes, she had a flurry of calls, during which I tried to process the new information she'd given me.

When Mrs. Scargill's calls abated, she said, "Pretty good log-keeping system, eh? We don't get every single ride, you know, although we get most of 'em."

I raised my eyebrows.

"Cowboy drivers," she said. "Some of 'em pick up a fare without reporting in. They make a bit extra on the side that way."

"Is Alf Gzowski on duty tonight?"

Mrs. Scargill shook her head, "Won't be in until eight o'clock tomorrow morning. Alf's on dayshift right now."

She was beginning to tell me about a special crystal she'd purchased in Las Vegas. It emitted an eerie glow when alien invaders were in proximity. I was actually quite interested to know what she'd do, should the crystal begin emitting. Her phone crackled again. "It'll be busy for the next hour," she said. "Clubs and discos are starting to close."

I blew Mrs. Scargill a kiss and went home.

CHAPTER SEVENTEEN

I woke up feeling as if an old sock was jammed down my throat. I drank a pint of water and spent five minutes with a tube of Colgate and a toothbrush before normalcy began to return. I put on a pair of much-washed, sun-bleached jeans, a polo shirt and dark blue tennis shoes, and went out to the loaner. Compared to the MG, it steered like a boat and was as responsive as a bad date.

I drove off the Warrior lands and headed east, toward the Johnson Street Bridge, the very heart of downtown Victoria. I ran into a traffic jam at Catherine Street. The bridge had been raised to let marine traffic traverse the narrows separating the Gorge Waterway from Victoria's Inner Harbour. I was stuck in traffic for 10 minutes. Alongside, to my right, the E & N Railroad's ancient red brick engine sheds were doing exactly what they had been doing for the last 100 years. Beyond, the dodgy high-rise condo development that had contributed to Jack Owens' and Janey Colby's grief raised its own proud head. Lou's Cafe was busy, too, when I arrived there just after eight o'clock.

Bernie Tapp was sitting at our usual table, staring out the window.

Lou—wearing a tall white chef's hat with a CAT logo on it— was doing a very creditable imitation of whirling dervishes near his hotplate. Sweat poured down his neck and inside the collar of his shirt. I ordered bacon, eggs, fried string-bean potatoes and whole-wheat toast, and filled my own coffee mug.

I sat across from Bernie. He looked me over and said, "Had a sleepless night?"

I said suspiciously, "Why?"

"Because you look like something the dog dragged in."

"Sometimes, your creative use of the English language really amazes me. 'Something that the dog dragged in.' Where do you come up with these gems?"

"Okay," Bernie said, "How about: Something that's been left out in the tropic sun then beaten with iron bars for eight hours?"

"Funny, that describes how *you* look."

"Yeah, probably," Bernie said. "But I look this way because I've been working all night. I haven't just crawled out of bed."

"I didn't know that DCIs worked long hours."

Bernie scowled.

I said, "What's up, Chief?"

"Midnight smash and grab," Bernie said. "And don't call me Chief."

Overnight, Bernie informed me, thieves had looted a ship-chandler's store after driving a stolen truck through its plate glass windows. "Third smash and grab this month," Bernie went on. "In and out in 10 minutes. They got away with canoes, kayaks, fishing gear, brass hardware, floater coats and on and on. The owner told Inspector Manners that she's lost stuff worth over a hundred grand."

"Does the inspector have any leads on who did it?"

"He thinks it must be an organized professional gang."

"Professional? How much skill does it take to drive a truck through a window?"

Bernie shrugged his shoulders. "A jewelry store was busted last week, probably by the same bunch. The insurance company is on the hook for over a million."

Bernie had been leaning across the table. His large hands, protruding from the cuffs of his long-sleeved shirt, were as big as hams. The yellow light pouring through the café window gave him a jaundiced look.

I stated, "I was at Pinky's last night."

"Silas," he said earnestly, "I hope you were wearing gumboots. Are you that hard up for a piece of ass?"

"*Piece of ass?* There you go again. Another lovely word picture painted by Bernardino Tapioca, master of the single entendre."

Bernie's stern visage softened. I said, "Speaking about lovely pictures, what do you know about Pinky's Back Room Club?"

"Everything I need to know, probably. Pinky set the racket up about a year ago. It's just an old-fashioned key club. The vice squad checked it out, saw what went on in there and thought it should be closed down. The crown prosecutor didn't see it that way. He told Vice there wasn't much they could do about a private club restricted to paid-up adult members. Amongst other things, it'd be an infringement of their Charter rights. Club members can do more or less what they like in the Back Room when the door's closed. As long as they don't do it in the street and frighten the horses, they're safe."

"Jane Colby was a member," I told him. "She was in the Back Room a few hours before we lost track of her. They were showing triple-X movies. One was homemade, perhaps by its distributor. It was presumably intended for offshore markets, but somebody goofed. The Back Room gang ended up seeing a movie they weren't supposed to. It might have been a peeping-tom movie, a clandestine shoot. Its leading and probably unwitting actors were Terry Colby and her uncle, Harley Rollins."

Bernie made a grunting noise deep in his throat. "We need to get our hands on that tape."

"That'd be nice. Doyle, Pinky's chief bartender, was on duty in the Back Room on the night in question. He told me the tape had been destroyed."

"Smart move, if true. Tapes are cheap though. If there's one, there'll be others. We just have to find one."

"I saw Henry Ferman leaving the Rainbow Motel a while back. He does a lot of business setting up CCTV equipment in gas stations, stuff like that."

"You think *he* made the movie?"

I shook my head. "I suspect Karl Berger."

Bernie was having trouble staying awake. He got up, grabbed our coffee mugs and went across the room to refill them. He brought them back and asked, "Who's Karl Berger?"

"He manages the Rainbow Motel."

"I must be losing it. Yeah. Karl Berger, I remember now. But you mean *ex* manager. The motel's being torn down." Bernie regarded me with a dissatisfied air and asked, "What makes you suspect Berger?"

"The last time I went around to the Rainbow Motel, Berger was messing around up a stepladder. It occurred to me even then, that he'd been removing hidden cameras."

"Motive, method and opportunity, Berger's got 'em all," Bernie said. "How about this: Berger is in the motel when Janey shows up. She's already put two and two together, so she knows or at least suspects that Berger made the movie. There's a showdown, Berger murders her to shut her mouth."

I told Bernie that my money was on Boss Rollins.

"Yeah, sure, but wasn't it a bodybuilder type who brained Owens? That describes Berger perfectly. Look, it fits: both Jane and Berger stay at the Rainbow Motel, so it's not a stretch for them to be sleeping together. Then things explode at Pinky's. Berger first attacks the ex-boyfriend, then he and Jane Colby go to the Rainbow, get into a lover's quarrel and he kills her."

Lou came over with breakfast and asked, "What we going to do about the Middle East? Things get any worse between Israel and Lebanon, there'll be an atomic war."

"I've got something deeper worrying me," Bernie said. "It's this puzzle: How come Tarzan was always clean shaven and could speak English?"

Lou, his hat tilted rakishly down to his nose, said, "Who?"

"Tarzan, the guy Johnny Weissmuller played in Saturday afternoon matinees when we were kids. He should have had a beard, communicated by grunts."

A workman seated across the café—probably a welder, wearing grimy coveralls pierced by dozens of tiny burn holes—shouted, "Hey, Lou! Where's my breakfast?"

Lou scuttled back to his grill.

Bernie said to me, "Well, whadda you think? Do you think Berger killed her?"

"He might have, but if he did, his motive's not very strong. For one thing, his reputation isn't worth protecting. What would he care if people found out he makes blue movies?"

"Yeah, I see your point. But together with the lover's quarrel angle, it's stronger. I'll bring him in for questioning anyway. Arrest him on suspicion, see where things go."

"Where it'll go, Bernie, is straight to the media. It's your first murder case since being promoted. If you're wrong about Berger, the media will be all over you. I can see the headlines now: "Victoria's New Detective Boss Implicated In Farce.""

Bernie's eyes glittered. He took a cell phone from his pocket and said, "I'm still gonna do it."

"Before you make that call, there's something else you should hear about first."

He put the cell phone down reluctantly. "Okay, shoot."

"Janey left Pinky's in a Blackbird cab driven by a man named Alf Gzowski. Somebody better talk to Gzowski as soon as possible."

"And you'd like that *somebody* to be *you* right? You'd like me to give you the go-ahead, do some more private digging, right?"

"Sure, why not. I'm not busy, and Inspector Manners has his hands full."

Bernie said without hesitation, "So? What you waiting for?"

Good question. What *was* I waiting for—for the oyster to give up its pearl, the Sphinx its secrets?"

Bernie said, "You're a damned good detective, Silas. Your talent's wasted, fooling around with neighbourhood policing schemes, so how about it? Move back to headquarters and work with me again. It'll be like old times."

"You, me and Nice Manners. One big happy crime-busting gang. It's tempting, in a way."

"There's an immediate opening on the squad that's yours if you want it. This may be your last chance for a while, don't blow it. I'll give you a couple more days to think it over. In the meantime, go ahead. Interview this cabbie. Just keep me posted."

I nodded.

Bernie picked up his cell phone again and punched the key-pad. Waiting for headquarters to respond he said to me, "If you need any help, from forensics or anybody else, better go through my office. And for chrissake, Silas, be careful."

He spoke to headquarters for a while; I didn't pay attention, particularly, to what was said. Bernie was about to leave the café when he suddenly remembered something. "By the way, there was a guy showed up at the hospital at Duncan with a broken jaw— Joseph Bickle, from Mowaht Bay."

"A Native man?"

"I don't know. He lives in a bunkhouse, not on the reserve."

Bernie turned away and walked through the door. I watched through the window as he trudged across the street toward Swans pub, turned the corner onto Store Street and was lost to sight.

AFTER BREAKFAST, I LEFT Lou's, went next door to my office and unlocked the door. When I opened the curtains, dozens of dead houseflies were prostrated on the windowsill. Half a dozen survivors crawled torpidly.

The office's housefly phenomenon has exercised my curiosity for years. For weeks at a time, sometimes, there isn't a single blue-bottle about the place, dead *or* alive. Then there'll be a Normandy Landing, with flies buzzing on my window panes, flies landing on my head, patrolling the coat rack, flitting in and out of the fireplace, parading along the frame surrounding Queen Victoria's photograph. I think they breed in dark spaces inside the walls.

I went out to the corridor, collected a vacuum cleaner from the building superintendent's closet and sucked every fly from sight. I was putting the vacuum back when the office phone jangled.

It was Alf Gzowski. He said, "I hear you want to talk to me."

"Correct, thanks for calling, sir. I want to ask you about a fare you picked up outside Pinky's recently."

"Oh yes? Sorry, I can't talk to you right now, because I'm outside the Empress Hotel, waiting to take somebody to the Schwartz Bay ferry terminal. I'll be free in about an hour."

"Can you come to my office on Pandora Street afterwards?"

"I'm at work, you know. I don't have unlimited spare time. How long will this take?"

"A bit of luck, not long."

"Fine, I'll come to your office, see you in an hour," he replied, then immediately changed his mind. "No, second thoughts, better make it an hour and a half."

I replaced the receiver, leaned back in my chair. After thinking for a minute, I picked the receiver up again, phoned headquarters and asked for Bjorn Matthiessen, in Vice.

When Bjorn came on I said, "What do you know about a guy called Karl Berger?"

"Never heard of him. What's he done?"

"I don't know, maybe nothing. He drives a Viper, probably spends more than he earns."

"Sounds exactly like me, except I don't drive a Viper."

"Is there much of a Blue Movie industry on Vancouver Island?"

"Nothing big. That's to say, nothing commercial. The competition's fierce. There's millions of underemployed bimbos and jocks out there. They call themselves actors, watch *Entertainment Tonight* and fantasize about getting into the movies. I mean, to them it's obvious that most of Hollywood's so-called stars have no talent. What they've got are boob jobs, hair extensions, personal trainers and contracts. Unfortunately, only one wannabe in a million actually makes it to Hollywood. The rest join amateur dramatic societies, or end up freelancing in front of a minicam, having sex with dogs, cats, goats and each other for peanuts in somebody's barn."

"Did you say *cats?*"

"Silas, you don't know the half of it," Bjorn said, ringing off with a laugh.

I looked at my wristwatch. It was nine in the morning. I got up and looked out the window. The street was jammed with traffic. Denise Halvorsen and Bob Fyles came into sight—weaving in and out between cars and pedestrians on hi-tech police-issue trail bikes. I locked up and traipsed across to Swans parking lot to pick up my loaner.

CHAPTER EIGHTEEN

Driving across town to the Rainbow Motel, I remembered noticing the Songhees condos—and in particular, the condo project that had failed badly, soaking up Jack Owens' and Jane Colby's money. Those condos started at close to a million and went up from there. Penthouses overlooking the Inner Harbour fetched millions. Something had gone seriously amiss with Janey's condo transaction, but in spite of that, her lawyer was now telling Owens he could relax, the pressure was off? How? Why? Jack Owens wasn't saying, and, as far as I knew, the Colby family's only substantial asset was the Fairfield house, which remained unsold and was owned by Janey's father.

Bernie Tapp's unmarked Interceptor was parked on the street outside the Rainbow Motel construction site, together with a prowlie with its roof flashers going. Since my last visit, the site had been almost completely cleared and was now being levelled. Sixteen-wheelers were delivering fill to an area by the water's edge. A construction trailer had been set up where the motel's boat shack formerly stood. A surveyor wearing a fluorescent vest was running transits. The motel building was still largely intact, although some doors and windows had been removed. Bare-chested labourers were sitting on the steps outside the front entrance, joshing back and forth as they took a break from work.

When I went past them to go inside, one of the workmen said, "Careful where you put your feet, pal. We've been tearing hardwood floors out."

I found Bernie Tapp up on a stepladder in the motel lobby, examining a hole in the suspended ceiling. A rookie constable I'd never met was supporting the ladder with one hand. When I entered, the constable waved me off with his free hand and said sourly, "Beat it, Siwash. We're busy."

The word *Siwash* denotes Native Indian and supports the vilifications applied universally to aboriginals living between Tierra del Fuego and the North Pole—ill educated, lazy, as trustworthy as jackals . . .

Bernie Tapp heard what was said and came down the ladder. He gave the constable an evil look but didn't say anything—maybe he wanted to see how I would handle the situation.

I am six feet four inches tall, 40 years old, with a muscular physique. To the best of my knowledge (it's a wise man that knows his own father) I am full-blooded Native, mostly Coast Salish. Maybe there's a bit of Blackfoot or Cree in me too, because I have a thin aquiline nose and my face is V shaped, rather than oval. Nobody's ever going to mistake me for a WASP, which is what the constable appeared to be. He gazed at me with angry blue eyes and made a small threatening movement. I stood my ground, which brought him up short. He was about to make things worse when I asked, "Find anything interesting up there, Chief Inspector?"

"I found what you thought we might find, Sergeant," Bernie said, a disgusted smile twisting his lips. Eyeing the constable up and down he said, "You can leave now, Constable. I'll deal with you back at headquarters."

The constable acted like he'd been kicked in the stomach. Flushing to the roots of his hair, he gave Bernie a sloppy salute and hurried off.

"I'll bust that racist swine," Bernie muttered.

"I have a better idea. Put him through sensitivity training. Then send him out to the Warrior Reserve to help Chief Alphonse with the kids."

Bernie nodded. "You handled it well, by the way," he said, reaching into his pocket for his pipe.

"Seen anything of Karl Berger?" I asked.

Bernie shook his head. "Karl took a powder. The construction boss hasn't seen him around here lately. Berger's not at his home and his Viper's gone. I've applied for a warrant to search his house. Maybe we'll get lucky and find that videotape."

I looked up to the ceiling and saw where another bundle of coloured electric wires had been snipped off.

Bernie lit his pipe with a kitchen match that he struck on his thumb. "How'd you make out with that cabbie—what's his name?"

"Gzowski. I'm seeing him in my office in an hour or so."

Bernie concentrated on his pipe for a minute. "You were right about hidden cameras. They'd been planted all over the building. We found two-way mirrors in some of the suites as well." He frowned and added, "Remember that chiropractor we busted last year—the one who had two-way mirrors in his examining rooms and in the women's washroom?"

I nodded.

Bernie sighed, shook his head, glanced at his wristwatch and said, "I was planning to see Henry Ferman next. Maybe I'll put that on hold. Talk to this cab driver first."

"Sure."

We went out of the building. While I'd been inside, a mobile catering van must have been and gone. Now the demo crew was drinking coffee from Styrofoam cups, eating doughnuts and clowning like frat boys, which, come of think of it, is what some of them probably were.

I watched Alf Gzowski park his cab in the no-stopping zone across the street from my office. Acting Detective Chief Inspector Tapp had usurped the chair behind my desk and was using my desk phone. I'd just been next door to Lou's café to pick up a tray of coffee and doughnuts. I put the tray on the desk. Bernie put the phone down and chewed his lip for a minute. He looked at me and said, "The Saanich Police just nicked Karl Berger. He was in the Schwartz Bay ferry lineup, with a ticket for Tsawwassen."

"Did they find any blue movies in his luggage?"

"No, but they found an ounce of cocaine."

Gzowski came in. He was a small, swarthy man with thinning black hair, a droopy moustache that added to his mournful air, and a mid-European accent. He was wearing the grubbiest black suit I've seen since Christmas, and brown shoes. Perched on his head was a chauffeur's cap with a brass number on it that had probably emigrated from Zagreb with its owner. Gzowski sat down on the visitors' chair and gazed hungrily at the coffee and doughnuts. "Go ahead," I told him. "Help yourself."

Gzowski seized a chocolate-cream doughnut and vacuumed it straight into his stomach. He ate the second one in two bites; cream dribbled out of his mouth and down his necktie.

Bernie said, "I understand, Mr. Gzowski, that you picked up a fare outside Pinky's a while back."

Burping, Gzowski reached for another doughnut.

I said, "To refresh your memory, sir. You picked up a woman, Jane Colby, outside Pinky's just over two weeks ago. It was a Friday night. There'd been a fight inside the bar."

Recollection dawned on Gzowski's face. "That her name, Colby? She was drunk, which isn't all that unusual for a Friday night. The reason I remember *her* is, when I got to Pinky's, there were cop cars and an ambulance blocking the street."

"Now that we've cleared that up," Bernie said, "do you remember where you took the lady?"

"I took her to the Rainbow Motel. When we arrived, the place was dark and it looked like it was closed. No lights on at all. When the lady got out of the cab, I was a bit worried. I didn't want to leave her on her own like that. What happened was I helped her. Held her arm, made sure she got to the front door. As it turned out, she had her own key. She let herself in, and that was that."

Bernie exchanged glances with me then said, "And what did you do next, Mr. Gzowski?"

"I went back to my cab and listened to the Canucks–Oilers replay."

"Who won?"

"Oilers, who do you think?" Gzowski replied. "Hernandez scored at the end of the third period. The game ended five-four."

Bernie smiled scornfully. "Approximately how long do you think you were parked outside the motel?"

"Quite a while, as it happened. I'd been busy all night, but there was a bit of a lull about then. I just stayed put, listening to the game."

"By 'quite a while,' do you mean half an hour? Maybe an hour?"

Gzowski put his head to one side and said uncertainly, "Maybe half an hour."

"Apart from listening to the game, did you notice anything unusual?"

"In the motel, you mean?"

"Inside, or outside," Bernie said patiently.

Gzowski laughed self-consciously. "I'd been drinking coffee all night. When the hockey game ended, I needed a piss. Generally, if there's a hotel or a restaurant handy, I just pop in and use their restrooms. I carry a plastic bottle around with me, just in case. But that night the street was quiet, there'd been a shower of rain, it was dark, there was nobody around. So I got out of the cab and was relieving myself against a tree when one of your constables saw me. Came round the corner from Superior Street and found me with my dick in my hand. He just completely lost it." Gzowski's indignation grew as he went on. "The officious little jerk threatened to charge me with gross indecency, for Christ's sake."

"Which constable are you talking about?"

"I don't know his name. Some blue-eyed rookie fresh out of the crib," Gzowski said angrily. "If he lives to be my age he'll know a bit more about aging prostates and be more considerate."

Bernie rubbed his chin with his fist and said, "Mr. Gzowski. You're probably the last person to have seen Jane Colby alive before she was murdered."

Gzowski had been lifting a coffee cup to his mouth. He started visibly and dumped hot coffee into his lap. "Jesus," he said. "You don't think I . . ."

"No, not at all. You're not a suspect," Bernie said. "I mean to say that you were probably the last person to see her alive except for the killer."

Gzowski, mopping his lap with a tissue, said, "I don't think I can tell you any more than I have already. After that episode with the constable, I went back to my cab. Then things got busy for a while, like they always do when all the clubs and cabarets close."

I said, "You mentioned that a *couple* of things happened?"

"Yeah, that's right," Gzowski said. "I picked my last fare up in Cadboro Bay. It was a routine call from the dispatcher to any driver in the vicinity of Cadboro Bay village. I was near the Uplands Golf Club, so I answered."

"Keep talking," I said.

"There's this guy waiting to be picked up on Cadboro Bay Road, that's all. So that's what I did, I picked him up. He was standing near Pepper's grocery store."

Gzowski stopped talking, took his cap off and scratched his head. He gave me a sidelong look and said, hesitantly, "This fare. I think he was a Native guy."

"You *think?*"

"That's right, I don't know, because here's the funny thing. I never saw his face. It was dark. He sat in the back seat of the cab."

I said innocently, "If it was dark, what made you think he was a Native?"

Gzowski moved uncomfortably. "Because of the way he talked, I guess. It was just an impression. It's like, you see a woman walking ahead of you on the sidewalk. You haven't seen her face, but you have an idea she's an Asian. Then when you catch up with her, it turns out she *is* an Asian."

I asked Gzowski where he'd taken his fare.

Gzowski was still uneasy. He looked at me directly, though, and said, "No offence, I didn't *want* to take him anywhere, to be honest. Some of your Native brethren have been known to throw up in the back of the cab or run off without paying. I'll be perfectly honest with you, sir. If I'd known he was a Native in the first place, I wouldn't have answered the call."

Bernie looked up at me. Neither of us spoke.

Across the street, a tow-truck driver was connecting a hook to Gzowski's cab.

Gzowski drank what was left in his coffee cup and remarked jovially, "It turned out okay though. Matter of fact, it turned out to be my best fare all night. I took him all the way to Mowaht Bay, dropped him off outside the Legion. There was $55 on the meter. He gave me two 50s and told me to keep the change."

Bernie said gloomily. "So he didn't throw up in your cab after all?"

"No, he did something nearly as bad though. He must have been soaked to the knees when he got in the cab, his shoes must have been sloshing water. He left a great soaking puddle on the carpets. Next day, when I found it, I thought he'd pissed himself. He hadn't though, the seat was dry. It was just the floor carpet was wet. I had to use a shop vac and a heater to dry it out."

Bernie beat a little tattoo on the table with his fingers and said, "This fare. You *think* he was a Native. Can you describe the way he was dressed?"

"Better dressed than usual, I would say, for a Native." Gzowski was blushing as soon as the words were out of his mouth. He gave me a conciliatory smile and said, "Excuse me, officer; sometimes I put my mouth in gear before the brain is engaged."

"Forget it," I said. "The main thing is, you wouldn't recognize this man again if you saw him?"

Gzowski shook his head. "No, I wouldn't. Apart from him getting in and out of the cab, when the dome light came on, I never got a look at him. A guy with long, dark hair. He was wearing a nice linen jacket, though. I did notice the jacket."

"What colour was the jacket?"

"Light coloured, maybe beige?"

I said, "Wait a minute."

I went outside, showed the tow-truck driver my badge and asked him to forget it. He refused.

I went back inside my office. With Gzowski's cab in tow, the truck started moving.

"Sorry about the interruption," I said.

"All right, to continue, Mr. Gzowski," Bernie prompted, "did you have any sense of how old your fare was? Old? Young?"

"Not quite middle-aged. Somewhere between 30 and 40."

Bernie told Gzowski to stay tuned, let him go, then sat for a minute fiddling with his pipe. When he had it going nicely, he blew smoke out the side of his mouth and said, "You think Gzowski is always that clumsy? Spilling coffee, squeezing doughnut cream over himself?"

I shrugged my shoulders and said, "The long arm of coincidence just stretched out and pointed a finger. It's funny that Gzowski picked up those two fares wouldn't you say?"

Bernie said, "It's time I paid Henry Ferman a visit."

"What about Karl Berger?"

"He can wait for now. I'll let him stew in the lockup for an hour or two."

"When you see him, ask him about that stolen speedboat, the one found on the beach at Cadboro Bay."

Bernie raised his eyebrows.

"Let me refresh your memory. Somebody stole a boat from the Rainbow Motel . . ."

"My memory doesn't need refreshing, pal. I may even be ahead of you."

"I hope you are, Bernie, because if this were my case, instead of yours, the guy I'd be talking to next is Harley Rollins. Find out if he stole his own boat, rammed a fishboat with it, then high tailed it to Cadboro Bay, where he ditched the boat, then called for a taxi."

"It's a good suggestion, but I've got a better one. *You're* the guy should interview Rollins next. The guy's already pissed at you. If you show up asking more questions, maybe he'll get mad, give something away that he shouldn't. Try not to get shot at this time."

THE SUN WAS HIGH AND ITS heat penetrated my shirt until I reached Fort Street and walked along the shady side. Looking east toward Rockland, I saw distant thunderheads. A rainbow sprouted up from Craigdarroch Castle and arched into the unseen. I turned right on Quadra Street, looped back downtown to the Inner Harbour and went into Jack Owens' office.

Owens' secretary, a nicely buffed professional woman who looked like an executive, remembered me from my previous visit. Her greeting was friendly, till I asked to see her boss. Her manner became vague, and she began to tell me that Owens was tied up indefinitely and was inviting me to make an appointment when Owens appeared in his doorway. He had a zombie-like blank stare and an untidy sleepless look, as if he'd been up all night. He was unshaven and his fingernails were bitten to the quick.

"Oh, it's you . . . I suppose you'd better come in. Sooner you're in, the sooner you're out, right?" he remarked, with an almost hysterical laugh then stepped clumsily aside to let me in. Going past, I got a whiff of his chemical halitosis.

He closed the door behind us and then spent several seconds adjusting the placement of a chair, before inviting me to sit in it. Had I done so, I would have ended up with my face in sunlight while he, in a chair behind the desk, had his own face in shadow. Perhaps he was hoping I wouldn't notice the glowing haunted look in his eyes. I put the chair back where it had been before and sat down.

He announced, "I've been expecting this call ever since I heard about Janey's murder."

I knew my grin was tight as I responded, "I'm sorry. It must have been a shock."

"Sorry?" he retorted. "You're a cop and never knew her. To you, she's just another number on another file."

"I'm a cop, which makes me some kind of a ghoul?"

Owens' lower jaw moved up and down, although no words came out of his mouth.

Love can be a hoax of the cruellest variety. At that moment, I presumed, Owens' suffering was intense, but his suffering would gradually diminish. In a year, two years, if he managed to extract his head from his ass, Jack Owens might be bestowing his affections upon somebody else. Janey Colby's situation was permanent. My interest in her wouldn't diminish till we found out who'd murdered her, and got a conviction.

The chair I was sitting in was uncomfortable. Its back-cushion sloped too much and it wasn't high enough for proper support. I moved my weight forward and rubbed my neck. Owens' eyes were soft and dull, his movements slow. To ensure his full attention I said sharply, "You were Jane Colby's financial adviser, were you not?"

He pulled himself up straight and sawed teeth across his lower lip until I thought he'd draw blood. For a brief flicker, his eyes weren't soft: they were hard and brilliant. He controlled his agitation and snapped, "Her financial adviser? That's one way of putting it."

"And as such, you had insight into her actual financial situation at the time of her death?"

"I suppose so," he retorted, fumbling into a drawer and bringing out a box of cigarettes.

"So tell me, because I want to know, *now*. What *was* her financial situation?"

The last time Owens had lit a cigarette in my presence, he'd apologized. This time, he didn't bother. He filled his lungs with smoke, blew an asymmetrical smoke ring and said, "Toward the end, Janey's finances took a turn for the better. She came into some money."

"Suddenly? An unexpected windfall perhaps?"

"Yes and no. It was something she'd been working on."

"Are we talking about the equity in Mr. Colby's house?"

"What's that supposed to mean?"

"Presumably," I explained, "if Mr. Colby borrowed on his equity, he might use some of it to help his daughter out. Fathers sometimes do such things."

Owens said sleepily, "I have nothing more to say. The relationship between me and my clients is privileged."

"This is a murder investigation," I snarled. "Nothing's privileged."

Getting up from my seat, I went around his desk. Owens was sitting on a chair fitted with castors. I put both hands on his chest and gave him a sudden shove that sent him sliding backwards several feet. Arms flailing, he came to a stop against a wall. Before Owens recovered, I started yanking drawers open. I found a bottle of liquid Ketamine and a needle rig in the bottom drawer of his desk.

"So that's what you've been having for breakfast. Special K," I snarled. "Where'd you get it? Pinky's?"

"You can go to hell," Owens said, still sprawled like a rag doll.

Ketamine was once a treatment for soldiers during the Vietnam War. Now a club or date drug, its legitimate use is as an animal tranquillizer. Known variously as Special K, ket, keller and wonk, Ketamine kicks in fast. Although a Ketamine high lasts less than an hour, impaired judgment and coordination can last a full day. Owens made an effort to stand. I pushed him back down and said, "Start talking, Jack, or you can kiss your professional life goodbye."

At that moment, he looked like a basket case, but there was residual violence in him. He managed to stand up and throw himself at me, his fingers going for my eyes. I grabbed a handful of his hair, did a half turn with my body and used my leg to sweep his feet out from under him. Owens crashed backwards to the carpet and banged his head, hard. What happened next made me feel sorry for him. Half inert, he covered his head with his arms and cried like a baby.

Owens' secretary came in. White-faced with consternation, hands to her mouth, she said furiously, "What on earth . . ."

"Your boss is ill," I informed her. "Bring him some strong black coffee, please."

Her eyes were on Owens. She didn't move.

I asked her, "How long has he been acting crazy?"

"Since yesterday," she snapped, pulling herself together. "What have you done to him?"

"Nothing, compared to what I might do, if I don't get co-operation from somebody in this office."

Belatedly, she seemed to realize how serious things were, for she produced a tentative smile and said, "Mr. Owens hasn't been himself lately . . . this is the first time I've seen him like this. What can I do to help?"

"Fetch some coffee."

I had spoken harshly. She pulled herself together and went out. Owens pulled himself together too, after a fashion. He crawled around the room for a while, slobbering and moaning, before climbing back into his chair and closing his eyes. I slapped his face—not too hard—and asked more questions. It doesn't matter what I said, because I didn't get intelligible answers.

When, after swallowing two cups of black coffee, Owens *did* start talking, I couldn't shut him up. Words, slurred and partially incomprehensible, tumbled out of his mouth. I asked Jack Owens to explain the change in Jane's fortunes.

"Janey had tons of money in the end," Owens told me, in a singsong voice. "Janey had money coming out of her yingyang. She was rolling in it, had hit the jackpot, right here, in the middle of River City, with a capital C, which rhymes with V, which is short for Victoria."

"Where did the money come from?"

"I told you," he burbled. "It came from right here, in the middle of River City."

After that, Owens lost control of his brain and I didn't get another comprehensible word from him. Eventually, breathing normally, he seemed to fall asleep. Maybe he was acting. I decided to let things drop for the moment. The secretary still hovered. I told her to keep a close watch on her boss and started to leave.

She said vehemently, "You should be ashamed of yourself."

"You'd rather he died with a needle in his arm?"

"Of course not," she said contemptuously.

"How long have you known about his drug use?" I asked.

She suddenly became very meek, but gave no answer.

"Keep an eye on him. I think he'll be okay, but if you become worried, call an ambulance. The medics will know what to do," I said, and started walking. She followed me into her own office and closed Owens' door, saying, "Just a minute."

I sensed the disgust behind her brittle smile. Unable or unwilling to meet my gaze, she said, "There's something perhaps you *should* know."

I waited.

"There's this man. John Doncaster. Mr. Doncaster invested heavily in Mr. Owens' projects. Mr. Doncaster has been putting pressure on Mr. Owens. I happen to know that Mr. Doncaster has threatened Mr. Owens with bodily harm if he doesn't get all of his money back. Doncaster and some other investors don't seem to realize that if they're patient they'll get their money back with interest."

Beneath the secretary's smooth veneer, I detected a flint-like hardness. I grinned at her and went out without speaking. Back on the street, I phoned Bernie Tapp. He wasn't answering. I left a message giving the gist of my recent encounter with Owens and suggested Bernie have somebody check out John Doncaster.

I DROVE ALONG THE DESERTED dirt road, beneath the trees, creating dust, traversing in daylight the same road that Alf Gzowski had travelled in the dark, until I reached the Mowaht Bay Legion Hall and parked in its weedy parking lot. Situated across the highway from the Sound, the hall was a wood frame building with a wide porch. Two old men, taking it easy on a shady bench, gave me the once-over as I went up the steps and inside.

One legionnaire was drinking alone in a corner. Two others were ineptly banging balls against the cushions of a full-sized snooker table, trying to make trick shots that seldom came off.

I sat at the bar. A narrow beam of sunlight streamed in through a small high window. Dust motes whirled endlessly in the window's yellow light like a mini universe. After a while, a toilet flushed in the W.C. and a barman appeared. Wiping his hands on an apron, he asked to see my membership card. I showed him my badge instead and ordered a Foster's. The barman took a bottle from a cooler, snapped the cap off and put it on the bar in front of me. I asked for a glass. The cold glass he brought glistened with condensation. Instead of filling the glass for me, he leaned against the back counter with his arms folded. I was thinking about half a dozen things at once, so it didn't occur to me for a minute that the bartender was giving me the evil eye.

When the snooker game ended, one player came to bar and said, "Same again, Frank."

The bartender detached himself from the counter, extracted a couple of Blues from the cooler and put them on the counter.

The snooker player was a middle-aged man in a well-tailored grey suit. He grinned amiably and asked me, "Fancy a game? Loser pays 10. Twenty if the winner makes any break above 50."

It seemed like a good option, considering the level of skill I'd been treated to so far, but that was the idea. I shook my head, left a five-dollar bill on the bar and went out. The barman said something I didn't catch. The pool sharks laughed.

Seen from outside, HANE Logging's bunkhouse and the legion hall appeared to have been built and designed by the same contractor and in the same era—that is to say, about 1940. I went up a similar set of steps, across another wide, shaded porch, pushed the bunkhouse's door open and went inside.

A long narrow corridor, with doors opening along each side, stretched the full length of the building. A white-bearded swamper, sloshing a wet mop back and forth across the gleaming linoleum floor, stopped work to stare at me. Joseph Bickle, one of the men I suspected of attacking me on the government wharf, lived in room number 11. Bernie had told me that Bickle lived in a bunkhouse in Mowaht Bay, and this was it. It was no surprise to learn that he worked for HANE. When I knocked on his door nobody answered. Apart from creaking sounds made by timbers expanding in the heat, the building was quiet.

The swamper cleared his throat and asked, "Who you looking for, Jack?"

"Joe Bickle."

"I haven't seen Joe since he got out of hospital."

"Know where I might find him?"

"No. If I do see him, who should I say was calling?"

"Tell him Norman was here," I said.

I went back to the loaner, collected the roll of small picks and keys that I carry in my toolbox, locked the car and then wandered around until I found a place in the shade where I could keep an eye on the bunkhouse. I was lucky. After less than half an hour, the swamper came down the bunkhouse steps and went across the street into the Bee Hive Cafe.

Bickle's door—like those in the rest of the building—was fitted with an old-fashioned lock. It took me about a minute—manipulating two L-shaped steel picks—before the latch bolt slid back and I entered. The room was dark and it smelled of beer and tobacco. About the size of a prison cell, it lacked plumbing. Its furniture included a chest of drawers, a dressing table with a small square mirror and a large cedar chest. The room's beige walls were plastered with dozens of unframed black and white photographs depicting, for the most part, the early days of B.C.'s coastal logging industry. Pictures of steam locomotives, steam tugs and steam donkeys of every variety stared out of history. Men, now dead for 100 years, felled massive trees with double-bitted axes. Bullocks, yoked together in teams of 20, dragged logs along greasy skid roads. Three- and four-masted sailing vessels were pictured alongside sawmills. I'd seen some of these pictures once before—aboard the *Mayan Girl*, in Tess Rollins' office.

The room was spotless. Bickle probably paid the swamper a few bucks a week to keep it that way. I poked around in drawers, entertaining the hope I might find something incriminating. The cedar chest contained cameras, lenses, tripods and other photographic paraphernalia. The thin mattress on Bickle's narrow iron bed rested on springs, which creaked when I sat on it. My eyes were drawn to a framed diploma on the opposite wall. On closer inspection, it turned out to be a Certificate of Competency, dated 1974, issued by The Chicago (Correspondence) Institute of Photographic Arts. The certificate attested that Joseph W. Bickle had satisfied the requirements of Examiners, and was Thereby, in their Opinion, Entitled to Practice the Art and Science of Public Photography.

Bickle had spent years making a photographic record of B.C.'s coastal logging industry, and I was struck by the technical excellence displayed. One photograph was conspicuous, precisely because of its dark, blurred image. The picture had been taken in natural light in an area of heavy bush. At first glance it appeared almost featureless, possibly even a double exposure. I got up off the bed for a better look. On closer examination, I saw that it was just one more photograph of yet another ancient steam logging-donkey. But I'd *seen* that particular steam donkey before—or one exactly like it—mouldering away in a grove of trees near Boss Rollins' house.

Footsteps sounded outside where someone climbed the bunk-house steps then moved toward me along the corridor. Someone knocked on Bickle's door and said, "You in there, Joe?"

It was the swamper. The doorknob rotated back and forth, as he tested the lock. I heard a few indistinct muttered words, followed by receding footsteps.

I removed Bickle's picture of the logging donkey from its frame, folded it carefully and stuffed it into my shirt pocket. When the building grew silent, I let myself out without relocking the door.

THE LOANER HAD BEEN STANDING in the sun for over an hour and was furnace-hot inside. I opened the windows and stood on the driver's side with the door wide open, pondering my options while the car's interior lost heat. Across the highway, waves glittered in the Sound, gold and black flecks in the afternoon light. Drift logs, bleached white by ages of sunlight, mouldered along the beaches—thousands of tons of wood, impregnated with sand and pebbles, riddled with teredo worms and commercially useless. The *Mayan Girl* lay at its usual berth in the government wharf. As I watched, two people emerged from a cabin door and stood together on the deck.

With sun in my eyes, I was unable to recognize either, until one descended the gangplank and sauntered ashore along a float. It was Tess Rollins, wearing a beige jacket and black slacks, a white shirt, white high heels and a straw hat the size of a garbage can lid. She got into a $200,000 Mercedes convertible and sat with the door open, one lovely leg out, the other leg in. She fumbled for keys. A minute later, she drove off toward the Mowaht Reserve.

Tess was already out of sight by the time I'd jumped in my car and set off in the same direction. Instead of driving onto the

Mowaht Bay Reserve, I pulled off the road near the place where I'd wrecked the MG, and parked. Overhead, trees with inter-mingling branches and leaves blocked the midday sun. The woods were silent, the filtered daylight green and surreal. I climbed that five-wire fence and hurried along the usual trail, which, that day, possessed for some reason the eerie quality of a place hitherto unexplored. It was as if I were seeing it for the first time. The trail led on till I saw a patch of sky. The trees thinned, and Boss Rollins' house became visible ahead. Tess's Mercedes was parked inside Boss's garage, alongside that big black Lincoln limo.

I settled myself comfortably behind a leafy rhododendron and waited. Birds that had grown silent at my approach resumed their singing. A blue jay gave out a series of harsh unmusical *shaaars* notes, then a thrush chimed in, its piping notes clear and sharp. After a while, Tess Rollins came out of the house, arm in arm with Boss. The siblings were about the same height, but they didn't much look like brother and sister. Tess, wearing her fashionable tailored outfit, appeared smooth and expensive, even elegant. Boss wore hillbilly coveralls and could have passed for a skid-row dere-lict. Out of earshot, they appeared to be arguing as they went into Boss's garage where Tess drew her brother's attention to some-thing involving the Mercedes' upholstery. After a short and appar-ently heated discussion, they returned to the house.

I backtracked through the woods to the site of the old log-ging-donkey. My arrival disturbed a pine siskin, perched on a stump eating a dandelion. It called out, a rough rising *Sreeeeee* note, before flying away. Things had changed there since my pre-vious visit. People had been partying. The area was littered with broken bottles and empty junk-food packages. Slivers of burnt bone, along with strips of scorched deer hide and charred meat lay in a fire pit.

I took Bickle's photo from my pocket, smoothed it out and

moved around until I was where the photographer had been when he took the shot. There I saw something that had gone unnoticed in Bickle's dimly lit room. The photograph was a time exposure, showing human or perhaps animal figures moving in circles around a campfire. That wasn't the only thing I noticed. The logging donkey had been tampered with. A flex-cable bicycle lock had replaced the weld formerly keeping the furnace door shut.

I was pondering this curious detail when the skin between my shoulder blades prickled. I felt a sudden dread. Somebody had just walked over my grave. Then chunks of bark, dust, birds' nests and small branches started to fall. Thunderous cracking noises sounded all around. I ran for my life and had travelled about 50 yards before a falling tree hit the ground behind me. Lashed by slender branches, I was shaken, but otherwise unhurt. Chunks of a great worm-eaten cottonwood lay scattered and broken across the trail.

I was dusting myself off when that sudden dread returned. Fighting panic, I followed a new path along the slope of a hill that wound down into a valley carved by water. A running stream had been dammed to make a pool, where a kneeling man was scooping water into his mouth. To reach the pool, I had to bypass an area of swampy ground, thick with bog orchids and skunk cabbages. Rotting trees lay collapsed, their damp pulpy trunks and branches a feast for putrid funguses like Dead Man's Fingers and Witches Chanterelle.

My feet made a crunching noise as I stepped across a dry twig, causing the kneeling man to look up. He was a large, barefoot, powerfully built Native wearing cutoff jeans and a straw hat. He was almost hairless, except for a mouse-like tuft in the exact centre of his very small head, and possessed the wet slack mouth, narrow eyes and the loose perpetual grin of an idiot.

"Hear that widdermaker?" he said. "Lucky you didn't get kilt."

"I'll bring a hard hat next time," I said, still trying to bring my panic and shaking hands under control.

"Powerful spirits guard this hill," the halfwit informed me. "Better not come here again. Boss Rollins don't like it when folks come this way." Round-shouldered, long arms swinging to his knees, he added, "I been pulling weeds inside the canoe."

It was an odd remark, because I didn't see a canoe.

The pool was almost circular, about a foot deep at the most. Muddy prints left by the idiot's feet showed along the margins here and there, but no animal prints. I thought this peculiar, until I noticed the spirit canoe. Built by shamans, spirit canoes are used in Soul-Recovery ceremonies—performances in which Coast Salish shamans board a mock canoe and journey in it to the land of the dead to bring back lost souls. Carved wooden manikins, placed inside the "canoe," act as guardian spirits for the shamans on their journey. This canoe was rudimentary. Its outline had been scratched on the earth with a stick. The manikins inside it were crude black and white figures, painted on boards and poked into the soft ground like fence posts.

The poor idiot had stepped inside the "canoe," and now he was clearing away weeds and fallen leaves, which, instead of throwing aside, he used to increase the height of the canoe's gunwales.

I asked, "What's your name?"

"Donny," he said, wiping sweat from his weak liquid eyes. "Do I know you, mister?"

I smiled. He didn't recognize me, but I recognized him: Donny was one of the men who had tried to kill me at the government wharf. I asked, "What are you doing, Donny?"

"Getting things ready. Boss says we're going, soon."

"Just you and the Boss?"

"There's a few of us been picked to go with him," he sniggered. "Boss's brother's coming with us as well."

It was after 4:30 when I arrived at the B.C. Land Registry offices on Blanshard Street in Victoria. I got inside the doors just before they closed for the day. After paying the title-search fee, I was attended by a clerk named Thurston.

I said, "I need to know who owns that Rainbow Motel property, on the Inner Harbour."

"Do you have the legal description?"

"Afraid not. If you show me a map, I can point it out."

He grinned and said, "Don't bother, I know where it is. Hang on while I fetch the plan."

He went away, returned a minute or two later, and spread the plan out on a counter. Thurston fiddled with a computer and announced, "The Rainbow Motel property is registered to HANE Logging, a legal entity."

CHAPTER NINETEEN

I went back to the loaner and used my cell phone to call Bernie Tapp. When he came on, I told him what I'd learned in Mowaht Bay and at the registry office. I'm not sure why, but I didn't tell Bernie about the earthquake—or spiritual manifestation, or whatever it was—that had shaken up the hill.

"I already know who owns the motel," Bernie said.

"How did you find out?"

"Asked the construction boss."

Bernie was a step ahead of me, something not unusual. I laughed self-consciously. "Did you get around to searching Karl Berger's house yet?"

His grunt denoted assent.

"Find anything interesting?"

"A bunch of triple-X videos and DVDs. We also found a couple of ounces of coke and a pint of Ketamine. Plus, about $10,000 cash. The money was in ice cream cartons in his fridge. We confiscated the drugs, the cash and a bunch of movies. Vice is looking the movies over now. So far, they haven't found the one allegedly showing Rollins humping his niece."

"*Allegedly?*"

"Well, so far, all we've got is a drug addict's uncorroborated testimony."

"Has Karl Berger been interrogated?"

"Yeah. Among other things, I asked Karl to explain why there was video surveillance equipment and one-way mirrors in the Rainbow Motel. He stonewalled, demanded a lawyer. We weren't getting anywhere, so we booked him. We're holding him overnight."

"On what charge?"

"Trafficking. He'll appear before a judge in the morning."

"Speaking of corroboration, what did you get out of Henry Ferman?"

"He was cagey at first. I had to lean on him a bit. Finally, he admitted selling videotape equipment to Karl Berger."

"He told me that already." It was nice to be a step ahead of Bernie once in a while.

"And you told *me* this?"

I smiled broadly. "I did."

"Well, Henry confirmed it by showing us his invoice books."

"By the way," I said. "Where is Karl's house?"

Bernie told me. Karl Berger lived on Cook Street, in an apartment building a few blocks away from the Dallas Road waterfront.

I said, "You got my message about John Doncaster?"

"Yeah, we're looking into it."

I put the cell phone back in my pocket. I realized I was hungry.

There are probably a thousand restaurants in Victoria, but I chose the Beagle, a busy pub in the Cook Street village. The Beagle's outdoor patio was infested with smokers. Inside, it was crowded with lapsed smokers who didn't seem to be having nearly as much fun as the patio crowd. I sat at the bar, bought a pint of draft Fosters and turned to survey the room. I was just emptying my first glass when a tall circular table the size of a serving tray became free.

I sat down on its tall accompanying stool and resumed my idle scrutiny of the couples, would-be couples, the singles who once were unhappy as half of a couple and the divorced singles like me who had been happily married once, but who hadn't known it till it was too late. And maybe I'd misjudged the whole situation and was the only guy in the place not actually enjoying himself. Something was bugging me, I just didn't know what.

A waitress brought me another Foster's and took my order for halibut and chips. I looked inward, thinking about HANE Logging and Tess Rollins. I asked myself if there could possibly be such a thing as a logging-donkey archetype. What I really needed was the works of Carl Jung—vest-pocket edition.

I suppose I must have eaten the fish and chips, and I probably drank three or four Foster's to go along with it. I ended up outside the Beagle's Cook Street entrance, surveying possibilities. It occurred to me that I was probably drunk, at least legally so. The Moka coffee shop was a couple of blocks north. I was thinking about something Donny had said to me earlier, back at Mowaht Bay, when my cell phone rang.

Somebody said, "Turn around, Silas, and look up. Look *waaaay* up."

Denise Halvorsen was standing on the fourth-floor balcony of a six-storey condominium. She leaned over her balcony, waved down to me and said, "If you fancy a nightcap, come on over. I'm in 403."

Denise buzzed me into her building. Suddenly, I was sober. I took an elevator up to the fourth floor. I put my finger on the bell push and held it there for one second. I heard soft footsteps. Door bolts slid open and there she stood, dressed in an unbelted white terrycloth robe worn over a silky blue nightie. Denise's long blonde hair—which when on duty she wore screwed up and pinned into a bun—now fell loosely over her neck and shoulders.

She kissed my cheek, sniffed and said, "Are you drunk?"

"I should be, otherwise I've been wasting my money."

Denise laughed and touched my arm. "Don't be shy, come on in. I was only reading."

"Reading in the dark on a balcony?"

"Taking a breath of air before going to bed."

"Are you on dayshift tomorrow?"

"Yes, but don't let it bother you."

I hesitated for a moment before following her into the spare bedroom she used as a parlour. Passing the master bedroom, I noticed white French provincial furniture. A lightweight pink duvet had been turned back on one side of her queen-size bed. The bedroom was intensely feminine. Her parlour contained mismatched oddments of good, possibly antique oak tables and chairs and cabinets. Denise stood with her back to a window overlooking Beacon Hill Park. She said, "I seem to recall you like single malt Scotch, but I've only got Bell's."

"That's okay, if you'll join me."

"Two Bell's coming up."

"That's one o'clock."

"What?" she replied, mystified.

"Two bells. A ship's bell is rung every half-hour after midnight."

"You're kidding."

"No, really. At 12:30, a quartermaster rings a bell once. At one o'clock, he rings it twice."

"Maybe you'd prefer navy rum instead?"

"Bell's is fine. Just a quick one and I'll be on my way."

"Make yourself at home, there's no rush. Drag that ottoman over and put your feet up."

She went across to the cabinet and fixed the drinks, humming to herself. She brought them back and sat down beside me, on the arm of the sofa. "Here's looking up your old address," she said happily, touching my glass with her own.

"What's that? An ancient Norwegian curse?"

"Dunno. It's what a guy said to me once. It seemed quite funny at the time."

A shapely and partially undraped female leg was inches away from my face. Denise smelled warm and freshly scrubbed.

She said, "The word in the station is out that Bernie Tapp's offered you your old job back on the detective squad. You're one lucky guy, Silas."

I looked up at her. When our eyes met, there was a gleam in Denise's eyes, and I suddenly realized something that ought to have been obvious for weeks: Denise was falling in love with me. Instantly, I became sober. Fool that I was, I'd stepped into a minefield. Somehow, the robe fell from her shoulders and landed on the floor. I stood up, but she was already reaching for me. I turned away, and a kiss intended for my lips ended on my cheek.

"Don't you know about Felicity?" I said softly.

She looked down. When her eyes met mine again, she was trembling slightly. "Did you know I was married?"

I raised my eyebrows, and she looked quickly away.

"Not *now*. I used to be. I grew up in Saskatoon, married my high-school sweetheart when I was 18. His name was Johan. I couldn't wait to show everybody my engagement ring. Johan had been a big man on a small campus, and everybody, especially my best friend, Alice, thought he was quite a catch. When we got back from our honeymoon, we rented a small apartment. Johan switched on the TV, broke out the chips and the beer, stretched out on a recliner with the remote in one hand and a bottle in the other. He suggested we start making babies right away."

"Sounds like a real lady-killer," I said.

"Oh yeah, a real lady-killer." She smiled. "Johan's dad owned a corner grocery. He stood to inherit it, 20 years down the line. In the meantime, Johan was practising shelf-stacking. Suddenly, as the saying goes, the scales dropped from my eyes. I left him watching *Entertainment Tonight* and made a run for it. He and I share the record for short Saskatchewan screw-ups. Now he's married to Alice. I hear they're very happy."

Denise's smile faded, and suddenly she was sobbing. I held her until she stopped. Then I left before something happened that we'd both regret. I took my second elevator ride, went outside and stood on Cook Street. I'd come close to making one serious error and didn't want to make another by driving under the influence. I started walking and was about half a block from the Pic-A-Flic video store when an empty taxi cruised by. I flagged it down and was getting into the back when a female voice called out, "Hello, Silas."

It was Tess Rollins. She was grinning at me from the sidewalk. She asked, "Going anywhere special?"

The cabbie turned around in his seat, looked me over, frowned and demanded, "Where to, soldier?"

I said, "Wait a minute," and got out of the cab. The cabbie gunned his motor—burning rubber as he took off.

Tess was grinning. "Good riddance," she said. "You need to go somewhere, we'll use my car."

I smiled, but I didn't like Tess's casual use of the possessive.

She said playfully, "I feel slightly aggrieved."

"With me, or just in general?"

"With you, because I thought you liked me. You came back to Mowaht Bay, but you didn't pay me a visit. That was very naughty."

"Who said I'd been back?"

"Does it matter? The fact is, you *were* there, right?"

"You're right, I was there. Briefly. How did you know?"

"Remember, I told you it's impossible to keep secrets in Mowaht Bay—it's too small."

"That's what you said, Tess, but it's not true, is it? Mowaht Bay's full of secrets."

She tucked my hand beneath her arm and raised her face to be kissed. I touched her cheek with my lips.

"My, my. Call that a kiss?" she asked, laughing out loud.

"I'm just surprised. Very surprised, running into you like this. What are you doing here?"

"I've been walking around, looking for *you*. I saw you earlier, in the Beagle. I was with some people; otherwise I'd have spoken to you then. You left before I had another chance," she said, bubbling over with apparent delight. "Come on, my car's parked near yours, behind the pub. Let's go somewhere, just you and me. We'll make a night of it."

I thought, *My car's parked near yours?* How did she know where my car was parked?

"Listen, Tess. It's lovely to see you, but I'm on duty now. I have to be going somewhere. Sorry."

"Liar, you're not on duty," she argued, her voice low. "Never mind, though. I'll let you go this time."

She gave my arm a little squeeze, turned and ran quickly across the street.

I hadn't been lying. I *was* back on duty. Now everything was different. I had said Mowaht Bay was full of secrets, but it was dawning on me only now, with absolute certainty, what it's greatest secret was: the second time I'd seen the logging donkey, I'd noticed that the weld on the door had been broken, then resealed with a bicycle lock. I cursed myself, I should have investigated it immediately. It was probably too late now. Or was it? I checked the time. This was crazy, it was nearly 12:30 at night. I almost called it off, thinking to wait for the morning, for daylight. But I couldn't escape the rising feeling of urgency. No, I had to go there tonight. A feeling told me that tomorrow morning would be too late.

I kept Tess in sight till she reached the Beagle's parking lot, got into her Mercedes and drove away. I drove to police headquarters. Mac Anderson, the attendant on duty in the tool crib that night, provided me with a bolt cutter, although he balked when I requested a bike lock.

"A bike lock?" he repeated.

"Correct. Not the U-bolt kind. The kind with a spiral cable that curls into a circle when you release tension."

"What do you think this place is? Wal-Mart?"

"Got one or not?"

Mac folded his arms, gazed into space and said, "I *own* one. Right now, it's out in the yard, locking my bike to a rack."

We went outside together. Mac took the lock off his bike, gave it to me and asked, "When can I expect it back?"

"Never. I'll give you a new one tomorrow."

Half an hour later I was steering the Chev along dirt roads. It was a warm night and I drove with the windows down. When I slowed for sharp curves, I heard waves, pounding the shores of Mowaht Sound. Little eyes, peering down from the branches overhead, reflected my headlamps. A barred owl, feasting on its kill in the middle of the road, swept up into the trees at my approach. Mowaht Bay's streets were deserted when I arrived there, about two in the morning. Apart from a few pole lamps on the government wharf, the township lay mostly in darkness. A motion detector lit up when I stopped in the Legion parking lot. The HANE bunkhouse was invisible in the dark. After thinking for five minutes, I drove on.

The woods were intensely dark when I parked in the bush near the Mowaht Bay Reserve.

I drank a couple of slugs from the glove-compartment mickey and put the bottle in my pocket. I switched on my flashlight, climbed the reserve's five-wire fence and floundered around in the dark forest till I picked up the game trail.

THE AREA AROUND BOSS ROLLINS' logging donkey had been cleaned up—just a little; there weren't quite as many empty bottles and other junk lying about as previously. I crossed to the logging donkey, positioned the flashlight and set to work with Mac's bolt cutter. It took me several minutes to sever the bike lock holding the furnace door shut. Instead of cutting cleanly, the bolt-cutter's blades merely flattened the multi-strand cable. I had to twist the cutter back and forth strenuously for a while, until the cable parted.

I was sweating when I dragged the rusty furnace door open and looked inside.

Designed to burn firewood, the furnace was now a rusty mausoleum; rodents and insects had feasted within it for years. My heart palpitating like an amphetamine junkie's, I gazed at the mummified remains of a man sitting upright on the fire grates, still thinly draped in the rotten, lace-like fragments of the jeans and red flannel shirt he had been wearing when somebody shot him.

Conquering revulsion, I crawled inside the furnace and checked in what was left of the mummy's tattered pockets. They were empty, but there was a jagged hole in the dead man's temple, where a .25 calibre bullet had penetrated. The bullet was still lodged in the corpse's lower mandible. I backed out of the furnace on my hands and knees. When my heartbeat returned to normal, I used my cell phone and called headquarters. Tony Seamann, the duty sergeant, wasn't familiar with the Mowaht Bay area, so it took a while to explain my situation, exactly where I was and how to get there. Before hanging up I said, "And listen, Tony. No sirens, that's important. Okay?"

"Got it," Seamann assured me. "No sirens."

I sat on a tree stump and finished the mickey. Alcohol didn't stop my racing thoughts, but it took my mind off that eyeless corpse.

The purple starlit night was full of sounds. A distant coyote answered an owl's hoot. Small night creatures went about their business in the dark. Water trickled along a creek. I left the empty mickey bottle on the stump, went back to the logging donkey and closed the furnace-door. Kneeling, I used Mac's bike lock and made the furnace as secure as I'd found it.

No sooner had the lock clicked shut than a voice said, "Stand up, turn around slow and raise your hands above your head."

I was kneeling on the donkey's deck, a foot or so above the ground. I stood up and spun around fast. Boss Rollins was standing below me, about four feet away. It was too dark to see the gun in his hand; otherwise I wouldn't have swung my flashlight at his head.

Rollins evaded my swing. He could have shot me, right then, but apparently he needed to keep me alive for a while before I joined that mummy in the furnace. He fired a bullet between my feet. I dropped the flashlight and raised my hands. The light went out, but Rollins didn't need it. He wasn't alone. Somebody else was with him, and had her own lamp. She focussed its powerful beam directly into my eyes, blinding me temporarily.

"Don't move!" Rollins commanded. "More tricks, and I'll beat your brains out."

I believed him and turned my face away from the light.

Rollins asked, "How did you know?"

"Know what?"

"How did you know that Neville was inside the furnace?"

"So that's brother Neville, is it?"

Rollins didn't answer.

I said, "I didn't know what was in there till 10 minutes ago. Finding your brother was a fluke. The first time I saw it, the logging donkey's furnace-door was welded shut. It was a nice piece of work. I guess *you* did it, right?"

Rollins grunted his assent.

I said, "It struck me as a bit unnecessary, somebody going to all that trouble, but I doubt I'd have given the matter any more thought, if I hadn't come back for a second look around. That's when I noticed that somebody had sawn through the weld and put a bike lock on the furnace door instead. I began to wonder what for. I'm still wondering."

I waited for him to say something, but he stayed silent.

"Seaweed's dangerous, you're wasting time," the person holding the lamp said coldly, speaking for the first time. "Deal with it now. You know what's needed."

It was Tess Rollins. I was already in a state of shock. Hearing Tess's voice nearly made my heart stop. I turned my head to gape at her, but that flashlight still blinded me.

Boss Rollins stepped close and lashed out with his gun while I was still looking over my shoulder. The blow was hard, and it landed on my jawbone. I took a nosedive. A knob of rusty iron came up off the deck, banged my head and nearly tore my ear off. Things went red, then black, and that was it.

I'd been cold-cocked.

I DON'T KNOW HOW LONG I was out. Not too long probably. I came to inside that rusty tomb, in pitch-blackness, sitting alongside a grinning mummy because the furnace was too short to lie down in. Fortunately for my state of mind, the furnace door wasn't completely shut. The Rollinses were standing outside, arguing, although I couldn't make out what they were saying. My head ached. My left ear was caked with dried blood, and it burned as if somebody had used a blowtorch on it. I started to inch out of the furnace, but the door, barely ajar, was too narrow for me to get through. When I shoved it wider, it creaked noisily. The Rollinses stopped arguing.

That's when we all heard the noise of approaching sirens. I managed to get out of the furnace before Boss started shooting; luckily, the sirens spooked him and his aim was off. Bullets ricocheted off metal as I made a run for it into the trees. The wailing sirens grew louder now as three police vehicles turned off the highway and raced toward us through the reserve. After a while, I heard more noises as the Rollinses drove off in the other direction in Tess's Mercedes. I reached Harley Rollins' house before the police did. I went inside to Rollins' bathroom, soaked one of his expensive white towels in warm water and wrapped it around my head.

Then I went outside and sat down on a lawn chair. Suddenly, my hands began to shake and my knees turned wobbly. Red and white lights began to flash intermittently between the trees as cars screamed toward me along the reserve's woodsy road, until blue and whites with RCMP markings arrived.

After 10 minutes of strenuous SWAT team athletics involving megaphones, bulletproof vests and trigger-happy shotgun-toting constables, the RCMP inspector in charge concluded that I might actually be the unarmed policeman I said I was, after which things calmed, a little.

CHAPTER TWENTY

I was sitting in Bernie Tapp's office with a band-aid the size of a birthday card plastered across my forehead. The ER surgeon who'd worked on my ear had left me with me with more stitches than a catcher's mitt. I was tired, groggy. My head ached, my back teeth ached, and I needed a drink. Twelve hours had passed since I'd opened that furnace door, and thoughts of spending eternity with Neville Rollins were still giving me goose bumps.

"We had no choice," Bernie Tapp was telling me. "The Mowaht Bay Indian Reserve is under RCMP jurisdiction. We had to notify them first. They insisted on handling matters themselves. Besides, they had a SWAT team handy and ready to go. We told 'em you didn't want sirens, but I guess they didn't listen."

Bernie had described a typical RCMP fiasco, one that had worked to my advantage. If I'd been forced to wait till police arrived quietly from Victoria, I'd be rooming with Neville by then. I cleared that grisly thought from my mind by asking, "Where are the Rollinses now?"

"Who knows? Your guess is as good as mine. The Mounties picked 'em up for questioning, kept 'em for a few hours, then apologized and turned 'em loose."

I was incredulous. "They didn't lay any charges?"

Bernie made a wry mouth. "Not yet. The Rollinses' story is

that you were trespassing by night on their private property. It was dark, and you hadn't identified yourself. The Rollinses didn't recognize you. They admit that things got a little bit out of hand, but it's your fault, they say. You acted suspiciously."

"What about that mummy? How did they explain that?"

"They didn't *try* to explain it," Bernie answered. "Neville went missing nearly 20 years ago. They insisted they had no idea he was in the furnace. Now that they *do* know, they want to be left alone so they can get on with their grieving in private. The Mounties found it hard to argue."

"Rubbish. But for those two grieving hypocrites, Neville would still be alive."

"Maybe. I haven't heard the rest of *your* story yet."

"In a minute. What about Harley Rollins' gun?"

"Oh yeah, the so-called gun. You told the RCMP that Harley was packing a .25. They had a good look around, but didn't find it. All they found was an empty mickey of rye, with your fingerprints on it. Harley Rollins says he's never owned a .25 in his life."

"The sonovabitch tried to kill me with a .25, so what about the bullets?" I asked. "Harley took three or four shots at me when I escaped the logging donkey."

Bernie shrugged. "Ever try to find a bullet in the woods?"

"It isn't impossible."

"For your benefit, they're still investigating. If a bullet hit a tree, they might find it and will let us know. In the meantime . . ." Bernie shook his head. "It's only your word against his."

"Even you don't believe me?" I asked.

"There's something wrong with this picture," Bernie said heartlessly. "First, you tell me, Tess Rollins did her best to *fuck* your brains out. Now, you tell me, Harley Rollins did his best to *blow* your brains out. So, with what's left of your brains, think this through again. Take your time, there's no hurry."

I took a deep breath and began to speak. Bernie listened politely, but he didn't seem impressed. When I'd said my piece, again, Bernie leaned back in his chair and twiddled his thumbs. He made a slight sucking sound with his lips and said, "Buddy, I think you've earned yourself a little convalescent leave. Take a few days off, why don't you?"

"Thanks very much."

"We seem to have reached a stalemate. If you have any more bright ideas, give me a ring. With a bit of luck, who knows? Maybe we'll crack this case yet."

I went home.

I woke after lunch, sweating in my bed and wondering which was worse—my pounding head, my aching molars or that sore ear. It was a close-run thing. I threw cotton bedsheets aside and put my feet on the floor. After a while, the world stopped spinning. When I reached up and touched my ear gently with my fingers, it felt swollen but intact. My only consolation was the bottle on my bedside table. I took a long swig to pacify my teeth, following which, after one unsuccessful attempt, I managed to stand. It was not my finest hour. I staggered outside to the privy and reached it without falling down. That rustic one-holer, situated in a cedar grove downwind of my cabin, is a very private place. I sat there for a while, posed like Rodin's *Thinker*, with the door open.

Fog blanketed the reserve; it was too dense to see anywhere but up, where the fog was thin enough to reveal the sun's diffused golden orb. Once, a low-flying float plane passed overhead. My headache slowly diminished and my teeth settled down, although I began to wonder if I had an infected ear. That led to dark musings about the dating possibilities available to one-eared bachelors. Such dates might be dismally few. I'd probably end up like

Henry Ferman, a figure of fun in a Brillo-pad wig. I returned to my cabin, poured another two fingers and sipped it while fixing coffee and bacon and eggs.

Last year, I had treated myself to wrought iron patio furniture, so I ate breakfast in my garden. Summertime, that little oasis is sunlit all day. As gardens go, it's small—a mere 20 feet square—surrounded by a cedar privacy hedge. The Garry oaks and arbutus trees make acidic soil, so for years, I've been digging seaweed in to sweeten it. Now, I grow dahlias with heads as big as cabbages, along with chrysanthemums, hollyhocks, pansies, begonias and a buddleia. The rest is lawn that I keep short with a hand mower. One of these days, maybe, I'll get around to building a small greenhouse in here.

When the fog burned off, a one-legged raven flew in and perched on a totem pole near the Warrior Longhouse. There was something in the raven's unwinking stare I didn't like. It was still glowering when somebody drove up and parked outside my hedge. A door slammed, and the raven flew off. I peered through a gap in the hedge, and there was a shiny S-Type Mercedes convertible. The garden gate opened and Tess Rollins swaggered in. *Unbelievable*, I thought.

She looked pretty good; her eyes were drawn as boldly as Tutankhamen's. She was dressed in a crisp white shirt that showed off sensational cleavage, shorts made out of some kind of shiny white rubber and white leather sandals. A leather bag draped her shoulder. It was a simple outfit that even I could recognize as ruinously expensive. She smelled of sandalwood and seemed uncharacteristically shy.

She smiled and acted as if yesterday had never happened, and I went along with it. After all, I reflected, if she tried any funny business I could always strangle her. I even gave her a brotherly kiss and a brief hug, carefully maintaining discreet airspace between our pelvic regions. Then we started to laugh and our tensions faded, although not entirely.

"You look wrecked," she observed, sitting on one of the chairs beside my table. "And I don't like the colour of that big fat ear. Is it *supposed* to be green?"

"Just passing?"

"I've got a few minutes to waste," she replied, taking a bunch of grapes from her bag. She handed them to me saying, "Forget what I said about your ear."

"You didn't soak these grapes in cyanide, did you?"

"Hell no," she said, popping one into her mouth.

The grapes were sweet and delicious. I ate a few, adjusted my chair till it faced hers and said, "So. What's up?"

"To tell you the truth, I'm feeling horny. I guess it was all that excitement last night. So I thought, What the hell, let bygones be bygones, right? So how about it?"

"How about what?"

"Don't be coy, Silas, you know exactly what I mean," she said, wiggling her tight little rubber-clad butt. "How'd you like to jump my bones?"

"I thought we'd left that merry-go-round. How about coffee instead—or perhaps you'd prefer a drink?"

"A drink would be a start. And another kiss to show there's no hard feelings?"

Laughing in spite of myself, I stood up. She stood as well, gently kissed my cheek and nibbled my good ear. Her voracious sexuality was repellent and attractive at the same time. She was trying to fondle my balls when I pulled away.

Grinning wickedly, she said, "Got any decent Chardonnay?"

I went inside my cabin, took out a bottle of homemade white plonk from my fridge and put it on a tray along with a couple of glasses. When I got back outside, Tess was using my outhouse.

She'd left her bag on the table so I opened it. It was chocablock with freshly minted $100 bills.

When Tess rejoined me, I gave her a glass of plonk, clinked it with my own glass and said, "Cheers."

"*Skol*. Did you like what you saw inside my bag?"

"You were keeping an eye on me from the privy?"

She gazed at me with steady dark eyes.

I grinned at her and said, "Sure, I love money. What's it for?"

"You, possibly, only it's not a gift. If you want the money, you'll have to earn it."

"To change the topic just slightly, do you know Pinky's?"

"That club on View Street?" she said, apparently a little puzzled. 'Yeah, I've been there a couple of times. It's not very upscale—I prefer the Bengal Room."

"Sometimes, income governs taste. Janey Colby spent the last night of her life in Pinky's."

"Did she?"

"You *know* she did."

"I hope she had fun," Tess said cheerfully, ignoring my comment. "Oh and by the way, I love this wine. Is it just me, or do I detect traces of eucalyptus, kerosene and wormwood?"

"Berries and English crumpets. According to witnesses, Janey was drunk. She'd been drinking heavily all night. More importantly, Janey had been watching triple-X movies in the back room. One movie featured her daughter having sex with your brother. Harley and Terry are blood kin, so it was incest."

Tess Rollins' happy mood faded noticeably. She moved uneasily in her chair and bit her upper lip, but didn't say anything.

I drank a little wine and went on, "It's time for a revisionist history."

Tess shook her head. "That might be okay, if I knew what 'revisionist' meant. Why don't you explain it to me in simple words?"

"I'm talking about the history of the Rollins family. There's *your* version, and then there's the truth."

Our glasses were empty. I emptied the bottle, filling them up. "You and your brothers were involved together in HANE Logging, a private company. When Jane Colby went missing, before I knew that Jane had been murdered, I started making inquiries in Mowaht Bay. That's where we first met, right?"

"I remember it vividly, and it was a lucky break for you. I saved your life, don't forget."

"Yes. I owed you one. Now we're even."

"And here I've been kidding myself that you were unique. But you *do* keep score. You're like every other man I've ever met."

I grinned at her with my head on one side. "You gave me a thumbnail history of Harley and his company. Your reasons for doing so weren't apparent to me then, but they are now. You told me that Harley Rollins founded HANE Logging while your other brother, Neville, was away at college. You were working as a hairdresser. Janey Colby was Harley's longtime girlfriend. You gave up hairdressing and joined Harley's company as a bookkeeper. Neville combined forces with Harley after graduating from UBC. Neville contributed greatly to HANE's success. Everything in the garden was lovely, until Harley Rollins found out that Neville was two-timing him with Janey. After that, according to you, things changed. Neville got Janey, but Harley made him pay for it by freezing him out of the company. You began to worry that Harley might freeze you out too, so you asked him to make you a partner. You ended up with a one-third interest in the entire operation."

Tess grinned and said, "What is it that you don't believe?"

"Harley never froze Neville out of HANE. You lied to me."

"How did I lie to you?"

"The Rainbow Motel property was, and still is, wholly owned

by HANE Logging. The principals in that company are Harley Rollins, Tess Rollins *and* Neville Rollins."

"How do you know that?"

"I searched the title."

"So what? Neville's dead. A dead man can't own anything."

That absurdity made me smile.

Tess drained her glass and said, "That's a cheap bottle of wine. Got anything better inside?"

I went into my cabin, came back with another bottle of home-made and refilled our glasses. Tess scowled when she saw the label, but steeled herself to drink an inch.

I sat down and looked at her. Tess still seemed quite composed. I said, "The actual facts are these: Your brother Harley founded a sawmill and ran it as a single proprietorship until Neville gradu-ated from UBC, when they created a private partnership. *That's* why it was called HANE—the brothers' combined the first two letters of Harley's name, and the first two letters of Neville's name. Originally, Harley owned two-thirds of the company. Neville owned one third. You, Tess, ended up owning half of Harley's share. Am I right?"

Tess nodded, but she was pretending to be more interested in her surroundings than in what I was saying. I went on, "Neville's marriage to Janey created bad feelings between the brothers. Harley tried to force Neville out, but Neville wouldn't budge. So Harley murdered him."

"No he didn't," Tess said flatly.

I smirked at her politely. "The way I figure it, Harley mur-dered Neville Rollins and put his body into a furnace."

Shaking her head in denial, Tess said softly, "It wasn't murder. It was an accident."

"How do you know?"

"The day it happened, Harley had called a directors' meeting at his house. I was there. Harley ordered Neville to sell his shares back to the company. Neville refused, they ended up arguing—fighting and smashing furniture, throwing things at each other. Neville was disgusted. Turned his back on Harley, left the house and started to walk away. Harley had a gun, a .25. Neville was 50 yards off when Harley fired a couple of shots. Kind of wild—they weren't intended to kill Neville or even hit him. Harley just wanted to scare him. You'd have to be a pretty good shot, to kill a man at 50 yards with a .25. Harley wasn't that good.

"By a fluke, one bullet struck Neville and it killed him instantly. It was terrible, awful. Harley went to pieces. We ought to have called the cops immediately, that's obvious now. But we lost our heads and shut Neville up inside that old logging donkey, told people that when Neville disappeared he had been working alone on a log boom. Everyone assumed he'd fallen into the water. Then we started a rumour that he'd been murdered, tried to blame Janey. Gradually, the fuss died down."

Tess took a long deep breath and her voice fell to a whisper. "Neville wasn't the only one who died that day. Something died inside Harley. He lost all interest in HANE Logging. Harley gave me another big piece of it and spent his time messing around with sorcerers, diving into the Gorge, trying to contact the Unknown World. Spooky stuff. HANE Logging went downhill fast. I took care of my money and ended up richer than Harley."

Tess reached for the bottle and refilled her glass without offering to fill mine. It wasn't rudeness—Tess was somewhere else.

I waited a minute and said, "Now we've got that settled, let's look at Karl Berger's part in this drama," I said, trying but failing to catch Tess's eye. "Karl wasn't just managing the Rainbow Motel. He had a sideline distributing triple-X movies. It was a marginal operation—too much competition—so Karl branched out, started making home movies. Harley didn't know it, but he was one of Karl's stars, as was Terry Colby."

Tess was staring up at the totem pole. The raven had gone; the sun was very hot. Tess said wistfully, "Poor little cow. Harley used to pick Terry up from her care home and take her to the motel. Nobody knew he was banging her. The nuns never suspected a thing."

"You knew about it?"

"Not at first."

"When did you find out?"

Tess dabbed her upper lip with her tongue and said absently, "When Janey told me."

"In other words, the same night Janey herself found out."

Tess nodded.

"Here's another screwy thing," I said. "Until almost the end of her life, Janey Colby didn't know that her dead husband was Harley's legal partner. I guess that during their short marriage she wasn't interested in learning just exactly where Neville's money came from. Obviously, she never asked. Many of her years were passed in drunken ignorance."

"All right, smartass," Tess snapped, a little edge to her voice now. "So tell me. How *did* Janey finally wise up?"

"Jack Owens and Janey had taken a beating on a failed condo scheme. They were having trouble meeting their obligations. To avoid bankruptcy, Owens delved into Janey's knotty financial affairs. He found out what I found out, that as Neville's widow, Jane was part-owner of everything you Rollinses own, including the Rainbow Motel—a chunk of waterfront real estate now worth millions." I gave Tess time to think that over, smiled at her and said, "Tell me. How did you handle it when Jane showed up demanding her share of the HANE money?"

Tess replied bitterly, "Believe it or not, I was very sweet with Janey. There wasn't much point in arguing because she had me by the short hairs. I fed Janey a few bucks to be going on with. Promised there'd be more when the Rainbow Motel came down and the new development progressed. She was satisfied."

"For a while."

"Right again, Silas. Janey was satisfied, if only temporarily. Janey was a heavy spender, and she started to up the ante."

"Up the ante?"

"That's what I said, isn't it? Janey upped the ante, wanted more and more, because she was greedy."

"Greedy? *You* tried to scam her out of a fortune, my dear. Janey became a nuisance, so you killed her."

Tess started to dispute the point, but suddenly changed her mind. Staring at her fingernails she said longingly, "I suppose there's no way we can just drop it, is there? I mean, we'd make a great team, you and me."

For the first time in minutes she looked directly into my eyes and said, "You're descended from a long line of nobility, Silas. Not so long ago, Coast Salish chiefs made their own laws. Now you enforce Whitey's laws, and for what? You earn $60–70,000 a year? Christ, I'm worth *millions*! Treat me right and we'll travel first class together for the rest of our lives. The money in that bag is yours if you want it."

I shook my head.

Tess came out of her chair, knelt at my feet, put both hands on my thighs and rested her head on my lap. I put my hand on her shoulder as she wept. Her voice muffled, she said, "I'm not glamorous, not like your girlfriend is. Or like the old Janey was. Janey was a cow, but she had plenty of boyfriends. My brothers and Jack Owens weren't the only guys who ran after Janey Colby. I was always jealous of her. Nobody ever loved *me*. Not for myself. Nobody. I was the ugly duckling, still am. Guys don't want me for myself, they want me for my money. It's different for men, men can look like apes, but if they're kind, if they treat people right, there's all kinds of women will love them and make them happy . . ." Her voice trailed away into dry sobs.

Tess was a murderer, and at that moment I felt sorry for her. But in a few minutes I was going to handcuff her and call a paddy wagon. She was going to spend the rest of her life behind bars, where her millions wouldn't matter. I said, "There *is* one loose end. Before Janey died, she had sex with somebody. Do you know who?"

"No. Karl Berger maybe? Janey was voracious, had a regular string of studs."

Tess got up unaided, went back to her chair and sat down. A little wine remained in the bottle on the table beside her. She poured it all into her glass, drank a little. Eyes brimming, trying to smile, she put the glass on the table and asked, "Are you going to arrest me, Silas?"

"Not quite yet."

"I was a fool, wasn't I, telling you everything?"

"They say that confession is good for the soul, and by the way, your confession didn't make much difference. I already knew that you killed Janey Colby."

"How? What made you think that?"

"It took a while. The taxi driver who picked up the Native in Cadboro Bay was sure he'd picked up a man, so I suspected Harley. But it bothered me that he never actually saw this man's face—and that this man was very well dressed." I paused for effect. "Harley always dresses like a bum. You're the fancy dresser, Tess. Plus, Harley didn't really care about money anymore. You *did*."

"Except that I'm not a man."

"But you have a low voice. Lower it more, deliberately, and you could sound like a man. You did the other night when you called me a liar after I told you I was off duty."

"So how did I kill her, then?"

"You drowned her. You took a steel cable from a speedboat and hooked it around Janey's neck. Then you got into the speedboat and towed Janey Colby off the Rainbow Motel's beach into the Inner Harbour. Unfortunately, you ran into another boat, so I know exactly what time you did it."

"Do you?"

"Yes. The Johnson Street Bridge operator noted the incident in his log. Afterwards, you beached the speedboat at Cadboro Bay and caught a taxi back home."

"I knew you were smart. I like smart men," Tess said, melancholy heavy in her voice, "but as long as we're being so open and confessional with each other, I've got another question."

"I don't guarantee to answer it."

"This white girlfriend of yours. Do you love her?"

Startled, I didn't say anything. I didn't need to. Tess inferred what she needed to know from the changed expression on my face.

She continued, "That night we ran into each other in the Cook Street Village. It wasn't an accident, Silas darling. I've been watching you for a while. I saw you go into her apartment building and I waited till you came out. I was going crazy, imagining what the two of you might be getting up to together. Did you make love to her?"

Tess had somehow made the mistake of thinking that Denise was Felicity!

I said, "Stop torturing yourself. There are more important things to deal with right now."

"What's more important than love? Death?"

I shrugged my shoulders.

Tess said, "Hate is stronger than love, and I hate that girlfriend of yours. Right now, I almost hate you, so here's something for you to wrestle with. For your girlfriend, it's all over."

"What are you talking about?"

"Harley's got her; he's going to kill her if he hasn't done so already," Tess said.

Her face expressionless, she reached under the patio table, brought out a .25 and stood up.

"You're not the only smart one, Silas. I've got brains too. I don't want to kill you, not ever, really. Right now I'm all messed up, though. I will kill you if I have to."

"Killing me won't improve your situation. The only thing you'll gain is a few miserable hours of running and hiding."

"Wrong, Silas, we've got it all figured out. Harley will take the fall for whatever's happened, not me."

"Does Harley know that yet?"

"It's his own idea, it's what Harley wants," Tess answered, not smiling. "He's taking some people with him as slaves, to serve him in the Unknown World."

We were standing 10 feet apart. Her face was half in shadow but sunlight shone in her hair and I realized once again how strangely attractive I had always found her. Tess had been look-ing at my lips instead of my eyes. Her own eyes were hooded, clouded. The upraised arm holding the gun lowered slightly, but when I moved she re-established her aim and said, "Take that cell phone out of your pocket and toss it over here."

I obeyed. She destroyed the phone by grinding it under her foot, then said, "Turn around, Silas, and head for your cabin. Keep your hands where I can see them. And remember, I'm ner-vous. If you do something stupid this gun might go off and you could end up with a bullet in you. That'd be a shame because in spite of the way things have turned out, I love you."

"You love me so much, you're willing to kill me?"

"*Willing* is the wrong word. We're descended from killers, you and me, and we'd be killers still, if it hadn't been legislated out of existence by the guys who killed our culture. Let's just say

I'm ready to do it if you force me to. Harley's different. He's got a slave-killer club with your name on it."

I said stupidly, "A slave-killer club?"

"Yeah, a real antique stone club, it weighs about 20 pounds. One tap on the head and brains pour out of your ears. The good news is, death is quick."

We went into my cabin. Tess Rollins ordered me to stand four feet away from a wall, lean forward and touch the wall with both hands. With my face turned away from her like that, I listened as Tess moved around. First, she closed the window blinds, after which she destroyed my desk phone and yanked the jack from its socket. I was thinking about slave-killers, and Denise, and feeling a bit sorry for myself.

"It's a shame things turned out this way," Tess lamented. "I kidded myself you'd take the money, go along with my proposition. We'd have made a great couple, Silas, and now it's too late."

"It's never too late to act sensibly. This is crazy."

"Crazy or not, I'm committed," she said. "Sure you won't take that money after all?"

"I can't."

"That's it then, there's no backup plan. I've got to get you into my car and have you drive us someplace."

"Where are we going?"

"You'll find out. Things might go better than you think."

I was still stretched out uncomfortably, with my arms stretched against the wall. I said, "I'm getting a backache. How about letting me stand up and straighten out for a bit?"

"Fine, you do that. Just make sure to keep your hands up, and don't move your feet or turn around."

Her voice told me that Tess was about 10 feet behind me. She said, "All right, let's go. Open the door, walk slowly through your garden and get into the driver's seat of my car."

"You want me to drive the krautwagen?"

"*Mercedes*, if you don't mind."

"Does the Mercedes have an automatic transmission?"

"No, it's a five-speed," she said, faintly mocking, "and don't pretend you can't drive it."

"Believe it or not, I can't," I lied. "I never did learn to operate a stick shift."

Laughing outright she said, "Your MG has a stick shift."

I shrugged my shoulders.

"Enough fooling around," Tess ordered. "Let's go. You know what I want. Make no sudden moves or I might pull this trigger."

I went slowly toward the door and, as Tess followed, I was trying to guess how close she was. Instead of opening the door immediately, I waited. She said, "Stop messing me about, Silas."

I could tell she was about six feet behind. My heart racing, I took a deep breath, reached out for the doorknob, then gave it a sharp inward swing. As the door slammed open I dropped to my haunches and threw myself backwards. Tess's gun went off and a bullet flew into the ceiling. Our collision sent Tess sliding across the floor in a swirl of arms and legs. She ended lying on her back, her head against a wall. She pulled herself up into a sitting position, the gun still firmly in her grasp. Grinning, speaking as lightly as if we were playing some sort of childhood game, she stared at me in the slatted light and said, "Silas, it's been fun. Now the fun is over because you've been a fool. You've lost me. You've lost your girlfriend. You'll never meet her again in this life. Harley will see to that."

Tess made herself more comfortable against the wall by shuffling her ass and raising her knees. I said, "One thing you ought to know. The woman you think is my girlfriend is actually a police constable. Her name is Denise Halvorsen. She lives in that six-storey condo on Cook Street."

"You're a liar."

I shook my head. Tess stared at me. As the import of my state-ment sank in, her jaw went slack. Then she put the muzzle of the gun into her mouth, and pulled the trigger. The gun clattered to the floor. Her eyes remained open. Her mouth stayed open wide enough to show the tips of her white teeth. Apart from a little trickle of blood collected at one corner of her mouth, Tess looked normal. The adrenaline rush that had kept me high faded. I was overwhelmed with a sadness that left me breathless, and I was crying real tears, whether in lament for Tess Rollins, for Denise, or for myself, when the door opened. Chief Alphonse came in. As he bent down to look at Tess, I said idiotically, "You're a bit late."

"It made a lot of noise, that little gun," the chief said, in the calm ironic voice of one who knows all about life's disasters, but is too wise to worry about them.

"The gun was big enough to kill her."

"Suicide is a lot easier than it used to be, but it still don't make sense," he remarked, gently closing Tess's eyelids. "Who is she?"

"Tess Rollins."

"Tess Rollins is in the land of the dead now," Chief Alphonse said, getting to his feet. "I'll say some prayers for her, make sure she sleeps in peace."

I hadn't moved since he'd entered the cabin. The chief locked the door, covered Tess with a rug and knelt beside her. When he finished praying, he made some medicine over her body with his hands and then seated himself at my kitchen table. He said, "You all right now?"

"No," I said, staring down at the rug-draped corpse. "According to Tess, Boss Rollins has kidnapped Denise Halvorsen and plans to kill her, take her to the Unknown World. Denise might even be dead already!"

CHAPTER TWENTY-ONE

We were in the loaner, travelling flat out along Mowaht Bay's unpaved road. Chief Alphonse was in the passenger seat beside me. "You might want to drive more carefully," the chief said mildly, as we raced an 18-wheeler toward a one-way bridge. Gravel thrown up by the truck's wheels peppered my windshield when I pulled out to pass. The 18-wheeler's horn thundered. We were doing close to a hundred when a pickup truck appeared right in front of us. The pickup truck's driver and I hit the brakes at the same time. The steering wheel jerked in my hands. I braced myself as the car went into a slide, yet somehow, we skidded to a stop, still on the road instead of hitting a tree or plunging into Mowaht Sound. As the pickup truck sped by, I caught a glimpse of its white-faced driver.

Out on the Sound, seagulls rose into the air. A massive freighter inched across the horizon. Closer in, a single Orca ploughed the waves. I closed my eyes and saw Tess, dead.

The chief took a pipe out of his pocket, put it into his mouth, then took it out again and said, "Time we got moving, Silas."

I restarted the engine and we went on. When we reached the reserve lands below Boss Rollins' house, I parked in the usual spot.

We got out of the car. The sun was straight overhead; my shirt was sticking to my back. I led Chief Alphonse across that five-wire fence. Below the trees, another foul-smelling greenish fog hovered above the ground. The fog thickened as we went deeper into forest. My throat tickled and my eyes watered. A smoker, Chief Alphonse was also sweating profusely. He started to cough. I stopped to give him a breather.

The chief stumbled into me from behind and tried to speak, but his face was purple. He leant forward, retching and coughing like a man in end-stage TB. Hands on his knees, he was still trying to tell me something when he collapsed face down on the earth. I turned him onto his back and was giving him mouth-to-mouth resuscitation, when harsh laughter echoed.

In that once-sacred wilderness, a spectral figure emerged from a patch of shrubbery. An almost transparent shroud-like garment hung from his shoulders; rope-like muscles and tendons ridged his emaciated body. This sudden apparition scared the hell out of me. The creature's thin lips twisted into a horrible smile before it dissolved like ectoplasm in that green enveloping fog.

The chief's eyes had opened. His face no longer purple, he was white to the lips instead, but he was awake, breathing on his own, because the stinking fog had evaporated, along with that ghost. As visibility improved, the circular stream-fed pool came into view. I helped Chief Alphonse to his feet and we went to take a closer look at the spirit canoe.

The chief seized my arm, because something was dodging toward us among the trees. It was the apparition. Silently, acting like a sleepwalker, or someone in a trance, the spectre came up, apparently without noticing us, and paused beside the pond. After giving the spirit canoe an approving glance, it resumed its erratic progress between the trees. The chief and I followed it to the logging donkey.

Anger replaced creeping dread as the spectre reached inside

the furnace and dragged Denise Halvorsen out by her heels. Limp, her face and uniform smudged with soot, she appeared lifeless.

"I've seen enough," I said, dry-mouthed and hoarse. "Let's grab him now."

"We can't grab him," the chief said, still marvelously unperturbed and unhurried. "You can't grab a ghost."

"That's not Denise's ghost. She's real."

"No she isn't," the chief said. "And look at that creature's hands."

Each hand had six fingers. I'd been nervous to begin with; this revelation spooked me even more. We saw Denise's inert body manhandled off the platform and carried off. Chief Alphonse and I followed, but lost sight of them in another rising fog. When we reached the pool, there was no sight of the spectre, or of Denise. The spirit canoe was destroyed, its manikin crew gone.

Chief Alphonse grabbed my arm and said, "It's a trick. We're at 'the Gorge,' but it's the wrong one."

Immediately, I understood. That whole area was a small representation of the Gorge Waterway where it passes below the Tillicum Road Bridge. The pool represented a placid version of the giant whirlpool created by every turn of the tide.

Just as we arrived back in Victoria, I thought to call Bernie Tapp and told him to meet me at the Gorge.

WE LEFT THE CAR ON Tillicum Road. Chief Alphonse led the way to the banks of the Gorge. Sitting on that high grassy cliff above the water, I sensed as never before the spirits that haunted this place. The ceremonies and rituals celebrated here by my ancestors were rooted in the surrounding rocks and trees, in the very waters of the Gorge itself. Moreover, these ceremonies would be repeated in perpetuity.

The tourists that sometimes walk in this area had gone for

the day; Chief Alphonse and I had the place to ourselves. Clouds obscured the moon. The tide had turned and small twigs, leaves and bits of driftwood drifted in lazy circles in that deep pool below the bridge, as the millions of gallons of water filling Portage Inlet drained back to the sea through this narrow channel.

The chief asked knowingly, "Are you scared?"

I looked at him.

"Don't be," he said. "We can't see anybody, but we're not alone. Part of what we once were is here with us, along with what's still to come. The powers that protected our ancestors will protect us."

Apart from the headlights of cars, flashing intermittently as they crossed the Tillicum Bridge, the night was now almost black. Onshore winds brought more clouds from the west. It began to rain and the night grew even darker. At a few minutes before midnight something moved among the rocks on the waterway's opposite bank. Looking closely, I saw a small figure darting across my line of sight. "It's a young boy," I said, as the figure went from view beneath the bridge abutments. "What's he doing out at this time of night?"

Chief Alphonse showed his teeth.

A police cruiser pulled to a stop on the Tillicum Bridge. Bernie Tapp appeared. Backlit by the cruiser's emergency flashers, he leaned against the bridge's concrete railing and peered down at the strengthening whirlpool. More police cars arrived, along with ambulances and a fire truck. Uniforms dispersed along the bridge to block traffic in both directions. The rain increased, trickles of mud slid down the banks. Trees shook their branches in the first faint breezes of a gathering storm. Soaked and shivering, the chief and I moved beneath a shelf of rock. High above, somebody handed Bernie a searchlight; he aimed it into the rapidly expanding whirlpool and along the banks of the waterway, where the child was captured in the light's conical beam. This time we saw him clearly, if fleetingly: he was wearing a cone-shaped grass hat and a long kilt-like garment.

Clouds thickened, thunder roared. The ground beneath us shook as lightning struck the bridge. The earth rumbled, and the boy fell tumbling into the whirlpool amid a landslide of pebbles, mud and small rocks. We saw him go under. The Chief, his hair blowing in the wind, was trying to tell me something, but the uproar drowned his words. The child reappeared, on our side of the water this time. Running toward us, I saw that he was not a child. He was a powerfully built dwarf, about a metre tall, with wet grey ragged locks hanging to his shoulders. His face and upper body were painted with black and white horizontal stripes—exactly like those spirit-canoe manikins.

Amazement became shock and horror as he pointed with a six-fingered hand: A large dark object was floating toward the bridge on the quickening tide. A police searchlight zeroed in on it, till the object drifted out of sight beneath the bridge. Moments later it reappeared. A searchlight found it again. Then another searchlight illuminated it, till it was lit like day. It was a canoe, with a high raised prow. Boss Rollins was manning a steering oar in the stern. We saw Denise Halvorsen, slumped across a thwart in the bows. Sagging behind her was the idiot, Donny. Neville Rollin's mummified corpse was propped upright beside Joe Bickle.

The dwarf opened his mouth to laugh, revealing blackened stumps of teeth and a long black tongue. Chief Alphonse, braver than I, reached out to touch him, but the dwarf drew back into darkness and dematerialized. The air stank of sulphur.

The chief put his mouth to my ear and shouted, "This is what it must have been like years ago, when Billy Cheachlacht was praying to Camossung. The same night that Boss Rollins stayed underwater for an age and came up with a dwarf. Billy

Cheachlacht told us the air stank like rotten eggs that night too. Spooky, hellish lightning strikes were falling all around."

The whirlpool was spinning faster every second. The hole at its centre grew wider and deeper. The canoe began to spin. Boss Rollins dropped his steering oar, picked up an axe and hacked a hole in the bottom of the canoe. As it filled and began to founder we realized that Denise, Donny and Bickle were still alive. Tied to the canoe as securely as Neville Rollins' skeleton, they struggled to escape.

I stood poised on a high rock ready to dive in, only the chief grabbed my arm and shouted something I couldn't or didn't want to hear. The outer rim of the whirlpool was now an enormous circle of greenish-white foam. Denise and the others were up to their waists in water when the canoe slid into the vortex and went under. The stern half of the canoe reappeared almost instantly on the whirlpool's outermost rim. Neville's grinning corpse was still aboard when the canoe smashed against Camossung's Rock.

Chief Alphonse was still hanging on to me. I shook loose and for what good I thought it might do for Denise dived into the whirlpool. Underwater it was cold, black, full of solid objects that pummelled my face and body and legs. I found it impossible to swim against the current and was drawn under and down to the bottom where something heavy fell onto me, driving the last bit of air from my lungs. I was drowning, at the last of my strength, when that *something* dragged me into the eye of the vortex.

Magically, the water warmed, visibility improved. Air, entrained in the vortex's giant hollow core, reduced my buoyancy. For a moment I was held upright in a spinning watery tube and was actually able to take a few breaths, before I landed with a thump on the bottom once more. The water mysteriously drained away. I found myself inside a dry, airy, underwater dome.

Was I going out of my head? No, because Denise Halvorsen

was inside that dome too, and Denise was real, alive, curled up comfortably on a bank of dry warm sand. When I called to her she smiled and sat up, but Neville Rollins interposed himself between us. I drew back in horror. Disappointed by my cowardice, Denise shook her head. Chastened, frightened out of my wits, I watched Boss Rollins emerge from a cave, along with Tess Rollins and that ghastly painted dwarf. Joseph Bickle appeared with a camera and sat on a rock, taking pictures. Donny's idiot laughter was the last thing I remembered, after I shoved Neville Rollins aside, took Denise into my arms and kissed her.

CHAPTER TWENTY-TWO

I was lying half-asleep in a strange bed. Somebody remarked pedantically, "Carl Jung's theory of the collective unconscious explains everything that happened. He taught us that none of us are isolated in time. We humans are part of what we once were, and what we shall be again."

I opened my eyes and realized that I was in a hospital. The room was dim. Bernie Tapp, Chief Alphonse and the man who had just spoken were standing around my bed.

"We don't need Jung to explain things to us. It just *is*, that's all," Chief Alphonse said, speaking in his slow, calm, measured way. "Everything that happened at the Tillicum Bridge has happened before. Coast Salish Spirit Questers have been diving into that whirlpool since time out of mind. Sometimes they come up, sometimes they drown. Silas is tough, he didn't drown."

"Maybe not," I chimed in. "I'm not real sure that's completely true, at present."

The three men got up from their chairs and came to my bedside—Chief Alphonse moving more slowly and stiffly than his companions.

The man who had spoken first took my wrist to check my pulse. "I'm Dr. McCall," he said. "You've been in a bad scrape. How do you feel now?"

"Not bad."

"I should say not. And don't worry. People emerging from coma are always slightly confused. Make no mistake, Mr. Seaweed. You *are* alive."

I said, "How is Denise doing?"

Bernie Tapp shook his head.

"We'll talk about that later," the doctor replied.

"Stop thinking and wracking your brain for once, and go back to sleep," Bernie said, helping me to sit up straighter and fluffing my pillows.

"Your vital signs are about normal now, Sergeant," Dr. McCall said, producing a pill. He handed it to me, along with a glass of water, and said, "Swallow this. You'll be out of this world in a minute."

I hesitated for a moment, until something small and malevolent appeared in my peripheral vision. A grey six-fingered hand was scratching at a windowpane. I swallowed the pill. Felicity Exeter walked into the room before I fell asleep.

WE BURIED DENISE AT HATLEY PARK. Five hundred uniformed marchers showed up; it's always a big deal when an officer dies on duty. New Westminster's police band piped us into the chapel with "The Flowers of the Forest." Chief Mallory gave the eulogy; Victoria's chief magistrist read the lesson.

Denise's father had memorized a few words of Kipling, and he recited them clearly and unbrokenly over his daughter's coffin.

> *You have heard the beat of the off-shore wind,*
> *And the thresh of the deep-sea rain;*
> *You have heard the song—how long! how long!*
> *Pull out on the trail again!*

> *Ha' done with the tents of Shem, dear lass,*
> *We've seen the seasons through,*
> *And it's time to turn on the old trail, our own trail,*
>   *the out trail,*
> *Pull out, pull out, on the Long Trail—the trail that*
>   *is always new!*

After hundreds of strong silent men from as far away as San Diego finished drying their eyes, after eight uniformed pallbearers took up her coffin, Vancouver's police band gave us "Scotland the Brave," and then led us to the tree under whose branches Denise would forever lie. It had rained, earlier. A slow kettledrummer beat the dirge when they lowered her into the damp ground.

Bernie Tapp and I waited until the last kilt had swished through the park gates, and the last faint skirls of "The Gathering of Locheil" had lamented away in the distance.

"You ready to talk about Tess Rollins now?" Bernie asked.

I came back from wherever I was.

Bernie went on, "Why did Tess have to kill Jane Colby? It doesn't make any sense."

"Tess wasn't as rich as everybody thought she was. She spent way more money than she could afford, and the Rainbow Motel was mortgaged to the max. Tess just didn't want to share what was left."

"So that's it? The motive was greed?"

"Yes, it's pathetic."

We were still there when the undertaker's men placed the last lilies on that heaped up mound of earth, and then trundled off in a cemetery buggy loaded with planks and ropes.

Bernie gazed at his muddy boots, cleared his throat and said, "They did her proud. I doubt if there'll be many mourners at that Rollins funeral in Mowaht Bay. Are you going, by the way?"

"No. The sooner I forget that fivesome, the better."

"Five?"

"Boss Rollins and Tess Rollins. Donny. Joe Bickle. Neville."

"Oh yeah, right. I'd forgotten about Neville," Bernie said. "Not that there's much of him left to bury. All they found was his skull and a couple of bones."

"There's one more. Jane Colby."

"She was buried last week. I went to her funeral. Only six or seven of us attended."

"And who were they?"

"Jane's dad. Terry. Four Crowe Street nuns and a drunken Irish bartender," Bernie said.

"How is Terry these days?"

"Pretty good. She's working part time at Safeway now." Looking down at his muddy boots he added, "My feet are cold. What say we go to headquarters, join in the wake?"

"No thanks. It'll be fun for a bit, but you know how it'll end. People will drink too much and start telling jokes."

"Sure they will, laughter's a relief valve. Nobody grieves forever. It's not healthy."

"You go then. I'm in no mood for jokes," I said, as we started walking. "I want to think about the way she was the last time I saw her."

"Which was?"

I pictured her in my mind's eye and said, "Denise was lying on a sandbank. I had my arms around her, and I was kissing her."

"Jesus, Silas, have you gone off your meds?"

"I've been off my meds for a week. I'm getting seven hours sleep every night. I'm as sane as you are."

"What you had your arms around, Silas, was the back end of a dugout canoe," Bernie said. "That's what saved you from drowning in the Gorge whirlpool. We had to pry your fingers loose before we could drag you ashore."

But that's not the way I remember it.

Felicity was in the Range Rover, waiting for me at the cemetery gate. I got in and said, "Home, James."

"There's something we must attend to first," she said.

SIR JOHN A. MACDONALD'S bronze statue had a fresh green shine after the rain. In the cool fall sunshine I could see all the way down Pandora Street to where an elderly lady in a large white hat was wheeling a poodle in a perambulator. Felicity parked outside Swans pub. Various tiny ideas were gnawing the inside of my puzzled head, otherwise full of B.C. air, when Felicity took a mahogany picnic hamper with a covered top from the back seat of her vehicle.

We let ourselves into my office.

"I'll open the blinds," Felicity said, putting the picnic hamper on my desk. "Why don't you just sit down?"

I sat behind the desk, admiring the hamper's shiny brass fittings.

Felicity went over to the filing cabinet, knelt down and came up holding a large oval plastic basin. PC's black ears showed above the basin's rim.

"Well, Silas. Guess what your clever cat's been doing?"

"Oh Lord," I said. "How many?"

"Eight, but you don't need to worry," she said, laying the basin on my blotter. "I can always use another couple of cats in my barn and the rest are spoken for."

PC jumped out of the basin, glared at me, then jumped to the floor and stalked out of the office, quivering with indignation.

"My goodness, eight little bits of mechanical fur," I said, looking into the basin. "Boys or girls?"

"Silly, you can't tell at this stage. A few of each, I expect."

"This calls for a toast," I said, reaching down for the office bottle and the Tim Horton mugs.

"Put those things away," Felicity said, reaching into the hamper for a bottle of bubbly. "We'll do this in style. You can propose the toast."

"To new beginnings?"

Felicity popped the cork. "New beginnings, that's perfect. You are clever, Silas."

ABOUT THE AUTHOR

STANLEY EVANS' previous novels are *Outlaw Gold, Snow-Coming Moon* and the first two books in the Silas Seaweed series: *Seaweed on the Street* and *Seaweed on Ice*. Stanley and his family live in Victoria, B.C.

ISBN 10: 1-894898-34-6
ISBN 13: 978-1-894898-34-8

ISBN 10: 1-894898-51-6
ISBN 13: 978-1-894898-51-5

"Makes great use of the West Coast aboriginal mythology and religion."
—*The Globe and Mail*

"The writing is wonderful native story telling. Characters are richly drawn . . . I enjoyed this so much that I'm looking for the others in the series."
—*Hamilton Spectator*